BLOODLINE OF THE ANCIENTS

ROAN ROSSER

Rainbow Dog

RAINBOW DOG BOOKS

Your free ebook is waiting

Sign up for my newsletter to get Jack's prequel story for free. Available at https://bit.ly/3J1twim

CONTENTS

PROLOGUE 1

1. Nice to Meet You, Evan 5

2. Learning to Hunt 11

3. Craving Vampires 22

4. The Basement 32

5. Blood Like Wine 38

6. Sleepwalking 43

7. Quiet as a Tomb 49

8. You Dated a Cougar? 51

9. A Night of Bliss 65

10. Vampire Mummy 70

11. Chained Up 78

12. Omaha 87

13. The Test of Control 92

14. Meeting the Pack 96

15. Salt Lake City 107

16. Brand New Vampire 111

17. Cats are Vindictive 120

18. Late Night Guest 126

19. Vampire Hunters 133

20. Fire 141

21. Aftermath   144

22. Sword of Damocles   151

23. Meet the Goddess   157

24. Drawn Like a Lodestone   167

25. Guardian of the Dead   173

Epilogue   177

Also By Roan Rosser   179

About the Author   180

PROLOGUE

COLD AND WET. IF anyone asked, that was how I'd describe the weather in London.

"So Jack, how was the flight over?" Cai asked me in a thick British accent. Cai was a local vampire, tasked with showing me around, and helping me with anything I need for the investigation.

"Long," I said, stifling a yawn behind my hand. "At least the PCA paid for first class."

Cai laughed. "True. Right here." She opened a steel door. A large sign on the door said "MORGUE".

A cool breeze heavy with the scent of disinfectants wafted out. "Showing me all the best sites, I see."

"Only the premium tourism package for our guest of honor from the states." Cai giggled. She walked past all the steel autopsy tables to the bank of body lockers and opened one. "Here it is." The table squealed loudly as she pulled it free.

The corpse was covered with a sheet, except for the feet, which were withered and dried, with a toe-tag. Cai folded the sheet back from the head and I stepped up on the other side.

The corpse's teeth were pulled back in a grimace, revealing two sharp vampire fangs. The brown, dry, desiccated skin was taut over the bones. I prodded the skin gently with one finger and it cracked and broke under even that slight pressure.

"The Portland office sent us pictures, of course," Cai said.

"But it's not the same," I finished the statement for her. "For what it's worth, I agree with your assessment. It's the same method of death as the one in Portland." I'd had a look at the vampire Everett had drained in Portland before flying out here. The council had ruled it an accident, since Everett was a new vampire.

More like self-defense, if you asked me.

"So it's the same killer," Cai stated with a frown. "But why come from Portland to London?"

I shook my head. "No, the killer in that case has an alibi for this one. But the method is the same."

"Method?" Cai shook her head, sending blond curls bouncing. "That's one answer I didn't get from your office. What could do this to a vampire?"

I blew out a breath and waved at her to cover the corpse back up, which she did. "Another vampire, one that can drain the blood of vampires. Where was he found? I'd like to see the place."

"She. And I'm sorry, we can't. She was a night security guard for the British Museum. She was killed there, or at least that's where they found the body. Luckily police thought it was a prank of some sort, so it didn't make the news before one of ours was able to retrieve the body."

"Where at the museum?"

"The hall of mummies."

"Ah, hence the prank theory by the cops. But I see your point. Not exactly going to be easy to get in there," I said as she led me back up to her office. "Any supernatural coworkers of hers that we could speak with?" I sat down in the plush visitor's chair in front of Cai's desk, and she took a seat behind the desk.

Cai shook her head. "That's the other problem. The only other vampire who was working that night has vanished. We fear the worst." She tapped at her computer for a moment, and then swiveled the monitor to show me his photo. A young Black vampire smiled out at me. The label on his file read "Kurt".

"I see." I made a few notes in my mini notebook that I was using to keep track of case files. "What day did you say this all happened on?" "Four nights ago." Cai turned her monitor back around.

I frowned, turning forward in my notebook to the timeline I'd been keeping. London was eight hours ahead, so here it would have been early morning during...

"The night after the explosion..." I murmured mostly to myself. Could the spell in Portland have been the trigger? The timing could have been coincidental, but my investigative gut told me there was a connection. I'd been studying to make detective when I'd "died" and had to relocate, so I didn't have a lot of real life experience to back up my hunch. I'd argued as much to Stacey when she'd given me this assignment; they needed someone with more experience, plus I was too close to Everett to be objective. But she'd been adamant, saying that was just what was needed. "Explosion?" Cai leaned towards me, resting her arms on the desk.

I jotted my thought down, then sighed and closed my notebook. "A spell that was set off in Portland. My partner was sacrificed to it, and I almost was as well. My boyfriend saved me, but he paid the price. He's being cared for by the mages right now. I should be by his side, but they won't let me see him until he's better."

"I'm sorry." Cai sounded sincere, her tone sorrowful and her smile sad.

I gave her a nod. "Thank you." I stared down at my hands, clasping them into fists, trying to hold back tears. Last time I'd seen Everett he'd been in a bloodlust frenzy. He'd terrified me, yet he'd been able to keep himself from eating me. I'd begged to go see him at the mages, but been denied. I think by giving me this job, Stacey was trying to distract me.

I discreetly wiped my eyes, and Cai was polite enough to not say anything if she noticed. "So, we can't visit the museum and we can't talk to witnesses. Where does that leave us?"

"We did manage to get the security tapes from that night at the museum. Pull your chair around here, and I'll show you the good parts." Cai rolled her chair over and gestured to me.

I obliged her, and she began playing the video.

The video was shot from above, and showed Kurt's backside, walking down a wide hallway with a tall, dark-haired, slim woman. They both wore security uniforms and carried flashlights, although neither had them on. Made sense; Everett had told me he saw better in the dark.

They walked down a hallway lined with Egyptian artifacts: statues, busts, pillars, and stone coffins carved with effigies. Something off-screen drew the attention of the two vampires. The video didn't have sound, but they ran off-screen, pointing. A few moments later, Kurt was thrown back into view. Blood now stained his uniform, a large splatter sprayed across the front and another splash, barely visible under his hand that he had clutched at the side of his neck. His fangs were down and his eyes glowed red. He lay partially in frame for a moment, eyes rolling back in his head as spasms shook his body, as if in a seizure. A few minutes later he was pulled back out of frame, and Cai clicked to end the video.

"That's the last time Kurt was seen. The girl's body was placed in a coffin in the display and found the next morning." Cai twisted her chair around to look at me.

"You think Kurt is dead as well." I leaned back in my chair, tapping my pen thoughtfully on my notebook.

Cai shrugged. "Unfortunately, yes. Kurt's an old vampire, powerful. If he's still missing...it doesn't bode well."

"How old was the girl?"

"Hold on." Cai got back on her computer and brought up her profile. "Mary? Not very old, couple of decades. Looks like Kurt was her maker. They were lovers."

I jotted down these facts in my notebook. Too early to glean anything from them.

"And the mummy?"

"What mummy?" Cai turned back to me, her eyebrows raising.

"The one that had been in the coffin before Mary's body was placed there. They didn't have an empty coffin on display, did they? Mummies are one of the main attractions."

Cai's eyes widened and she spun back to her computer. "Let me bring up the police report again." She typed furiously for a moment, then fell back, tugging on one of the blond curls. "Shit, you're right. The mummy from the coffin was also reported missing. I saw it before, but dismissed it as inconsequential. You think it's important?"

"I don't know." I sighed and noted the fact down to my growing list of questions. "But I don't think it's a coincidence. Can you get me all the information you have on the mummy?"

"Not much in the police report other than the mummy was from Egypt, dated to the late Middle Kingdom, but I can get the info from the museum for you tomorrow after it opens. Is it important?" Cai leaned her elbows on the desk.

"I don't know." I unthinkingly clicked my pen. "But it doesn't strike me as a coincidence that Everett's problems began with an ancient Egyptian amulet and there's a missing mummy, also from ancient Egypt."

CHAPTER 1

NICE TO MEET YOU, EVAN

I PACED THE GROUND floor, sick to death of this place, and I'd only been here a week. A knock on the door broke me out of my reverie. I wondered who it was; the house for new vampires was deep in the woods on a hundred acres of land down a private road, so we didn't get many visitors.

I was tempted to use my vampire speed to go to the door, but I was already thirsty, and doing that would make me thirstier. We were supposed to go hunting tonight, my first hunting trip. I was both nervous and excited.

Hand on the doorknob, I stopped and looked over my shoulder at the stairs leading up to the second floor. Upstairs I could hear Lin talking on the phone. As the house elder, she was the only one who was supposed to answer the door, but frankly, I thought that rule was a bit dumb. Still, she could come down at any time.

"Who is it?" I said.

"Jack." Jack's baritone came through the door loud and clear. "Here to drop off supplies."

"Jack!" I yelled, flinging the door open before he'd even gotten midway through his sentence and spreading my arms wide for a hug.

Jack stood on the porch, grinning underneath his neatly trimmed mustache. His black hair and beard also looked freshly trimmed, and my fingers twitched with desire to run through the thick locks. He wore a crisp red button-up, slacks, and loafers. I pouted when I saw his hands were full of a bankers box with a cooler stacked on top. I dropped my arms and stepped aside so he could come in, closing my eyes for a moment as he passed me to savor the smell of his cologne. All this to come see me?

"Where's Lin?" Jack asked as he came inside. "You're not supposed to answer the door alone, Ev." Still, he flashed me a smile and a wink on his way to the kitchen.

I shut the door behind him and then trailed after him, licking my lips at the smell of him. In the last week of only interacting with vampires, and I'd forgotten the warmth of the living. It radiated off him, calling to me. My fangs ached, trying to come down. I'd gotten better about controlling them in the last week of practice.

I'd had lots of time to practice at that since there wasn't much else to do here. Lin even had me doing exercises in the mirror. It was creepy the way my eyes changed with the fangs.

I began to understand why newbies were sequestered. At least a little.

I leaned on the kitchen door frame and crossed my arms, watching as Jack began filling the freezer with bottles of blood from the cooler. "The elder is busy upstairs. I'm sure she wouldn't mind."

Jack barked out a laugh. "Don't let Lin hear you call her that."

I stuck out my tongue at him. "I know, but why are you doing the delivery? You don't live anywhere near here." I gave him a crooked smile. "Could it be you wanted to see me?"

"As for my reasons for visiting..." He finished and shut the freezer door, setting aside the empty cooler on the counter. "That might just be you." He winked and picked up the cardboard banker's box from the floor, holding it out to me. "And to give you this."

Frowning, I shoved off with my shoulder and straightened to take it from him. "What is it?" The plain brown box didn't give any clue as to what was inside. It wasn't very heavy, but it wasn't light either.

"Just a few things that I thought you'd like." He shrugged and dug his hands into his pockets as he stepped back from me.

I scowled and tossed the box onto the counter. All I'd wanted to do since he came in here was run my hands down his chest, and maybe kiss him. Or the other way around. I wasn't picky. But I got the feeling he was avoiding me.

Jack frowned and crossed his arms, looking from me to the box. "I have something to talk to you about, but Lin should be here for this too. Can you go get her?"

"Sure, but first, can I get a hug?" I stood and opened my arms, moving towards him. Jack shook his head and held up his hands, palm out.

"Whoa there." Jack settled away from me hands still up. "I see the way you're clenching your jaw. Have you had anything to eat tonight?"

I stepped back to where I'd been and scowled, looking away from him and crossing my arms to hug myself. "No," I growled. If I'd still been human my stomach would've rumbled; as it was, my mouth felt dry and my throat itched. I licked my lips.

"Well, I brought more bottles," Jack said, stepping towards the fridge.

I stopped him with look and a shake of my head. "No, Lin is supposed to take me hunting tonight."

Jack pursed his lips, but stepped back. Footsteps sounded on the wood floor behind me, and I turned my head to look at Lin as she came into the kitchen.

She'd curled the ends of her long black hair, one sweeping lock of which fell forward across her face. Her mauve dress was backless with ruffled sleeve caps, the skirt hitting just above her knees. It was very cute, but I wondered why she'd gone to such lengths just to take me hunting. Between the two of them I felt a bit underdressed in my jeans and T-shirt.

Lin scowled, wrinkling her perfect purple lipstick, when she saw Jack and put her hands on her hips before rounding on me. "You're not supposed to be answering the door, Everett."

Before I could protest, Jack stepped up beside me. "I let myself in. The door was unlocked."

I grabbed Jack's hand and gave it a grateful squeeze, dropping it when Lin glanced my way.

"And put that disgusting thing away." Her nose wrinkled as she looked me up and down, the same expression she got every time she caught site of the gold Egyptian amulet that I wore on a chain around my neck. Lin waved one manicured finger at my chest.

Trying to keep down a growl, I tucked the gold amulet into my shirt, so that the bare metal rested against my chest. The feel of it had been making my skin crawl lately, but both Lin and Trevor objected every time they saw it. Yet I didn't feel comfortable putting it in my pocket where it could fall out or get pickpocketed, and wearing an undershirt still felt too much like wearing a binder.

Lin shifted her attention back to Jack. "The delivery's supposed to be made by a vampire." Her scowl deepened.

"We're shorthanded. You have a problem, take it up with Stacy." Jack crossed his arms and leveled looked down at Lin who, despite her being nearly a foot shorter than Jack, had moved into his personal space and was trying to intimidate him.

"You can bet I will. I'm sure this was just an excuse to see your boyfriend," Lin snapped, narrowing her eyes but taking a step back from Jack.

Jack shrugged and made a noncommittal grunt. "Can't deny that. Anyway, anything else you need before I leave?" He stepped up next to me and wrapped his arm around my waist in a sideways hug.

I had to close my eyes and clench my jaw against the warmth of his sudden and unexpected touch. Once I was sure my fangs were under control, I leaned against him and put my arm around his back.

Lin huffed, and I knew I was going to pay for this later. But it was worth it to hug Jack.

"You were supposed to bring his new ID," Lin snapped.

I opened my eyes to see Lin pointing at me.

Jack's arm stiffened around me, holding me tighter. It seemed Lin ruffled his feathers as bad as she did mine. "In the box."

Lin looked at me, and then glanced at the box in an unspoken order. I sighed and slipped out of Jack's embrace to go over to the banker's box that I'd abandoned on the kitchen's island. I popped the top off and propped it against the box. A tan manila folder sat directly on top. I picked it up, revealing a plush tiger underneath of it. I picked the tiger up with my other hand and playfully thrust its mouth at Jack, making growling noises.

Jack took the tiger from me, tossing it underhand back into the box. "You weren't supposed to see that till I left," Jack said with a laugh. I smiled back at him, immediately getting the inside joke. I was his fierce Tiger. It was a sweet gift.

I stuck my tongue out at him as I open up the folder. Inside were a bunch of official-looking documents, as well as a laminated driver's license. I picked up the license to take a closer look at it. The picture was mine, but the name... "Evan Truman? Who's that?"

Lin stalked up and snatched the folder from me. "That's you."

"She's right." Jack thrust out a hand towards me for handshake. I transferred the license to my other hand and shook the offered hand, feeling a bit baffled. "Nice to meet you, Evan," Jack said.

"Um, what?" I said, blinking. "But I like the name Everett. That's why I chose it, after all."

Jack gave me a sympathetic smile and pulled me into a hug. I wrapped my arms around his back and breathed deep of his scent as the buttons of his shirt pressed against my face. After a moment more Jack released me and stepped back, moving his hands up to rest on my shoulders. "I know. I made your case with Stacy about keeping it, but she was adamant it had to change after the way your face and old name had been splashed all over the news."

I scowled and crossed my arms, feeling the edges of the license in my palm. I was tempted to tear it up—I probably could too—but was stopped by Jack's understanding sympathy. He'd had to go through the same thing. Instead, I huffed and looked down at my feet. "They could've at least asked me for input."

Jack shook his head. "Takes a while to make fake documents. We had to decide your name while you were still under sedation with the mages. I chose Evan because it was pretty close to Everett. It was either that or Rhett, like Ev-rhett," he emphasized the end of my name. "But I thought you'd like Evan better."

That made my lips twitch into the beginning of a smile. I glanced up at him from under my hair; it'd been a while since I'd had a haircut, and it was getting shaggy. "Thanks."

Jack glanced over at Lin, which made me look at her too. Her legs were spread and her hands on her were on her hips. She was glaring at Jack.

"Any news on finding Everett's maker?" Lin flipped the long lock of hair out of her eyes and gave Jack a sideways look. "I'm more than done babysitting someone else's whelp."

Jack frowned at her, his hands tightening into fists at his side. "You'd be willing to give Everett's training over to the vampire who hurt him? And who probably breaks every other rule that the PCA put in place to keep us safe?"

Lin huffed, putting her hands back on her hips and flipping her black hair, a lock of which had fallen in her face again, with a twist of her neck. "That's not what I mean. I just meant this isn't what I signed up for."

She glared at me. I wanted to shrink back, hide behind Jack, but I took a deep breath and met her gaze. Jack was right. It wasn't my fault that this had happened to me, and I refused to let her ribbing get to me.

"It wasn't what I signed up for either, but I'm making due." My eyes bored into hers and she looked away with a frown.

Jack shook his head. "Back to your question, no, we're no closer. Stacy called off the search. We suspect they are no longer in Portland."

"They might just be laying low until the search dies down," Lin said, voicing the question that had been bouncing around my head.

Jack glanced down at me and rubbed my shoulder. "A vampire was found dead in London two weeks ago. Murdered. We suspect the killer is a vampire of Everett's bloodline."

I blinked. "My bloodline? What makes you so sure of—" Then it hit me, and I blanched. "Oh."

Lin's eyes widened and she put a hand over her mouth. "You're not saying... they were drained?"

Jack's mouth hardened into a thin line and he nodded. "Totally dry. Just like the vampire here that Everett accidentally killed."

I hadn't known what I was doing, but I'd still killed him. I hugged myself and closed my eyes.

"Has he, they, changed anyone else?" I asked.

Jack's warm hand gave my shoulder a reassuring squeeze. "Not as far as we know, no."

"Good," I said forcefully, and opened my eyes to look over at Jack. Jack gave me a smile, which I returned with a half-hearted one of my own, before taking his hand off my shoulder.

Jack turned back to Lin. "In any case, we'll keep you updated. And Stacy is looking for someone to take over for you, but so far there aren't any volunteers."

"Volunteers?" Lin sniffed and rolled her eyes. "Of course not. Who wants to mentor someone they don't know, and might not get along with, for ten years? Usually you only take this job so you can be the one to turn a loved one and show them the ropes. On top of that, as soon as they find out about this one—" She jerked a thumb at me. "—any smart vampire would turn tail and run the other way."

I rubbed my elbow and stared at the floor. She was probably right.

Lin's cellphone jingled with an incoming cell message. She dug in her purse to pull out her phone and checked the message before stuffing it back in her purse. "Enough chit-chat. I'm thirsty."

"I can see I've overstayed my welcome." Jack stepped in front of me and leaned over me. I turned my face up to meet his, hoping for a goodbye kiss, but to my disappointment he planted his lips on my forehead.

"I miss you," I said softly.

"Me too, Everett. I'll talk to Lin about maybe getting you out here for a date night," he whispered, then rested his forehead against mine briefly before straightening. He glanced at Lin, his lips twitching to a smile that quickly faded. "Nice to see you, Lin."

Lin ushered him out the door. Jack stopped on the porch and turned around wave at me. "Bye." He paused. "Evan."

I flipped him off and stuck out my tongue at him right before the door shut. His roar of laughter was audible even through the closed door.

Chapter 2

Learning to Hunt

Lin parked down the street down from the bar on the corner. Harsh neon lights glittered off the puddles in the parking lot left by the rainstorm we'd had this afternoon, and laughter and cigarette smoke drifted to us on the night breeze.

I got out of the backseat and stretched, breathing deep at my first taste of the out-of-doors in a week. Lin slammed her door and walked around to join Trevor and me on the sidewalk.

Trevor, the other newbie vampire who lived at the house, wore a light denim jean jacket covered in tattered patches from local bands. Pins lined the edges of the front collar. His dyed-black hair was shaved into a fohawk, and he had a pierced eyebrow that glittered in the neon lights from the bar.

He had his hands balled into the pockets and his shoulders hunched as if he were cold. I licked my lips and shivered, understanding how he was feeling. As a vampire I no longer really noticed the temperature outside. That didn't mean I no longer felt cold, however. The longer I went between drinking blood, the colder I felt.

Worse, the bottled stuff didn't keep me warm nearly as long as when I drank from the source. This last week had left me freezing and ravenous to bite someone. Trevor and Lin, both stuck in the house with me, had to be feeling the same.

Lin held up a hand to stop the two of us as we started for the bar.

"Everett," she said, and I looked at her expectantly. "I know Jack was joking around about your new name, but from now on you'll need to start using it."

"Why?" Trevor gave Lin a curious look. "They let me keep using Trevor." He pulled out his wallet and flipped it to show me his ID.

"Terry?" I read out loud and giggled. "Really?"

Trevor grimaced and put his wallet away. "Ugh, I know."

"Evan," Lin emphasized the name as she looked at me, "is a special case. His face and old name were splashed all over the news recently. Yes it was in Portland and we're in Eugene, and yes we faked his death, but we don't want to chance him being connected with that Everett. Estacada is still close enough to Portland that you need to be careful."

I bit my lip and nodded. I didn't like it, but I could see her reasoning. I wondered, if that were the case, why not send me somewhere far away? But I didn't want to give them the idea by asking about it.

"Don't worry, you can go back to your original name in forty or fifty years or so, once the heat dies down." Lin gave me a big smile that I think was supposed to be reassuring.

"Gee, is that all?" I muttered as I followed her into the bar. I wasn't sure if she was joking or not.

We walked past a crowd of four people smoking outside the front door. One of the girls in the group gave Trevor a little smile and wave as we walked through their cloud of smoke. He pulled a hand from his pocket and gave her a little three finger wave. Lin ignored it all, intent on the door.

Inside was half-full. The stools at the long, wraparound bar were empty except for two at the end. Small groups were scattered around at the round tables. Lin led us towards one of the larger tables in the corner that sat six or seven, which was already occupied by two men.

When they saw Lin one of them waved at her, his face lighting up in a grin and his eyes sparkling as he caught sight of her. I couldn't tell how tall he was sitting in the booth, but his thin, sleeveless T-shirt did little to hide his muscled chest. His brown hair was artfully spiked to look messy, but I knew from experience that a look a lot of effort. His muscle shirt had the logo of a Portland CrossFit gym on it.

"How was the drive, Stephen?" Lin asked as she go to the table.

"Not too bad," Stephen said, winking at Lin. "Especially when the reward for getting here is seeing you."

Lin laughed and slid into the booth to peck him on the cheek. He put an arm around her shoulder and she cuddled up to him. "Hey, babe. Trevor." He bobbed his head at Trevor as he sat at the booth next to the other boy, then looked at me. "And you must be Everett. The guy who stole my spot."

He was still grinning, but the smile didn't reach his eyes.

I ignored the jab. "Evan now." I slid in next to Trevor and then offered a hand across the table towards Lin's boyfriend. "Pleased to meet you." Now that I was closer, I could see the scars covering both sides of neck. The sight made my mouth dry. I tightened my jaw. Embarrassed, I glanced away, to Stephen's companion. He looked a lot like Lin's boyfriend, but with darker, longer hair that went to his shoulder, and not as many bite marks.

"I'm Stephen." Lin's boyfriend reached across and shook my hand. I almost gasped at how warm his skin was on mine, and my mouth felt drier than ever. My fangs descended, and I jerked my hand out of his and clasped my hands over my mouth, closing my eyes to hide the red eyes that I knew came with the fangs.

Lin muttered, "Honestly, Ever—Evan. If you can't control yourself we'll have to leave."

"Sorry. I'm really thirsty," I said through my hand. I took a deep breath, concentrating on bringing my fangs back up. "I've got it, see?" I lowered my hand, opened my eyes, and smiled at Lin to show her my normal, human teeth and irises.

"You'd better," Lin growled and narrowed her eyes at me. "This is the first time I've seen my boyfriend in a week."

I glared right back. "I hadn't seen Jack in just as long, and you made him leave after only a few minutes."

Lin shrugged and smiled, batting her eyelashes. I scowled and slumped back into the booth.

Stephen's friend held his hand out towards me. "I'm Lance. Nice to meet you."

Despite my bravado, I wasn't sure I could keep my fangs under control at another touch. "Nice to meet you," I said, keeping my hands clasped in my lap.

After a few awkward moments when it became clear I wasn't going to shake his hand, Lance looked disappointed and sat back to take a swig of the beer in front of him. Maybe that would help take the edge off the dryness until I found someone to bite.

"Lin, can I have some money to get myself one of those?" I pointed at the beers.

Lin wrinkled her nose and stared at me.

"That's not a good idea—" Trevor began.

"No, no, it's fine." Lin cut him off with a wave of her hand. She got out her wallet and fished a twenty out of it. "Knock yourself out." I snatched the bill before she could change her mind and slid out of the booth.

At the bar, I caught the eye of the bushy, bearded bartender. While I waited for him to finish serving the couple on the end of the bar, I leaned on the counter and took a look around. Might as well see what was on the menu for tonight. I chuckled at my own joke.

The crowd skewed older, which made sense for a weeknight. This sports bar, with the lines of pool tables and televisions lining the walls, would be packed on the weekends. Most of the people in the bar already looked pretty drunk, and raucous laughter and slurred conversation almost drowned out the awful music.

I frowned at all the groups. I didn't see anyone drinking alone; I figured they would be the best targets to bite. But then again, what did I know? I'd never even be able to pick up a guy or girl before. Man. I was going to be the worst vampire. I sighed.

The bartender came over, crossing his arms and frowning at me. "You old enough to be in here?"

I suppressed a groan and handed my new fake ID to the man. I got that a lot. When I passed, people thought I was fourteen, at most.

The bartender examined it with a critical eye before handing it back to me with a shake of his head. "They get younger every year. What can I get you?"

"Two of your most popular drink." One for me, one to butter up Lance, see if I could get an easy meal out of him. I set the twenty on the bar. I left a few dollars as a tip and took the two drinks back.

When I got back, Lin and Stephen were making out, and Trevor had scooted almost all the way out of the booth. Lance had drifted around too, and sat right up next to Trevor, talking at him while Trevor studiously ignored him to play with his phone. Lance's mug sat in the middle of the table, already empty. Perfect.

"Hey, make room." I frowned at Trevor, my hands both full of beer.

"Here." Trevor stood up and moved aside.

The subject of his monologue suddenly gone, Lance stopped talking and looked around, then slid back around to the middle. I set the beers down and slid into the booth, pulling the glasses along the table with me, making sure to get over far enough to leave room for Trevor to sit down.

"Hey, thanks." Lance took the beer from me and took a long drink from it.

I sighed and eyed Lin and Stephen, running my hands around the sweating pint. I'd thought I'd be getting at least a few tips on hunting before being left on my own for dinner. Then again... I smiled and leaned close to Lance, shivering as I felt his warmth this close to him. My fangs ached. "No problem. Hey, you want to slip away together for a few?"

I tried to look at his face as I talked, but my gaze kept drifting lower, to the pulsing vein on his neck that throbbed as he took another gulp.

Lance set down his glass and grinned at me. "I thought you'd never ask. Let's go." He scooted closer. I grinned back and moved to ask Trevor to let us out.

I hadn't thought Lin and Stephen had been paying attention to us, but they broke apart and Stephan grabbed Lance's arm. "No, he's not for you," Stephen snapped.

"He's for Trevor. You need to practice hunting," Lin said, settling back against Stephan's chest.

Lance pouted. "He's not interested."

"I told you I like girls, Lin." Trevor waved across the room and stood. "And my meal just got here. I'll see you all later." Trever stood and trotted away to meet the girl who'd been outside smoking when we came in.

"Lin, I'm so thirsty. Haven't you ever heard the phrase, 'Don't shop hungry'?" I swallowed and licked my lips as Lance leaned close to me. I could see the outline of his veins under his skin beating in time with his heartbeat.

"No." Lin gave me a sideways glance and an evil smile. "The point of this exercise is to practice your control."

"I thought it was so you could teach me how to hunt."

Lin let out a low laugh. "If you're so thirsty, why not drink your beer?"

"Lin, that's probably not a good—" Stephen began as I took a sip.

Lin smacked his chest with the back of her hand. "Shush."

The beer sloshed around in my cup, its malty scent making me wrinkle my nose as I lifted it to my mouth and took a swig. I gagged at the taste. It was so nasty I couldn't even get myself to swallow and, coughing and sputtering, I spit beer all over the table and my lap. Even then I couldn't get the taste out of my mouth and continued to dry heave hunched over. Lance started pounding me on the back like I was choking until I managed to wave him away.

I sat back up, still coughing, to see Lin doubled over in silent laughter, tears spilling down her face.

"That was vile." I wanted to stick out my tongue and scrape at it to try to get the taste out of my mouth, except I didn't want to give Lin further ammunition to laugh at me. I shoved my pint of beer away.

Wait. I remembered the way my favorite flavor of Gatorade had tasted rotten, just like the beer. A scowl spread across my face as I slid out of the booth. I stomped away, using my anger like a mask to try to hide the tears I felt threatening behind my eyes.

I headed towards the back hall, where I'd seen a sign for the restrooms. My stomach roiled. I didn't feel like I was going to throw up, but I wanted a moment of privacy.

The swinging door to the men's room banged against the wall at my touch. I winced; I hadn't meant to shove it quite that hard. A man stood at the urinals and he looked around at the loud thud. I fled past him into one of the two empty stalls and slammed the door behind me. Leaning back on the door, I bent over and put my hands over my face, letting the tears start to fall. I missed Jack. I missed the sun. And I missed being able to do normal human things like having a beer with friends. Not that I considered Lin or Trevor friends, but maybe, hopefully, eventually I would, or this was going to be a long few years.

A pounding fist on the door of my stall, vibrating the door against my back, brought me back to myself. I wiped my sleeve across my face and turned around to open it. The man from the urinals was there, giving me a sympathetic frown.

My mouth went dry at how close he was. The warmth of his breath on my face.

"Hey, you okay?" He was short and pale, wearing an expensive-brand button-down and a lot of large, tacky gold jewelry. Flaunting new wealth.

Because of the lingering chance of tears, and the fact that if I opened my mouth I knew I wouldn't be able to stop my fangs from coming out, I just nodded.

"You must have been really out of it, miss. You came into the wrong bathroom. This is the men's room."

"I'm a guy," I snapped, glaring at him. As I'd feared, my fangs popped out, slurring my words.

The man let out a disbelieving laugh, his eyes widening. I saw red. Before I could think too hard about it, I grabbed the man by the front of his shirt and yanked him into the stall with me. I used my hip to swing the door shut while I pressed the man up against the side of the stall. He let out a startled cry and tried to push away, but with my vampire strength he was no match for me. I shoved him back and to the side, so that he fell into a sitting position on the toilet seat. I let myself be pulled along with him and tumbled into his lap, embracing him like a lover.

Mouth hovering over the pulse of his neck, I took a brief moment to breath in the scent of him and bask in it before sinking my teeth into the side of his neck. I moaned as the taste of the blood danced along my tongue, driving away the last remnants of the sour beer. Despite Lin's failure tonight, she had at least given me a few tips on the drive over—ways to time how long I should feed so I didn't take too much from my victim. But with the man's pulse pounding against my cheek, and my head swimming with the overwhelming taste of the blood, I lost track of time almost immediately.

The squeak of the swinging door to the men's room brought me back to myself. When I retracted my fangs and sat back up, the man was unconscious. The stall door had swung open behind me and was resting against my back. The stall was so tiny that meant only a small gap was left between the door and the frame, not enough that whoever had come in could see into the stall, but still I mentally cursed at myself for being so careless as to not make sure the door was latched before feeding.

His eyelids fluttered and he slumped back as I climbed backwards off of him, licking my lips, pressing the door closed with my body. Crossing my arms, I frowned as I regarded my meal. It didn't feel right leaving him here.

A shadow darkened the gap at the bottom of the stall as whoever had come in took up position at one of the urinals next to the stall. A belt buckle rattled, then a zipper unzipped, and finally water splashed on the porcelain. Of the entire line of four urinals in here, he'd chosen the one closest to the stall.

I looked at the shadow, then at my feet and the feet of my victim clearly visible to anyone outside, and remembered where I'd been when the person had entered the bathroom, and how long it had taken them to travel from the door to the urinal—a distance of less than a few paces. Great. They probably thought we were in here getting it on. I suppressed a sigh. Better than them knowing the truth, but still, I didn't want to get banned on my first visit here.

I bent down and pulled my victim's arm around my shoulder, holding it in place with one hand and using my other arm to lift him up. Not bad. Probably looked like I was helping a drunk friend walk. The effects of vampire venom did look a lot like intoxication. As I hoisted him to his feet, the jostling woke him up enough that he blearily opened his eyes and began shuffling his feet as I dragged him out of the stall.

Ignoring the man at the urinal, I "helped" my victim out of the bathroom and down the hall back into the bar's main room. Lin, Stephen, and Lance were still at the booth—Lin and Stephen back to making out while it looked like Lance well on his way to drinking the entire contents of the bar, judging by the empty mugs scattered across the table.

"Lin," I hissed as I half-carried, half-dragged my victim up to the booth. "Lin!"

Only when Lin pulled away, licking her lips, and Stephen pressed a napkin to the side of his neck did I realize that she'd been feeding on him, not kissing him as I'd thought. It was impressive, actually.

She smiled at me as I reached the booth, her lips red and her cheeks flush. "See, that wasn't so hard, was it?"

I stopped and blinked at her, then glanced over at the man I carried. Blood trickled down his neck from two needle-like puncture wounds on his throat. Surprisingly little blood. Hopefully because the bite was so small, and not because he didn't have enough left to bleed. She was right though. I'd been so worried about not being able to flirt with a victim, or being able to lure them away from the crowd. Yet it had taken me less than a minute after leaving the table to find a meal. "I guess not," I admitted.

I pushed my victim onto the booth seat. He blinked at me and said something in a slurry mumble that I didn't catch.

Lin pulled a square bandage out of her purse and slid it across the table at me. "Put that on his neck. Good idea to keep these in your pur—" She eyed me. "Wallet, or whatever."

"Thanks." I opened the bandage and stuck the thing on his neck over my bite marks. It was one of those clear, invisible bandages. Once I stuck it on you could barely see it against his skin.

I licked my lips. Biting the man had helped, but I still felt thirsty.

A woman wearing tight-fitting jeans and lots of jewelry came over to our table. "Gregory, do you know these people?" Her gaze was fixed on the man I had carried out of the restroom. I stood up and offered her my hand.

"No, actually. I'm Evan. I found him passed out drunk in the restroom. I helped him out, but he's too drunk to talk."

Frowning, the woman ignored my hand and sat down next to Gregory. Blinking, Gregory mumbled something and slumped over into her lap.

"I don't understand," the woman said, running her hand through his short-cropped hair. "He'd only had one beer so far." Shrugging helplessly, I turned to Lin.

"Some men just can't handle their alcohol." Lin gave an airy smile and waved her hand dismissively. For all her sink or swim teaching methods, I had to give Lin props for having my back.

Gregory's wife, judging by the gigantic, gaudy diamond on her ring finger, shook her head in disbelief then grabbed Gregory by the shoulder. "Wake up, Hon. You're plastered. Let's go home."

Gregory snorted awake and the woman helped him sit up.

Shit, I needed to get his contact info. Vampire venom could be very addictive. One bite might not be enough to get a victim addicted, but it had before—with Kevin, the former dirty cop who'd worked for the woman who'd been trying to kill me. One bite had been enough to get him to change sides, willing to risk his life in order to help me. I realized I'd forgotten to ask Jack about how Kevin was doing. I hadn't seen him since that night in the park.

"Let me help you out to the car," I said, reaching to grab Gregory's other arm as he slid out of the booth after the woman.

"No!" The woman slapped my hand away. "You've done enough." She draped Gregory's arm around her shoulders, much as I had done, and started helping him towards the door. I trailed a few steps after them, trying to figure out excuse to ask for their number.

The woman glanced back at me with a frown. When she reached the door, she stopped in front of the bouncer who sat on a stool just inside the door, and whispered something to him. The bouncer moved between me and the woman. I watched helplessly as the woman and Gregory stumbled out the door together. Shit.

"Lin, I messed up. I didn't get his contact info," I said with a shake of my head as I slid back into the booth next to Lance.

Lin sighed. "You need to work on your technique. What happens if he gets addicted?"

I groaned. "I know. I get the feeling that I came off as creepy serial killer. And I know, I know. I've seen it before. Maybe I can leave a note with the bartender, in case he comes back looking for me."

"Good idea. Bartender's one of ours."

I stared at her, mouth dropping open. "The bartender's a vampire?"

Lin nodded. "One of the reasons I picked this bar for your first hunt. In fact, most of the local supernaturals frequent this place because of that. I don't see anyone else in here tonight, but before we leave I'll introduce you to the bartender, at least."

"That'd be nice." It would. So far I only knew Lin, Trevor, and Stacy. Of the three, none of them really seemed to like me. I licked my lips and eyed Lance. My mouth and throat weren't as dry as they had been, but I still wanted more. "Anyway, I'm still really thirsty."

Lin looked at me with disbelief, her eyes widening. "Are you kidding? You almost took too much from that guy, yet you're still thirsty?" I nodded.

Lin frowned, her eyebrows coming together. She didn't answer right away. Her gaze flicked down to the table in thought. Finally she glanced back up at me, and then over at Lance, who was halfway through his fifth beer. "As long as he still wants to, I guess. Knock yourself out." "Heck yes." Lance thrust his arm at me across the table.

Lin shook her head. "Not there. And don't try to duck under the table to bite him. That looks like something else entirely, and I don't want to get kicked out."

I snorted at that and shook my head. "I'm not that dumb, Lin."

"You wanted instruction, I'm giving you instruction." Lin glared at me.

"Okay, okay. I'm sorry." I put my hands up a gesture of surrender. "What do you recommend, oh wise teacher?"

Lin rolled her eyes. "Don't get cute, Evan." She tapped her throat. "Make out, then turn it into something else. Like what I did with—"

"I have a boyfriend," I said, cutting her off, my voice probably a bit harsher and louder than I should have and my cheeks flaming.

"So do I." Lin jerked a thumb at Stephen. "I do this all the time, with all sorts of men. Stephen doesn't mind. It's not cheating—just misdirection."

Stephen's tight expression, lips pressed together into a thin line at her words, told another story. I shifted uncomfortably. Still felt like cheating to me.

Lin huffed and crossed her arms. "Look. I've been around a while. I know you don't believe me, but I'm trying to help you. Take my advice or not, but I'm just trying to help you from making the same mistakes that I did." With that, Lin stood and pulled Stephen out of the booth with her. They made their way over to one of the pool tables and began setting up a game.

That left me and Lance alone together at the booth. Lance scooted towards me and put a hand on my leg. I pushed his hand off with maybe a bit more force than necessary. "Look, Lance. I'll bite you, but don't make this more than it is."

Lance shrugged and leaned down towards me for kiss. I licked my dry lips, concentrating to make sure my fangs stayed up as I tilted my head back to meet his mouth with mine. He was so warm underneath me I couldn't keep my fangs up, but if anything my fangs pricking his lips made Lance even more excited. He moaned into my mouth and wrapped an arm around my back, pulling my closer. I didn't like how much he was touching me, but my thirst kept me from cutting off the kiss or pulling away. Lance pulled away for air, so I took the opportunity to move my mouth down to his jaw. Lance obliged me by throwing his head back with a low moan.

I sank my fangs in and drank deeply for several moments. Lance shuddered underneath me, clearly enjoying himself. My hand on his pants felt something hard pressed against it. Enjoying himself way too much.

The gold amulet on my chest, which I'd kept hidden under my shirt since the sight seemed to make the other vampires uncomfortable, seemed warmer than it had been, enough to draw my attention to it even with the delicious taste of the blood dancing on my tongue. Each person had their own unique taste that I didn't have the words to describe. Biting two people in such quick succession just highlighted it. The last of Gregory's taste in my mouth was quickly replaced with the taste of Lance.

In my initial bliss I forgot to count seconds, but I figured it had been long enough. I pulled away, licking at the few drops that came out after I retracted my fangs.

Lance's blood had helped, but as I scooted back away from him, my throat still felt dry and my fangs still ached to bite into something else. Like Gregory, Lance tasted just fine. Yet, I craved something else.

He sunk back into the plush bench with a contented sigh, pressing a napkin against his neck where I'd bit him. Lin and Stephen returned, each carrying two glasses of water. Stephen slid into the booth next to Lance, and had to nudge Lance before he opened his eyes and took the glass of water.

Lin, rather than sitting back down next to Stephen, took a seat next to me and slid her second water down the table to sit it in front of me.

"Something the matter?" Lin turned sideways in the booth to regard me. She tucked her leg up on the bench, which pulled up her skirt to almost indecent heights, but she didn't seem to notice. But as she'd pointed out, she was old, and I guessed the move was calculated to distract me. Or throw me off balance.

I was determined not to let her get to me, and instead picked up the glass of water, focusing my attention on it as I tilted it around so that the water sloshed against the sides as I spoke. I twisted the glass around in a circle, enjoying the little wet ring it made on the coaster. "I still want to bite something. They took the edge off, but it's like there was something missing." I shook my head, unable to articulate just what it was that was missing from their blood, and instead took a sip of the water to cover my discomfort.

Lin tapped her own glass with a manicured fingernail in thought. "Some bloodlines get cravings for specific thing, or person or type of person," she said slowly. "Perhaps yours does as well."

"So I just have to feel this thirsty until I figure out what I'm craving?" I stared down morosely into my glass of water.

Lin gave me a sympathetic look and nodded. "Afraid so. Best I can tell you is to try to remember who you bit previously that satisfied you the most, and start there. Think about it, and when we go out tomorrow night we can look for someone specific."

I sighed. "Thanks, Lin. I'll try."

CHAPTER 3

CRAVING VAMPIRES

BACK AT THE HOUSE, we all went our separate ways. I took the banker's box that Jack had left for me up to my room to go through it. Underneath the stuffed tiger, which I put in a place of honor on my nightstand, was a sealed envelope with my name on it.

I popped the seal on the envelope and pulled out the paper inside. It was a letter from Jack.

"Everett, or I guess I should say Evan now? I talked Stacy into letting me do the supply runs up to the house from now on, so I should be able to see you at least every few weeks. She's even going to talk to Lin about us having a date night for two. In the meantime, I got you a few toys to keep you occupied."

I stopped reading and lowered the letter, my eyebrows pulling together in confusion.

Toys?

Discarding the letter on the bed, I dug into the banker's box. The letter had been sitting on a plain brown paper bag that had pink crepe paper stuffed into the top. I took out the paper bag intending to open it, but then I squealed in delight at what its removal revealed underneath.

Forgetting about the bag, I discarded it unexamined on the bed to pull out the Playstation Vita system box. I hugged it to my chest, excited by the prospect of being able to play games during the long hours of the day when I couldn't sleep. Maybe I could ask him for an e-reader next.

I still hadn't gotten up the courage to ask Lin about what happened to her and Trevor at daylight. But, when I was pacing restlessly around my room during the last week, I hadn't heard a peep or any sign of activity or movement from the other upstairs rooms where Lin and Trevor slept. I knew by now not to rely on the movies, but I still couldn't help but wonder if the other vampires lost consciousness as soon as the sun went up. The lack of sound from the rest of the house seemed to back that up.

Grinning wide, I set the Vita box aside and picked the letter back up.

> "I don't know if you play games, but I know while we were at the safe house you mentioned being bored during the day. I also got to a few games I thought you might like, but if you want something specific or need anything else tell me the next time I drop supplies off and I'll try and get it for you.
>
> Love, Jack
>
> PS, I've already friended my profile on the system."

Friended? Why would that matter? It wasn't as if Lin would let me get online. New vampires were kept in isolation after being changed, a rule I'd been told existed to keep new vampires from revealing they were still alive to old loved ones, as well as to give them time to adjust to their new existence without outside interference.

I stared down at the letter, frowning. Was Jack trying to tell me something secretly, suspecting that Lin might read the letter as well? A valid fear. I read the letter again, slower, but nothing jumped out.

While I thought about it, I unpacked the Vita from its box. I put the charger on my dresser, but on a whim I tried to turn it on right away. The screen flashed on right away to show a full battery. Jack had already charged it and downloaded a bunch of games, which was why I hadn't seen any game cases. I went to friends to see he'd already set up a profile for me, and as he said, already friended me.

I went to settings and searched for an open Wi-Fi connection, hoping to get lucky, but the only one that showed up belonged to the house and was password-protected. The house was in the middle of the woods, surrounded by trees on all sides, several miles down a dead-end road, so it wasn't so surprising that there were no other Wi-Fi signals. I sighed and plugged the Vita in to charge.

Turning back around, I caught sight of the brown bag I'd abandoned. I sat down and picked it up, placing it on my lap. I tossed away the pink crepe paper, to reveal... a brand new dildo and fascination sleeve. Startled, I cried out, my face feeling like it was on fire.

The door to my bedroom squeaked as it began to open. Hands shaking, I dropped the bag between my knees and kicked it under the bed with my heel.

Lin stood in my doorway, her hand still on the knob. "Everything okay in here?"

My face was still blazing, but I swallowed and tried to play it cool. I nodded. "Yes, just going through the presents Jack got me, and one of them startled me, that's all."

"Oh." Lin's eyes roved over the empty Vita box and letter discarded on my bed. "It's almost sunrise, so get all this cleaned up and get ready for bed."

"Alright." I started picking up the garbage under Lin's watchful eye. While I cleaned, she walked over to my dresser and picked up the Vita.

She turned it over in her hands, clearly baffled. She ended up holding it backwards and upside down. "What is it?"

"It's a game system." I threw the garbage away and joined her by the dresser. "Here." I placed her hands on the sides so the screen faced her and pressed the power button to turn it on. "See?" I touched a finger to a random icon to start a game.

"It's not a phone? It looks like one." She tilted her head and wrinkled her brow as she examined it.

"Nope, just games. Ask Trevor."

"I will." She raised her voice and yelled, "Trevor!"

A moment later, Trevor's door opened and he stepped out into the hall. "Yeah?" He was shirtless and barefoot, revealing a large tattoo of a pirate ship across his chest. He was actually pretty adorable, in a skinny guy grunge kinda way.

She held up my Vita in one hand towards him. "What's this?"

"Oh, cool!" Trevor came in and took it from her. I tried to quell my rising anger at them all handling my present from Jack. I took a deep breath and counted to ten.

"What is it?" Lin repeated as Trevor pressed the home button and began scrolling through my games.

"Oh." He glanced up briefly. "You play games on it. Where'd it come from anyway?"

"Jack gave it to Evan." Lin bobbed her head my direction. "Can you use it as a phone too?"

"No." Trevor shook his head and reluctantly handed the Vita back to Lin when she held out her hand for it. "You can send messages on it, but only if you get online, which he can't without the Wi-Fi password."

"Technology changes so fast lately," Lin said, looking down in awe at the machine. "I only understood about half of what you said. But it doesn't break the rules, if I understand you correctly, right?"

"Right," Trevor confirmed. He looked at me. "Can I play it sometime?"

"Sure. I'll make you a profile." I grinned as Lin handed the Vita to me.

"What else did he get you?" Lin asked abruptly.

"Well, you saw the tiger already..." I trailed off as she stalked across the room, knelt, and pulled out the bag I'd stashed under the bed. "Don't—"

Still kneeling on the floor, she cut me off with a glare. I shut up, my face heating up again as she pulled it open and peered inside.

Lin gasped and stiffened. I bent over the bed, grabbing for the bag, but Lin managed to shake herself out of shock enough to pull it from my grasp. She upended it onto the bed, sending the sleeve, dildo, mini-bullet vibrator and its wireless controller, and a large tube of lube tumbling across the bed.

"What the hell?" Trevor half-yelled, half-laughed, picking up the bullet vibe.

"That's mine," I snapped, grabbing it from him, or at least trying to. Trevor was a lot taller than me and held it up out of my reach. Scowling, I pointed at the door. "Both of you, out!"

Lin got to her feet, still staring down at the toys strewn across my bed. She waved a hand across the bed, looking up at me. "No, first we are going to talk about this. Jack gave you these?"

"Yes, why?" I crossed my arms and shifted from foot to foot. This was not the conversation I wanted to have right now. I was still struggling my feeling of thirst. "You sound very...accusatory. There's nothing wrong with my boyfriend giving me a few sex toys."

"That's not the problem. It's..." Lin made little circles in the air. "These toys are for women."

Now my ears were getting hot too. "People with vulvas," I muttered.

"Whatever." Lin rolled her eyes. "That still doesn't explain why he gave them to you."

I sighed. I'd been hoping to go stealth here. Looks like the cat was out of the bag. Still, I couldn't look at Trevor or Lin as I spoke. "Yes, it does. I'm trans."

I risked a glance up at the two of them. Lin and Trevor were both staring at me with open mouths.

"Wait, you mean..." Trevor furrowed his brow. "I don't know what that means. You look like a guy... Are you saying you want to be a girl? Cause, no offense, I think you'd make a really ugly girl."

"What?" I whirled to glare at Trevor, balling my hands into fists. "No. Look, I was assigned female at birth, but I transitioned." I huffed and shook out my hands, turning my back on Trevor to try to keep myself from strangling him.

Trevor made a strangled noise. "You mean you don't have a p—"

"Shut up!" I whirled back around and pointed at the door. "Get out of my room, now."

"Evan—" Lin started.

"Don't call me that!" I yelled. "Get out, all of you."

"We need to talk about this," Lin said, putting a hand on the side of my arm.

"No, we don't." I shook her off, and stalked around the bed to where Lin had just been and crossed my arms.

"Fine, we'll leave," Lin said. There was a pause, and the sound of rustling and feet on carpet.

"I'm going, I'm going," Trevor said. "Here's your thing back."

My door creaked, but didn't click shut. Lin spoke. "I'm sorry, I didn't know. I didn't mean to out you like that to Trevor."

I kept my arms crossed and didn't say anything. My door creaked again and clicked shut.

I WOKE UP AFTER dark to Lin pounding on my door. Shaking off the lingering effects of my dreams containing Gregory's and Lance's memories, I opened my eyes. I enjoyed being a cis-guy, if only in my literal dreams, although it always made me feel even more aware of what I was missing while awake. The dreams had been random snippets of memories, bouncing back and forth between the two men, which had been a bit disconcerting.

I struggled out from under my covers and answered the door. Lin had already dressed. Her clothes were more casual than last night, jeans and a T-shirt, and she'd pulled her long hair back into a ponytail with a ribbon. "Living room in ten. We need to talk about where we're going to go hunting tonight."

Her eyes went to my chest. I'd gone to sleep without a shirt on, and it hung free on my chest, glittering in the light coming in from the hall. I put a hand over it protectively.

"I'll dress and be right there," I told her before shutting the door. At least I tried to. Lin held up her hand and stopped it.

Although I was still angry at Lin about last night, I tried to keep my expression neutral. "Is there something else?"

Lin bit her lip for a moment before speaking. "I just want to apologize for last night. I didn't know."

My shoulders slumped. "It's my fault. I asked Stacy not to tell you. I wanted to be stealth." I paused. She might not know what that meant. "Um, that means I didn't want people to know I was trans."

"I know what it means." Lin cocked her hip. "I've been around a long time, and trans people are not new. It doesn't bother me."

"Thanks." I offered her a wan smile. "And for the record, I didn't know Jack was going to give me those."

"Noted." One edge of her lip twitched. "You'll have to give me a review of that dildo."

"Not gonna happen, Lin," I said in a sing-song as I finished shutting the door in her face.

Through the door I heard Lin laugh, so I guessed there were no hard feelings.

Truth was, I was a bit disappointed, but not with Lin. I'd only been on testosterone two years, which was why a lot of people, like the bartender, thought I was a teenager when I passed. The longer on T, the more you looked your own age as a guy, just like a teenager going through puberty. But when I'd asked Stacy about getting my T prescription refilled, she told me I could, but it wouldn't do anything. My appearance was set now. Twenty-five yet perpetually a teenager.

I threw on a casual outfit—T-shirt, jeans, and a hoodie—before heading downstairs. My mouth felt like sandpaper and my throat scratchy, like when I'd been human and had a cold. So thirsty.

When I got downstairs, Trevor and Lin were both already in the living room waiting for me.

Lin began talking before I even finished sitting down on the couch. "Evan, have you thought about what I asked you yesterday, about what you might be craving?"

Honestly, that question had been the last thing on my mind after last night's pre-dawn drama. I shifted on the couch and stared at my knees, face drawn in thought.

The windows in the living room were opened, and the thick black sun blocking curtains had been tied back to let the warm summer evening breeze blow through the house. Trevor sat on the other side of the couch, closer to the windows. I took a deep breath as I thought. His scent came to me on the breeze and the moment it hit me, my fangs wanted to come down. I had to clench my jaw to keep them up, but I couldn't stop myself from turning to stare at Trevor.

Out of the corner of my eye, I saw Lin raise her eyebrows. "Is something wrong?"

"Sitting next to Trevor is making me thirsty." I licked my lips, unable to take my eyes off Trevor's throat, although I was able to tear my gaze away long enough to at least glance at Lin as I started speaking.

Lin and Trevor both stared at me. Finally Lin, with a deep frown on her face asked, "Why?"

"What do you mean, why?" I was so thirsty it was hard to think. I leaned closer to Trevor, inhaling deeply. His rich, spicy scent made me flutter with ecstasy and my fangs came down. "Because he smells delicious, that's why."

He didn't have the burning warmth like Gregory and Lance from last night. If they'd been a campfire, Trevor's draw was more like that of banked coals. Where the campfire was almost too hot, the coals' subtle heat invited you to drift closer, the warmth enveloping me like a blanket.

"Shit," Lin spat out, all the color draining from her face.

Trevor recoiled from me, scrambling over to the opposite side of the couch as far from me as he could get. His sudden movement had me lunging after him before I could think. Chasing him across the room, the amulet burning against my chest, I couldn't think about anything else except sinking my teeth into Trevor's neck.

Lin flashed across the room, her fist cocked back, and cracked me across the face. I went twirling backwards, landing face first down on the couch. The edge of the couch pressed into my stomach, my knees and legs splayed behind me on the carpet. It hadn't hurt, but the shock of it was enough to bring me back to myself.

Groaning, I pulled myself up onto the couch into a sitting position, putting my hands over my face so I didn't have to see Lin and Trevor's expressions. "Shit, I'm sorry. He ran and I just... reacted." I slumped, sliding down into the couch and pulling my knees to my chest.

Lin sighed. "Guess that answers my question."

"What? How?" Trevor growled. "Why did he chase me and why did he say I smelled delicious? Vampires can't drink from other vampires."

"I'm different," I mumbled through my hands. A shudder racked me and my stomach twisted. Another secret out. I was feeling very alone. I'd cried myself to sleep last night, and today was already looking worse. All I wanted to do was sink into Jack's arms and have him hold me.

Lin nodded. "I'm not taking you hunting for vampires."

"So then, what are we going to do?" I wiped a stray tear away, or maybe more than one, and pushed myself up. I wrapped my arms around my knees and kept my eyes downcast, licking my lips again. My mouth felt like sandpaper. "Maybe I can bite you or Trevor then."

Lin and Trevor stood on the far side of the living room near the windows. Trevor was almost hiding behind her. Lin scowled and tugged on her ponytail, then pointed at me. "You stay right there. I need to call Stacy." She stalked out of the room, pulling an old flip phone out of her pocket as she went.

Trevor shot me a panicked look and dashed after her. "Lin, don't leave me alone with him!"

I stayed where I was, trying not to cry, while Lin talked to someone on the phone in the kitchen. Finally I heard her phone click closed, and then she and Trevor came back into the room. Lin did not look happy, judging from the deep scowl she wore.

"Stacy agrees with you." She paused and looked at Trevor then back at me. "She thinks Trevor or I should feed you."

Trevor stayed standing in the foyer, looking uncomfortable with his arms wrapped around his stomach and his shoulders hunched. Lin began pacing back and forth at the entrance to the living room.

I shrugged. "So what's the big deal? What's your objection to feeding me?"

Lin's pacing was making me jumpy—not a good combination with how thirsty I was. Vampires were predators, and every time she turned her back on me I had to restrain myself from striking out at her, like I had earlier with Trevor.

"I mean, you'd already know it won't kill me," I continued.

Lin stopped her pacing and wrinkled her nose while looking at me. "Just the thought of it makes me feel like prey. I've been the predator going after prey for so long." She shook her head. "Just no."

I shifted my attention to Trevor. "What about you?"

Trevor frowned over at me. "I do kind of miss the euphoria of being bitten, but your venom wouldn't give me that."

I grinned. "Actually, it would. When I bit Stacy before—"

Lin reeled backwards. "You bit Stacy?" She gasped and put a hand over her heart.

I shifted on the couch, wondering why that was such a big deal. "Yeah, and like I was trying to say, she was slurring her words and stumbling around like she was drunk. It reminded me of what happens to the humans I bite."

Trevor looked thoughtful at that, but Lin looked even more horrified. "You can bite me," Trevor said.

"Absolutely not." Lin thrust out her hands palm up. "I'm responsible for Trevor, and if anything happens it will be on my head."

"You're responsible for me too," I pointed out. "And if I don't figure this out soon, I don't know how much longer I can keep control." As if to emphasize my point, my fangs came down unbidden. I concentrated for a moment to bring them back up.

· Lin crossed her arms and huffed. "Fine. I'll feed you." I perked up at this, but she kept speaking, giving me a hard look. "On my terms." She turned on her heel and stalked towards the kitchen.

I jumped to my feet, eager to get started, and followed Lin.

While vampires didn't need to eat, our visitors did. Plus, it made the house more believable that actual humans lived here to have a kitchen fully stocked with the usual tools: pots, pans, utensils, knives, plates, cups, and all the rest.

Lin had me stand by the center island while she went over to the butcher block and pulled out a large carving knife, pointing at Trevor with the tip of the knife. "Trevor, go upstairs. I'll call you when you can come down."

"But—"

"Go, and lock the door. If he—" She waved the knife in my direction. "—frenzies, I don't want to have to protect you."

Trevor had a stare down with her for a moment before throwing up his hands. "Alright, alright. I'm going." He left and the stairs creaked as he went upstairs.

Trevor gone, Lin set the knife down on the island block and went over to the cupboards. She got out one of the glass tumblers that we kept for guests, and placed it next to the knife. I could see where she was going with this and stifled my disappointment. I craved to sink my teeth into something, but I wasn't going to argue with her if this is how she wanted to give me blood.

Lin stood opposite me, leaving the kitchen island between us as a kind of buffer, I guessed. As she picked up the knife, I grabbed the edge of the counter to stop the trembling in my hands, but I couldn't stop my fangs from coming down again when she put the knife against her arm.

I tensed as she pulled the knife crossed her forearm, and the sickly sweet scent of vampire blood filled the room. I moaned, my eyes fixed on her arm, and only by locking all my muscles did I keep myself from lunging across the island at her.

Only a few drops of blood fell into the tumbler before her wound closed over. She slashed again. The marble counter top cracked under my hands as I fought to stay still. My fangs cut into my lower lip, but I barely felt it; my eyes were locked on the blood rolling down the edge of the knife and into the tumbler. Lin had to cut herself over and over again, her arm healing almost too fast for the blood to come out.

After what felt like an eternity, Lin stopped cutting and used her hand not holding the knife to push the glass across to me. It was only half full, but I wasn't going to complain.

I snatched it up and downed it in less than a gulp. I shuddered at the taste, how cold it was, but still I wished there was more. Despite how little had been in the glass, I felt less thirsty than I had after eating two people.

My eyes were half-lidded with pleasure as I ran my tongue around the inside of my mouth to get every droplet of flavor. Lin's blood had so much more complexity and depth than Gregory's or Lance's. It satisfied me in a way that the humans' blood never did.

Without thinking about it, my left hand went into the collar of my shirt and grabbed the chain for my amulet, pulling it over my head with one smooth motion. I dropped the amulet into the empty tumbler.

The tumbler let out a hiss and exploded, sending shards of glass flying.

"Evan, what did you do?" Lin yelled, ducking and backing away from the island until she hit the kitchen counter by the fridge. Her fangs were down, her eyes glowed red, and her lips were pealed back in a snarl.

"I don't know," I said, picking glass shards out of my arm while staring down at the amulet lying on the marble. The area around the amulet was blackened and cracked, and black smoke curled up from the area.

I vaguely remembered the action of taking off my amulet, but not of willing myself to do that. It had been like my arm moved of its own volition.

I blinked down at the amulet and then looked back up at Lin. She hadn't moved, and her eyes were locked on my amulet. "Get that thing away from me."

"I—"

"NOW!" Lin screamed.

I rolled my eyes and picked up the amulet by its chain to drape it back over my neck. After a moment's hesitation I reached down to touch the face of the amulet, running my fingertips over the stylized vampire fangs of the face, but yanked my hands back almost immediately. It had felt like the fangs had stung me. I turned and fled upstairs to my room.

Chapter 4

The Basement

THERE WAS A SOFT knock at my door. I took the pillow off my face and sat up, putting my legs off the side of the bed to face the door.

"Come in," I groaned, hunching my shoulders and staring down at my dangling legs. I saw the amulet flashing and quickly stuffed it down my shirt as the door began to open.

Lin stuck her head in. "How are you feeling?"

Frowning, I straightened to blink up at her. "I'm fine. It's done something similar before when it came in contact with vampire blood. I shouldn't have done that. I honestly don't know what came over me."

"About that." Lin stepped fully inside and shut the door behind her. "Could you really not feel the..." Lin twirled her hands, clearly searching for the right word. "...darkness emanating from it?"

I shook my head, my mind whirling. Darkness? More like heat.

"Usually it's low-grade," Lin came over, turning my desk chair to face me then sitting down. "It's better when we can't see it, but even now I can still feel it. Why do you think Trevor and I have been avoiding you as much as possible?"

I regarded her warily. "I thought you were mad at me for taking your boyfriend's spot."

"Well, yes." Lin folded her hands in her lap. "But that feeling swirling around you all the time certainly isn't helping things. Have you considered giving the amulet over to the council?"

I ran my free hand through my hair, trying to decide how to describe it. "I can't, Lin. Without it, it's hard to think. I..." I trailed off and fell silent and bit my lip, remembering.

Lin nodded for me to go on, giving me an encouraging smile.

"That's when I bit Stacy. Everyone around me looked like a meal, and all I could think about was getting it back." My eyes lost focus as I remembered.

Lin said in a soft voice, one corner of her lip turned down into half a frown, "That sounds a lot like what everyone goes through when they first turn."

"It does?" My eyes snapped back into focus and I looked at Lin.

Lin sighed. "Yes. I wish you had more experience with vampires. Have you been in the basement yet?"

I let out a short laugh at the abrupt change of topic. "This house doesn't have a basement." I should know; I'd spent the last week exploring every nook and cranny of the two-story farmhouse. Except of course for Lin and Trevor's bedrooms, but they were both on the second floor. I knew where every door on the main floor led.

"It does, and if you have another incident like earlier tonight, where you go after me or Trevor, you'll get an up-close look at it." Lin stood, smoothing out her shirt carefully, and then left my room without another word.

Scowling, I pulled the amulet off and dumped it in the drawer of my nightstand, but left the drawer open. I could see it there, I told myself. My anxiety spiked as I stepped away to sit on the bed. I locked my eyes on it and told myself it was fine, I could pick it up again whenever I wanted.

The voice pipped up in the back of my head. "Mine."

I stared at the amulet, getting a sinking feeling in my stomach. The feeling of possessiveness came along with the word, and I'd attributed it to the amulet. I began to think I'd misunderstood. What if it wasn't telling me that the amulet was mine? What if it was talking to me? Telling me that I belonged to it? I shivered.

So thirsty. I licked my lips. I'd been hiding upstairs since the incident with the cup. Lin's blood had helped with my craving for vampire blood, but hadn't been enough to satisfy me. I kind of wanted to go downstairs and warm up a bag of blood, but I also didn't want to see either Lin or Trevor right now. It was almost dawn anyway, so instead I curled up on the bed with a game, leaving the amulet where it was.

I had a hard time concentrating with the amulet so far away from me, but I wanted to see if I could learn to live without it. Still, I ended up tossing and turning until almost noon, when I gave up and put the amulet back on so I could sleep.

THE NEXT NIGHT WHEN I woke up from dreams of Lin's memories-snippets from her last trip to China. Wouldn't it be fun if I could speak Chinese now, like her? In the dream I understood it, but probably because it was Lin's memory. I stayed holed up in my room, alternating reading a book and fiddling with my Vita, trying to guess the Wi-Fi password without any success so I could message Jack.

Lin knocked a few hours later, but didn't open the door, instead just speaking through it.

"Staying in tonight. Blood in the freezer." Lin paused. "If you need anything, I'll be in the living room."

I sighed, but tried to keep my warring anger and depression from seeping too much into my voice. "Thanks, Lin."

I looked at the overflowing basket of laundry in the corner of my room, and decided to work on that for the evening. When I took it downstairs to the washer and dryer in the garage, I studiously avoiding looking at Lin or Trevor in the living room.

At one point I heard a knock downstairs on the front door, and voices. I crept down the hall and peered through the banister railing that looked down over the foyer and front door. Lin invited the two men at the door inside, and led them into the living room out of my sight.

My mouth felt dry and I licked my lips in longing. I wished I could order dinner in, and thought about asking Lin if I could call Kevin to see if he could come over.

When I took my next trip down to put my laundry in the dryer, the two men were passed out on the floor, asleep. The sharp tang of blood drew me closer, until Lin stopped me with a glare. She and Trevor were playing chess on the coffee table.

"They can't give any more safely. If you're thirsty there's blood in the freezer," she told me, her voice bland.

"So you said, but—"

Lin cut me off with a slash of her hand and a glare. "No."

I glared right back at her. "C'mon, that stuff is nasty. You two got to eat fresh blood. Let me call Kevin. I've bit him before. I know he'd come."

"Look, no one likes it, but you need to practice your control. Being thirsty is a thing that happens, and you need to be able to deal with it."

Lin moved a white pawn, knocking down one of Trevor's black knights. "Besides, you drank enough for three vampires a few nights ago, and had my blood last night."

I made a face and didn't bother arguing further. Sighing, I went into the kitchen. It was better than nothing, but only barely.

The other thing I hated about it was that when it was all I had to drink, I didn't relive my victim's memories in my dreams. I'd really come to look forward to them, because it could allow me to see and feel the sun.

My next trip down an hour later to get my now-dry clothes, I decided to leave the amulet in my room on my bed. I wanted to see if could make it just five minutes with it out of my sight. Downstairs, the men were gone and the living room empty. As I came back up with my clothing, Trevor came out of his room.

I hefted my basket, resting it on my hip, and moved to the side so that he could pass me in the hall, but instead he stopped in front of me.

"Hey, Trevor." I ducked my head and began edging around him to my room, trying to concentrate on keeping my fangs up. Just seeing him had started the voice in my head, the one that was louder without the dampening of the amulet.

Trevor backed up to his door to let me pass. "Hey, Everett." He paused. "Evan, I mean. Can I borrow your Vita?"

I set down my basket to open my door, then turned to answer him. As I opened my mouth and took a breath to reply, I caught his scent. The spicy tang of him short-circuited my thought process and my fangs came out. I couldn't think of anything but biting him and the voice, quieter now that I was so close to the amulet, was still almost overwhelming. With a growl, I lunged at Trevor's throat.

Trevor fell back with a yell, grabbing my throat with one hand and holding me at arm's length. We both fell over, me on top. I gnashed my jaws, fighting to get to him. I couldn't think of anything else but sinking my teeth into him.

"What's that racket—" Lin threw her door open and froze. "Shit!"

"Lin, help! He's really strong!" Trevor yelled. Even with both hands keeping me at arm's length, I was getting closer to biting him with every second. Only the fact that he was using his legs to keep me in the air, robbing me of leverage, had kept me from already biting him.

Lin flashed down the hall and punched me in the head, snapping my neck to the side hard enough to break it with an audible crunch. I fell limp, unable to move. Trevor tossed me aside and scrambled back. I landed on my back on the carpet, groaning as my body healed.

It hurt. A lot.

While I was lying there twitching, Lin landed on me and flipped me over onto my stomach, pressing my face into the beige carpet with one knee.

"Go open the basement room!" Lin yelled at Trevor.

I screamed as my neck straightened itself back out with another snap. As soon as it did, I could feel the rest of my body again. "Lin, I'm back. I won't attack you anymore."

"Don't care. You were warned," Lin snarled, twisting my arms up painfully high behind my back. "Now up." She stood, pulling me up with her, and began dragging me down the hallway.

"No, Lin, my amulet!" I kicked and writhed in her grip. Being pulled away from it was like torture.

Snarling, Lin stopped and pressed me up face-first against the wall. "You took it off?"

"You said—" Tears pricked my eyes and anxiety closed my throat up. Or maybe it was thirst. I licked my lips, swallowed, and tried again. "I wanted to see if I could live without it."

"Next time check with me before doing something like that, got it?" Lin dragged me back towards my room and up to my bed. She let go of my left hand. "Put it on. I'd do it, but I don't want to touch the nasty thing."

Hand shaking, I picked it up by the chain and stuffed into the pocket of my jeans. As soon as I had it secured, Lin grabbed my wrist and twisted my arm back.

"March."

She pushed me ahead of her down the stairs, through the foyer, and into the kitchen. Trevor waited for us inside the pantry.

I'd opened it once my first day here. The boxes that lined the shelves had clearly been placed there in an attempt to stage the kitchen, but ironically they broke the illusion of this being a lived-in house. Not only were they caked with dust, but the packaging was dated, and some were yellowed with age.

But now, the shelving on the back had been swung backwards to reveal a wooden staircase that led down into darkness. A stench wafted up from below, so strong my stomach lurched and I recoiled, feet sliding on the linoleum as Lin pushed me forward from behind.

As she pushed me down the stairs, the smell strengthened until my eyes began to water.

"How can you stand that smell?" I said, gagging.

"You're a vampire. You don't have to breathe unless you want to." She said softly into my ear, then snorted. "Yuck."

My mouth dropped open and I almost missed the next step. It had never occurred to me to try to stop breathing.

The smell assaulting my nostrils was bad enough that I made a conscious attempt to do what Lin was suggesting. It was hard, however. When I held my breath, my brain screamed at me that I was going to die. Worse, the moment my concentration wavered—which it did quite a few times since the stairs were narrow, old, and rickety—I would find myself breathing again out of habit as I tried to keep my feet.

At the bottom of the stairs, most of the basement had been bricked off, leaving a narrow hallway that ended in a solid steel door. The door was propped open, held there by a thick brick doorstop.

Lin force-marched me forward. The room was dark inside, but enough light leaked in from the hall that with my vampire eyesight, I could still make out what sat in shadow.

A large square drain in the center of the floor had dark-red stains leading to it. Here, the nauseating smell was accompanied by the harsh bite of bleach and other cleaners.

The room was spartan. The only furniture was a bare mattress in the corner, under a pair of restraints bolted into the wall. A toilet sat near the mattress, close enough it looked like the restraints could reach. Shower curtains hung from the ceiling on sliding tracks around the toilet, partially obscuring it. Nothing else was in the room.

The concrete walls, especially around the mattress, were covered with deep gashes clustered in groups of five, like fingernail marks.

With a yell, Lin shoved me inside. I stumbled and landed on my stomach. Before I could scramble to my feet, the steel door slammed shut behind me and locked with a clang that echoed through the entire basement.

CHAPTER 5

BLOOD LIKE WINE

I'D GOTTEN THE CALL to head to New York City while I was on my way back to the office after seeing Everett, and hopped on the last red-eye flight out of Portland. I stifled a yawn behind one hand, waving at the vampire with my other. I hadn't slept on the plane, instead using the time to read up on the two New York victims and the witnesses' accounts.

Two more vampires had gone missing just the night before, and like London, one had turned up dead-drained dry and the other was missing. My guide tonight met me in front of the nightclub, Blood Like Wine where the missing vampires had last been seen.

"Jack Smith," I introduced myself to my guide, holding out my hand. I recognized Birch from their profile picture.

"Jack, welcome. Birch Gorney." Birch had short-cropped hair, and wore a red velvet cloak over a brocade vest, looking like he'd stepped right out of a stereotypical vampire movie. The thing that ruined the look was the Bluetooth earpiece clipped over one ear. He shook my hand firmly, and then waved at the entrance to the nightclub behind him. "Shall we?"

From the outside, I never would have guessed the door led to a bar. It was plain black, halfway down a dirty brick alleyway, with no signs or advertisements to indicate where it led. The walls on either side were covered with layers of graffiti. If the place had any windows, they had been long since bricked over.

Blood Like Wine was a vampire bar. A discrete club that catered mainly to vampires, almost more of a social club than a true bar; Birch had to call in a few favors to even get them to agree to let me inside.

It was early evening still, just after dark, and although the club was technically open, Birch said it didn't usually get a crowd until after midnight at the earliest.

Even though I'd been invited, I still felt a bit of trepidation as I followed Birch inside. Vampires found shapeshifters delicious, and outside of neutral territory like the PCA offices, I'd be considered fair game, even if this was official PCA business.

Inside, I found a tastefully decorated space that reminded me of pictures I'd seen of Victorian gentlemen's clubs. Lots of polished, carved wood and plush furniture. The floor was covered in layers of overlaid rugs, and the bar, which wrapped around the back corner, was made of gleaming marble. An old Victrola set on the bar played a record of some slow ballad in a language I was unfamiliar with. As he'd promised, the place was empty except for two aproned figures behind the bar.

Birch led me over to the bar and popped the needle off the record, abruptly cutting off the wailing lament. Both bartenders froze what they were doing, their heads whipping around to stare at us with red eyes. Birch gave them an easy smile. "Haley." He clapped me on the shoulder. "This is Jack, the PCA investigator working with me."

Haley nodded at the other vampire and he left, going through a swinging door to the back. She gave me a slow once-over as she wiped her hands on a towel, so I returned the favor. She didn't even look old enough to be in a bar, let alone own one. I'd have pegged her as eighteen as most. Under her apron she wore a peasant-style blouse and a loose skirt that swirled around her ankles. She'd been the last one to see the two vampires alive. Finally, she put down the towel and came around the bar to take a seat at one of the small four-person tables. We followed her and sat.

"I'm not sure what else I can tell you," Haley said, relaxing back in the chair. "And believe me, I'd like to help. Dolf and Ada were two of my best customers; they'd been coming here since I founded the place, and they'll be missed."

"Is this the man you saw them talking to?" I pulled out my notebook and flipped to the page where I'd jotted down my thoughts. Birch had interviewed Haley yesterday after they'd found Ada's body, and included the transcript in the file he'd sent me. One thing had jumped out at me: her description of one of the people Dolf and Ada had been talking with before they left the club could have been Kurt, but I needed to be sure. I'd stuck a photo of Kurt there as a bookmark, and now slid it across the table towards Haley.

Haley sat up and leaned forward to study the picture with a frown. After a moment she pushed the photo back towards me. "Yes, that's him. Spoke with a British accent. They left the club with him. As far as I'm aware, it was his first time here."

Birch sat up in alarm when Haley positively identified Kurt. He took the photo and studied it with a frown while I wrote.

"About what time did the three of them leave together?" That had been in Birch's transcript, but it never hurt to double-check.

"Four of them," Haley said. "And around three-thirty, I think?"

I paused in my notetaking and looked up, frowning. "I don't recall a fourth person mentioned in the account you gave Birch yesterday."

Haley rolled her eyes. "A human. Inconsequential."

I laced my fingers together on the table and focused all of my attention on her. "I'll be the judge of that. Describe them."

Haley ignored me, turning to Birch. "Are you kidding me here?"

"Just answer his questions, Haley." Birch slid Kurt's photo back to me.

Haley huffed and slumped in her seat. "A really old woman, a centenarian at least. Skin like dried leather, short. Wore very expensive, designer clothing, and a straight-haired black wig."

I frowned and nodded, noting this down. Very odd. "Do you know what prompted them to leave with Kurt and this old woman?"

"Sure." Haley shrugged and pulled a cigarette out of one of the pockets of her apron, lighting it up as she talked. The smoke drifted my way and I almost gagged at how strong it was. Not a cigarette, but cloves. "Ada came up to get them all drinks. Said the old woman wanted to die being eaten by vampires. Offered to pay them, even."

I let out a laugh of disbelief. "What, really?"

Haley raised one eyebrow at me, white smoke trickling from her nostrils. "Not that farfetched. The modern vampire craze has been great for easy meals."

"Alright." I tapped the end of my pen on my book. "But if she was already with Kurt, why would they need Ada and Dolf?"

Haley glanced at Birch, who nodded in agreement. "You don't know much about vampires, do you?"

I sighed. "I only first shifted a year ago, so I'm still learning. Tell me."

Birch answered this time. "A vampire only needs a bit of blood each night. Taking enough to drain them dry is hard, if not impossible, for one alone."

That made sense then. "Makes sure the job gets done," I said.

Both vampires nodded, and Haley made a show of looking at her watch. "Look, I need to finish setting up."

"Just a few more questions," I assured her, giving her my most professional smile. "I'd like to get copies of all the security camera footage from that night. They weren't in the files I was given."

Haley snorted and took another drag from her clove. "Cameras? You're joking."

I fell silent for a moment before it hit me. I imagined quite a few lives had been lost here. "Right... Last question then. Do you know how Kurt found out about this place?" I ignored the immediate and obvious question of why he'd apparently voluntarily left London for New York City without burying his wife, who he'd been married to for over a hundred years.

Given the timeframe of nine days since Kurt had last been seen in London, he'd immediately hopped on a boat. The trip averaged around seven days, so he'd had at least one night in New York before Dolf and Ada had been killed.

Haley shrugged. "I don't advertise, but if he asked around, almost any vampire in New York could have told him about my place."

"I take it that it's not unusual to see humans in here then? I noticed you don't have a bouncer. What if someone, a human for instance, just stumbles in off the street?" I nodded towards the door.

Haley threw back her head and laughed. "Are you kidding? Highlight of the night whenever that happens. It's like a feeding frenzy in here."

I tried not to grimace, but Haley must have caught some small tell.

"Don't judge, wolf-boy."

"I'm not. My boyfriend is a vampire." I let the insult roll over me, not bothering to correct her. I was here to try to track down Everett's maker, not get in fights with the locals. I put down my pencil and held up my hands in gesture of surrender. "I'm just trying to understand. So, this old human woman with Kurt didn't stand out?

"Oh, no, that's quite common. Since they're spoken for, so to speak, they're left alone." She paused. "But there have been a few incidents, so I do encourage my guests to never leave their food unattended."

I frowned, but nodded. While in my human form, I could almost never tell a vampire from a human or a shapeshifter, but from the way Haley spoke, it was obvious to the vampires. I'd have to ask Everett about it next time I saw him, but Haley seemed certain the woman was human. So, where was the vampire who'd drained Kurt's wife and Ada? Why would Kurt be helping him by bringing him more victims?

The front door opened with a squeal and a gaggle of three people came in, chatting amicably.

"If that's all..." Haley stood without waiting for confirmation and headed back towards the bar.

"Yes, we should go," Birch said, gesturing at me to get up. I too had caught the excited looks I was drawing from the newcomers, so I stood and followed him outside.

In the alley, Birch made a beeline for the main street, but I followed after him more slowly, scanning the walls on either side about ten feet up.

"There." I grabbed Birch's cape to stop him, pointing at the telltale black bulb above the door to the bodega that was across the street from the alley that led to Blood Like Wine.

"What?" He glared at me.

"A camera. We should ask them about it, see if it caught a picture of them leaving the bar."

"Why? We already know what they all look like." Birch shrugged his cape out of my hand.

"It's clear that Kurt was leading the two of them into an ambush. And maybe the vampire I'm after, the one that killed these other vampires, was waiting for them outside. Plus, I'd like to see if I can find out who the human was, and that'll be easier with a picture."

"Why?" he asked again. "She was obviously just bait." Still, Birch adjusted his direction to cross the road towards the bodega with me.

"Perhaps," I agreed, but something about Haley's description of her gnawed at me.

Investigating was so much easier with a vampire. All Birch had to do was look the store manager in the eyes to hypnotize her, and she gave us the video tape from two nights ago, no fuss. The camera angle focused on the front door, but you could see the mouth of the alley in the background.

Unfortunately the tape had been erased and re-recorded over so many times that the picture quality was degraded, but we did manage to get one still that showed the group exiting the alley. No sign of them meeting anyone. This eater-of-vampires probably met them at a predetermined location away from the bar.

I got one blurry picture of the old woman, but the image quality wasn't good enough to get any kind of ID on her. Birch and I canvased the morgues for a body matching our description, and came up empty—which also didn't mean much. In the end, I flew back to Portland with more questions than answers.

Chapter 6

SLEEPWALKING

Two nights later things had settled back down. Lin agreed to let me out of the basement after talking with Stacy. I had to promise to keep the amulet on my person whenever I left the bedroom, and in return Stacy said she'd come over and let me bite her every few weeks until I could get my cravings under control.

Still, Lin and Trevor had avoided me even more than usual after I'd been released. When I'd come up to the second floor, I'd caught sight of Trevor peeking out at me through his cracked door. When he saw me, he slammed the door shut and I heard the click of the lock. I didn't really blame him.

I'd gone into my own room and shut the door behind me, staying in there the rest of the night. A bit after dawn I was reading a book, when I heard footsteps down the hallway and then the squeak of someone going down the stairs. A moment later the front door opened and I heard low voices.

There was more creaking as two people came up the stairs this time, speaking in low voices. I leaned my ear against the door.

"Are you sure we won't get caught?" a man said. I recognized the voice as Stephen's.

"Yes, I told you," Lin replied in a whisper. "Baby vampires conk out at sunrise. They'll never even know you were here."

Their voices faded as they entered Lin's room and shut the door.

I crept back to bed, my suspicions confirmed. I pulled the pillow over my head as the rhythmic creaking started and finally fell asleep.

I WOKE STANDING IN front of Trevor's door with my hand on the doorknob. My fangs were down, pressing into my lips.

"Evan?" someone said from farther down the hall.

I dropped my hand to my side and concentrated on bringing my fangs up. It was hard. I was so thirsty, but after a moment I got them to go up and I turned towards the voice.

Stephen stood there wearing pajamas, an empty glass in one hand.

We both stared at each other moment in silence. Stephen spoke first. "You know it's the middle of the day, right?"

I stared at him a moment longer, trying to figure out how I'd gotten out into the hall and what I was doing in front of Trevor's door. "Is it?"

I walked the few steps over to the door to my bedroom and opened it. My covers had been tossed back, and one of my pillows lay on the other side of the room.

Stephen came closer, glancing into my dark room and then at Trevor's door across the hall. His eyebrows raised, and he looked back at me with an unspoken question.

I bit my lip. "I must have gotten confused." I started closing the door, but Stephen put his hand up and stopped it midway.

"Actually," Stephen said, "I'm glad I finally got a chance to talk to you."

"Me too. I want to apologize for taking your spot. I—"

"No, I want to thank you." Stephen grinned. "I'd been having some second thoughts, but Lin wanted it so badly. I'm glad you gave me more time to think it over."

"Second thoughts?" I blinked, then nodded. "Yeah, I get it. Being a vampire really isn't all that. Except for the 'being alive when I would otherwise be dead' part."

Stephen chuckled. "I'm glad someone understands. Lin just doesn't get it when I talk about downsides. She doesn't think there are any."

I winced and glanced down the hall at Lin's closed door.

Stephen let out a small laugh. "Don't worry, she's asleep."

I relaxed. "Good."

"If you're up anyway, you're welcome to come downstairs and hang out with Lance and me."

"Lance is here too?" I grinned. He'd tasted good. I wondered if he'd let me bite him again. "I'd love that. I'll be right down."

I'd gone to bed wearing nothing but pajama bottoms, so I threw on a shirt to cover the amulet, grabbed my Vita, and headed downstairs. When I got there, Lance and Stephen were both sitting on the couch eating McDonald's.

The curtains were drawn, but a small sliver of sunlight bisected most of the room. I inched around it, careful not to let it touch my skin. This was my first time seeing daylight since I'd turned. I thought I'd be scared of it, but instead I felt drawn to it. The light was so bright and warm, even this close to me. It drew me to it, despite the warnings everyone had given me about vampires and sunlight. Although I was very curious to know what would happen if I put my hand into the sun, the warnings had been dire enough that I avoided it.

Stephen had taken off the bandage on his neck, and in the bright room the wound on his neck looked nasty. He caught me staring at it and reached up to gingerly touch his neck and shrug.

"It looks worse than it feels." He grinned, and a look of bliss came over his face. "Besides, it was worth it."

I nodded, not sure what else to say. I had never been bitten before I was changed, so I didn't truly understand the appeal.

Lance nodded his agreement, his mouth full of hamburger.

"Why'd you bring Lance?" I asked, trying to make small talk. I still found it awkard to be the only one in the room not eating. To distract myself, I thought back to my sleepwalking, and why I'd been outside Trevor's door. And why my fangs had been down. If I bit Trevor or Lin in my sleep, Lin would lock me in the basement forever.

"Being bit, it's a bit like taking drugs." Stephen laughed.

"Better!" Lance added with a giggle.

"Safer if you don't drive for a while after." Stephen threw a pillow at Lance.

I nodded like I knew what they were talking about and decided to change the subject. "So, Stephen, what is it you do when you aren't hanging out with vampires?"

"Lance and I work at a CrossFit gym downtown."

Well that explained one thing, at least. I'd always wanted to look like that, but all the overtime at work plus hunting the storeroom for things to steal hadn't left me much free time for things like working out. I glanced at Lance's chest with not a little bit of jealousy. My gaze slid to Lance's neck. I shook myself and gritted my teeth.

"I never did hear the full story of what happened," Stephen said into the silence.

"With me?" I pointed to myself and Stephen and Lance both nodded. "Not much to tell. Got jumped leaving work, woke up a vampire. Don't even know what my maker looks like."

"Crazy." Stephen looked at me with wide eyes.

"How'd you meet Lin anyway? Not like vampires go to the gym," I asked.

"Lance is in a metal band. They're actually really great." Stephen pointed to him, and Lance beamed at me. "I met Lin at one of his shows."

I quirked a smile. I bet concerts were a great hunting ground. "Wow. Maybe I can get Lin to take me to your next gig."

"That'd be awesome," Lance said around a bite of hamburger.

The overpowering smell of the hamburger and fries was making me a bit queasy, so I decided not to ask Lance about biting him.

"Hey, Evan," Lance said, waving his cellphone. "I'm not getting a signal out here. You got the Wi-Fi password?" I shook my head.

"No, sorry."

Lance frowned in disappointment.

"You know a lot of older vampires aren't tech savvy," Stephen said. "I bet it's something stupid like 'password'."

"No, I already tried that." I slumped back. "I've been trying to guess the password for days." A thought struck me. "Have you seen the modem? If they never changed it from the default, the password would be on the sticker on the box."

Lance cocked his head. "You live here. You don't know where it is?"

"I haven't seen it," I said.

Stephen jumped up suddenly. "I have. Be right back."

He ran out of the living room and up the stairs, taking them two at a time. Of course, Lin's room. Lance munched on fries while we waited for Stephen to return.

A few moments later he came back down the steps. "Success!" He held up his phone before flopping back down on the couch next to Lance.

I got into the settings of the Vita and entered the password as Stephen read it aloud. As promised, a moment later I got a little connected ding. Giggling, I sent Jack a message. "Ta-da!"

Jack responded with a laughing emoji about twenty minutes later. I'd missed talking with Jack, and while texting wouldn't be the same as hearing his voice, at least I now had a way to communicate with him.

A loud slurping from Stephen as he sucked down the last of his drink reminded me that I still had guests.

"You, uh, won't tell anyone we were here, right?" Stephen said as he and Lance gathered up their garbage.

"Your secret is safe with me." I held up my Vita. "As long as you don't tell Lin about this being online."

Stephen laughed and made a zipping motion across his mouth.

THE NEXT NIGHT, THE landline phone rang, startling me. Lin answered, and then called me down after she hung up.

She was waiting for me in the kitchen, her arms crossed and tapping her foot impatiently, and began speaking as soon as I crossed the foyer.

"That was Stacy. We're all a bit on edge, so she's letting Jack take you to a party tomorrow night."

I gnawed on my lip and hugged myself. "That sounds fun, but is that a good idea?"

Lin scowled, tossing her ponytail. "I don't think so, but Stacy overruled me. Said we need a break from each other."

I sighed. "I do miss Jack."

"He'll pick you up during the day, so you can get there on time." Lin stalked out of the room.

"During the day? How—"

"You'll see," she shouted back over her shoulder. "Oh, and I'll take you hunting tonight. Need to make sure you aren't thirsty before your field trip. So get ready."

The hunting trip was a bit tense, but Lin was true to her word and helped me to get a meal. This time I was even able to get his phone number, and Lin gave me a few tips on what to say when I called later this week to feel out if they were a good candidate to bite again. We got back to the house a bit before dawn.

"Get dressed for the party before you go to bed," Lin told me as we split up in the hall, me heading for my room and her to hers. "Jack will be by a few hours before dark to get you."

"Sure, thanks. And tell Trevor he can play my Vita tomorrow while I'm gone." I offered her a smile before going into my room.

Lin was wrong. I didn't want to sleep in my clothes; if I did they'd be all wrinkled by the time I woke up. Besides, I'd been up and about plenty during the day. Hanging out with Stephen and Lance hadn't been the only time I'd been awake at that time, but normally I just stayed in my room.

Just in case I had trouble waking up to my alarm, I put the stuffed tiger Jack had given me in the hallway directly outside my door. That way Jack could come in and wake me up.

As I changed into my pajamas, I decided to sleep without the amulet on, to continue my exercises to try to wean myself off relying on it. Lin had said not to take it off outside my room, but I'd put it back on before I left.

I put it into the drawer of the nightstand, and closed it for good measure. The moment I could no longer see it, panic surged through me, and I had to close my eyes, gripping the sheets of the bed tight as I counted backwards from twenty until I calmed down a little. It's right there in the drawer. I could reach out and take it back anytime I'd like. It's safe. It's close.

I still shook with the need to take it back, but when I finished repeating my mantra, I felt well enough to open my eyes and relax my grip. However, I couldn't get myself to turn away from the drawer, and found myself staring at the nightstand, even as I lay down and pulled my sheets up to my neck. Still, I prided myself in my accomplishment of leaving it where it was as I drifted off to sleep.

CHAPTER 7

QUIET AS A TOMB

WHEN I ARRIVED AT the vampire house to pick up Everett, I left the keys in the van and propped open the van's rear door. I'd backed into the garage, and while a tiny bit of light shone through where the rolling garage door didn't quite meet up with the frame anymore, it should be safe enough.

Inside, the house was quiet as a tomb. I snickered at the thought. Too accurate by far.

As I entered the foyer, I could hear faint beeping coming from somewhere above.

The blinds and living room curtains were open, and the afternoon sunlight slanted through the room. The light didn't reach the foyer, but I didn't want to take chances, so I went over and twisted the blinds and curtains closed before heading up the stairs.

The beeping grew louder as I ascended. Stacy had given me directions to Everett's room, but I still smiled when I noticed the plush tiger sitting outside his door like a guardian.

I picked up the tiger before knocking loudly on Everett's door. The beeping was definitely coming from his room.

"Everett. Evan, sorry. Still getting used to that. You awake?" I waited a moment or two, the silence filled by the steady beeping blare of the alarm, then knocked again and followed it with another call of, "Evan?"

A door farther down the hall opened, and I jumped and whirled around towards the noise. Lin stood there, wearing only an oversized t-shirt, her hair mused and her eyes blazing red.

"What's that awful racket?" she snarled, drawing back her lips to bare her fangs at me.

"The beeping?" I pointed to Everett's door. "I think it's his alarm."

"Well, shut it up fast." She stepped back and slammed her door.

Sighing, I gave up waiting for Everett to answer, not wanting to take on a pissed-off, sleep-deprived vampire during the day when I couldn't transform. "Ev, I'm coming in."

The room was pitch black inside; the only light there was came from the hall, and it only illuminated the foot of the bed. I felt along the wall inside the door until I found the light switch and flicked it on.

With the lights on, it was evident why the room had been so dark: where the window should have been was instead a plywood box that stuck out six inches into the room. It blocked light from entering, but allowed the window to have curtains on the inside to complete the illusion from outside that this was a normal house.

Everett didn't react as I walked around the bed and shut off the blaring alarm. That done and Lin placated, I leaned over Everett and shook his shoulder gently.

I shuddered as I prodded him. He was so unnaturally still. None of the small, slight movements you see in the living. It had shocked me the one time we'd slept together. Everett had fallen asleep in my arms, and to all my senses it had felt like I was cuddling a corpse. He'd stopped breathing, stopped moving, and gone completely limp. Even his skin under my hands felt cooler, though that might have just been my imagination.

Everett didn't respond, so I shook him harder. His body flopped to the side and I jumped back, biting back a curse.

"Looks like I have to carry him down after all," I said out loud, mostly to break the oppressive silence of the house.

I set the tiger on the nightstand next to the clock and flipped back the covers over Everett, then groaned. Pajamas. I looked around the room, but didn't see that he'd set out an outfit. Well, he better not complain about whatever I picked for him.

CHAPTER 8

YOU DATED A COUGAR?

I WOKE UP ON my back in the dark, but this was not my bed and something fuzzy was tucked in the crook of my arm. It was so dark, even my vampire vision couldn't make out anything.

I groaned, remembering my alarm. Not only had a slept right through it, I hadn't even woken up when Jack arrived. He must have carried me out and put me in this box, for some reason.

Experimentally, I pushed up on the lid above my face, but it didn't budge. Balling my hand up, I knocked on lid above me. "Jack! Jack!"

A speaker crackled near my head. "Ev, you're awake! We're almost to Portland."

Now that Jack said that, I recognized the hum of wheels on highway asphalt beneath me and the rock to one side as Jack changed lanes. I was beginning to panic, but I swallowed it down. "I'd feel better if I could get out of here."

"Push the button to unlock it. It's on the same side of the box as where I put your tiger."

"Okay." The tiger pressed into my side as I reached that arm out and felt along, until my questing fingers found a large round button near my shoulder. I pressed it in and was rewarded with a loud click and the lid popped open on that side, letting in a thin beam of lighter gloom.

I pushed the lid the rest of the way open and sat up to look around. I was inside a small panel van. Wooden tie-downs ran down both sides of the space, although they were currently empty. I lay in what looked like a long, over-sized tool chest from the outside. Weak light came through the tinted windows in the back doors. A partition with a sliding door, currently closed, separated the front driver's seat from the back.

Jack's voice came out of a speaker behind me, and I twisted around to look at the source. A two-way radio lay by where my head had been. I picked it up and climbed the rest of the way out, flipped the lid closed, and sat on it while Jack spoke.

"If I got pulled over, I didn't want to try to explain why I was hauling a dead body around. That's why that coffin is there."

I set the stuffed tiger in my lap and ran a hand through my hair, then lifted the radio to my mouth to speak into it. "Oh, that's why it was latched too."

"Exactly." There was a pause, and I braced my feet on the floor and grabbed the lid with my other hand as the van rocked. "Anyway, I picked out some clothes for you. Go ahead and get changed. Should be dark by the time we get to my friend's house."

"Oh, right." I looked down at my pajamas. I found my clothes in a pile next to the coffin-toolbox, along with my shoes.

I stripped off my pajama top and dropped it on the floor, then looked down at my chest to again admire how it looked now. Wait. Something was missing. I clutched at my neck, picturing taking the amulet off, and...

"Shit." Now that I'd noticed its absence, I could feel the subtle tug of the magic on my senses growing fainter by the second as the van barreled farther and farther away from it. "Shit!" I repeated louder. My hands began shaking.

"What's wrong?" Jack's voice came through the radio and startled me.

Crap. If I told Jack about my missing amulet, he'd insist on turning around to get it. But it was an hour drive each way, so we'd probably miss most of the party. That was even if Lin let me go back out again if she found out why we'd come back. I chewed on my lip staring down at the tiger, my mind whirling.

"Everett, what's wrong?" Jack repeated, a bit of panic slipping through. I sighed and hugged the stuffed tiger, not sure how to respond to that. "Nothing. Everything. Why couldn't I wake up for you? I even set an alarm." I felt guilty being so dependent on Jack for everything. Tears pricked my eyes.

"It's not a big deal, Ev."

We rode in silence for a few minutes. I got dressed, and then Jack said, "Sun's far enough down you can come right up front with me if you want."

I swallowed and licked my dry lips. "I better not. I'm really thirsty and you're driving. Did you bring any..." I paused and licked my lips again. I hated saying it, and I hated the thought of drinking them, but I hated the thought of feeding off Jack more. "... bottles?"

"No, I didn't. I figured you'd be sick of them by now; you were always making faces at them before. Stacy and Lin both assured me you had enough control to safely feed on somebody at the party."

My stomach twisted. The only reason I was okay was that I couldn't see or smell Jack through the partition. No. I shook my head. All my control couldn't have come from the amulet. I could do this. "I am pretty sick of them." I forced a laugh, hoping Jack wouldn't hear panic in my voice.

"Well, hang on five more minutes. We're almost there." I felt the van slowing as we got off the freeway. I rode in silence until Jack parked.

There was a click from the front partition, and the sliding door opened to reveal Jack. My eyes locked on him and I stood, dropping the stuffed tiger. My fangs came down unbidden. Where Jack's skin wasn't covered by his clothes, his veins seemed to pulse red in my sight in time with his heartbeat. Jack froze mid-step and slowly lowered his foot, not taking his eyes off me.

My throat burned with the need for his blood. I forced my eyes higher, to his face, and internally repeated, He's my boyfriend not food, he's my boyfriend not food.

"Can't go out with your fangs down," Jack said in a low, soothing voice.

"Thirsty," I whispered, through my clenched jaw. I had to take a breath to get enough air to say that, and the smell of his aftershave on my tongue made me shudder.

"Here," Jack said, slowly moving his left arm towards me, and rolling back his sleeve with his other hand. "Take a little from me to tide you over till we get to the party."

The movement drew my eyes away from his face, and I was caught by the bright spot at the crook of his elbow where the blood pulsed close to the surface. "Boyfriend, not food," I growled out between my fangs.

"It's okay. I give you permission." Jack took a slow, sliding step towards me until he was clear the sliding partition. Still presenting his left arm to me, he reached behind himself and slid the door closed. The swift movement of the door seemed to snap me out of my frozen state. I dashed across the four or five steps separating us in a blink of an eye, slamming my body into Jack's and hurling us both into the side of the van. The wheels creaked as it rocked from the impact.

Jack was taller and heavier than me, but I had caught him by surprise. I had one hand pressed up under his chin, pressing his neck against the door. My other hand was around the wrist of the arm he'd been presenting me, pinning his arm to the wall. My mouth hovered over the crook of his elbow, but I was able to stop myself before I bit down. I froze there, trembling with the effort of not biting him. I held my breath, remembering what Lin had said about not needing to breathe. It helped.

I could feel Jack's heart hammering in his chest against my shoulder. But he didn't try to fight me; in fact, he relaxed underneath me.

"Don't worry," he assured me in a low voice. "I can protect myself from you if I need to."

I pulled my head back a finger span and twisted my neck to look up at him. He was smiling down at me. I risked a quick breath so I could talk.

"Venom. Sure?" Even my quick inhale had been a mistake. His scent danced along my tongue.

"I'm immune, remember?" He tilted his head towards the arm I had pinned. "Just try not to bite hard, okay?"

I didn't respond, but leaned towards his elbow and sunk my fangs in where the red pulse was the brightest. Jack made a small sound between a whimper and a gasp, but otherwise he didn't move. Blood welled into my mouth and I eagerly sucked it up. Jack tasted earthier, and wilder, then the humans I'd been eating. I almost gagged, but I was too thirsty to be picky.

Still, I was only able to force down a few swallows before I retracted my fangs and stepped away from him. I dropped my eyes and whirled around so I didn't have to see his face. I walked across the van and picked up the tiger, hugging it to my chest and closing my eyes. I hated how weak I'd been. I should have protested more—or refused altogether—but it had assuaged one fear, that I'd see him as nothing more than a meal like I had with the humans I'd hunted the last few days.

I heard Jack move, and opened my eyes, keeping my head down and looking at him only in my peripheral vision. He knelt down and pulled a plastic first aid kit box from the van's sidewall, got out a bandage, and stuck it onto his arm.

Jack replaced the kit, and then came over and wrapped me in a hug from behind, putting his arms overtop mine and resting his hands on my elbows. "What's wrong?" he asked softly, his warm breath tickling the hair on the top of my head.

"I bit you," I whispered. "I'm sorry."

"Don't apologize for what you are." Jack's tone was hard, and he tightened his arms around me. "I gave you permission. Are you sure you got enough? You didn't take much."

I shook my head. "I'm still thirsty, but it was enough to tide me over until we get to the party."

"Do you want to take more?" His breath tickled the top of my head.

I giggled. "No offense, but no. I don't actually like the way you taste."

"Really?" He chuckled. "That's odd. Did you know the reason that vampires and shapeshifters were at each other's throats historically is because most vampires find us irresistible?"

I twisted around in Jack's arms so I could look up at him. "I find that hard to believe."

"That's what I heard, anyway." Jack shrugged. "I did have something else to ask you."

"Ask away," I said, leaning back against his chest.

"Can you tell a vampire from a human on sight?"

"What?" I twisted to look up at him. "Why?"

"Stacy's had me investigating something, and it came up. Can you tell?" He ran a hand down my arm.

I bit my lip in thought. "When my fangs are down, for sure. Other than that?" I shrugged. "Sometimes?"

"But not all the time?"

I nodded. "Lin said the bartender at the bar we went to my first night out is a vampire, but I didn't notice."

"Interesting." He made a humming noise. "Anyway, you feel a lot warmer now, and your color is better. You ready to go?"

I nodded and opened the van's back door to jump out onto the street. Outside, it was twilight. We were just off Mississippi Avenue in the trendy district. Shoppers out enjoying the warm weather streamed by on the sidewalks, and the steady hum of traffic from the road drowned out their overlapping conversations. I had to close my eyes and grip the van door as a couple walked by on the sidewalk next to me. My head swam, and my fangs ached to come down.

I felt the van rock as Jack jumped out, and felt his warmth next to me.

"You'll have to let go so I can shut the door, Ev," he said gently. I opened my eyes and gave him a wan smile, loosening my grip and dropping my hand. He raised his eyebrows at me as he swung the door closed. "You sure you okay?"

I nodded vigorously, but didn't say anything, distracted by a woman walking by. Her quick movements made me want to chase after her, and I imagined sinking my teeth into her neck where her skin flashed at me teasingly through the folds of her thin, decorative scarf.

Jack took my elbow and guided me up to the sidewalk as I craned my head to watch the woman until she walked around the corner. All the movement and colors and sights and sounds left me dizzy. My head swiveled this way and that, trying to watch it all, but I was quickly distracted by something else. My gaze flitted about like a hummingbird as he led me down the sidewalk. What had the amulet been suppressing besides my thirst?

"Are you sure everything's okay? Stacy told me you were sent to live with Lin to learn control, but you seem less in control now than when I first met you."

I didn't look at Jack, instead pulling my arm from his and putting both my hands in my pants pockets. "Yes, I'm fine. I just... guess I got too used to the quiet and lack of people." I glanced up and over without lifting my head. Jack frowned, but didn't press more. I clenched my fingers to keep myself from grabbing at my chest where the amulet should have been.

THE PARTY INSIDE THE house Jack led me to had spilled over into the front yard, where people were lounging around on deck chairs and kitchen chairs that had been dragged outside to enjoy the balmy Portland summer night.

I had to swallow down my fangs at feeling all the warm bodies around me. I'd have to find someone to bite fast, but we didn't even make it into the house before Jack was greeted by a person smoking on the front porch.

"Jack, you made it!" The speaker was a tall, thin man with the goatee, dark hair with a green streak dyed into the middle, and thick glasses. A swirling tattoo could just be seen poking out from the front of his T-shirt. "Eric," Jack said with a smile and wave as we went up the front steps.

Eric opened his arms for a hug, but Jack shook his head and pointed to the lit cigarette. "Don't want to risk ash on my shirt." I stood a step behind Jack, suddenly realizing that I didn't even know the names of any of Jack's friends. Awkward. Jack reached behind to gently grab my arm and tugged me forward. "Eric, meet my boyfriend, Evan. Evan, Eric."

Eric's eyebrows raised and he took a long drag off the cigarette, giving me an appraising once-over as I awkwardly held my hand up for a handshake. He blew his long stream of smoke out of the side of his mouth before gingerly reaching down and briefly touching his hand to mine. "So you're the infamous boyfriend."

I gave an awkward laugh and looked over at Jack. "Infamous, huh?"

Jack gave a sheepish half smile and shrugged, blushing slightly. "You went out of town right after we started dating. People started to think I was making you up."

I laughed again, this one more genuine. "Oh."

Eric joined in on this one. "Glad to finally meet you, anyway."

"Me too. So, Eric, Jack hasn't told me anything about you. How did you meet?"

I could tell this was going to be good because Jack turned bright red under his mustache and beard. Eric flicked ash off the balcony and grinned. Eric leaned toward me conspiratorially. "Gay hookup app—"

"It wasn't like that," Jack said in a rush, cutting Eric off.

I held up my hands palm out against my chest. "No business of mine who you hooked up with before we were dating."

"It was exactly like that." Eric straightened and took another puff of his cigarette.

Eric didn't exactly strike me as Jack's type, not after what I'd seen of Andre in Jack's memory. Then again, I didn't look anything like Andre either. And I'd been telling the truth; it didn't particularly bother me what Jack had done before we got together.

"Well," Jack said, "we just got here, so I'm going to go introduce Evan around."

"Foods laid out in the dining room," Eric called after us. "Talk to you more later. Enjoy the party!"

I waved goodbye to Eric as Jack hustled me away through the open door into the house. Eric gave me a wave with the hand that held the cigarette, and winked at me before I lost sight of him.

Jack made a beeline to the kitchen table, where bowls of chips and snacks were set out along with plates and utensils.

While Jack filled a plate, I said, "You're probably thirsty, after..."

"Parched," Jack said.

"I'll go grab you a drink from the kitchen. What do you want?" I asked.

Jack paused in the act of scooping up chips and turned to regard me. "You sure you'll be alright on your own?"

"Yeah, I am." I grinned to show him my normal teeth. "The walk over here helped." I was still thirsty, so I was going to have to find someone soon. But I should be alright for the walk there and back.

"Water if you can find it, or juice. I'll leave it up to you, as long as it's nonalcoholic. The last thing you want to do is be drinking after donating blood."

I blushed and hurried off with a nod. Donating blood. I liked that.

When I got to the kitchen, I found a note stuck to the fridge with an arrow pointing to the counter.

Cold beer and sodas in the fridge.

Alcohol is out on the counter along with cups.

I opened the fridge, and the cool blast of air to my face helped to drive my bloodlust down. Inside I didn't find any juice, but there was water and sports drinks. I got out one of the sports drinks for Jack and a water for me, and shut the fridge.

Someone walked behind me before I turned around, close enough that they almost brushed my back. I got a whiff of something as I started to turn, a rich smoky smell that I associated with vampires, and suddenly my fangs came down.

I clenched my eyes shut and whirled back towards the fridge, knowing that my irises now would be tinged with red, and pressed my hands over my mouth, forgetting about the cold bottles I still held. The cold plastic against my fangs and lips made me cry out in surprise.

"You alright?" a woman asked from behind me.

"Fine," I mumbled around my fangs, keeping my eyes squeezed shut and the bottles over my mouth.

There was an awkward pause, then she said, "You wanna move over then? The rest of us need drinks too."

"Sorry." I shuffled to the left when a wave of euphoria washed over me. My legs went limp and my head spun. I fell backwards into the woman, shudders of pleasure racking me from head to toe. The woman and I tumbled to the floor together.

I dropped my bottles, and they bounced off the floor and rolled away into the sea of feet and legs. But I hardly cared. Warmth spread out through me, driving away the eternal cold of being a vampire. I arched my back, balled my fists, and curled my toes in pleasure, letting out another involuntary cry.

A moment later, the feeling passed and I went limp, my eyelids still fluttering as I came back to myself. My thirst was gone, and I felt warm all over, like I'd just fed.

I opened my eyes to screams of terror from the woman who I'd fallen into. She'd landed on her butt and scrambled back away from me like a crab. When she saw me looking at her, her eyes widened even more and her scream increased in pitch that made me wince.

My eyes caught on her throat. The way she had her head thrown back arched her neck, presenting me a straight shot to the large vein pulsing there. My fangs pressed into my lip. I clapped a hand over my mouth and screwed my eyes shut.

"Evan!" Jack's voice cut through her screams.

"Here!" I called through my hand.

The woman's scream trailed off as she ran out of breath, and then I heard the squeak of shoes on linoleum as people crowded around to comfort her.

"What happened?" someone asked.

"Sorry, I—" I began to say, but hands grabbed me under my armpits and pulled me to my feet.

"Evan, it's me. What happened?" Jack said. "What's wrong?"

I was concentrating, doing all the tricks I knew, but my fangs remained stubbornly down. I glumly thought back to the night I'd spent with Jack, when I'd had the same problem, and he'd jokingly compared them to an unwanted erection. The comparison was more apt than he knew. Perhaps another reason young vampires were isolated, until like a teenage boy, they could keep their teeth where they belonged.

"I dropped the drinks," I said softly, close to tears.

"Don't worry about that right now. You feel flushed." Jack put a hand to my forehead. "Did you..."

I shook my head and said in a whisper, "I had a seizure or something, and then my fangs came down and won't go back up."

"Too many people, I bet. Guess this was a bad idea. C'mon." His hand took hold of my free one and tugged me forward gently.

I resisted him. "No," I hissed. "I can do this."

The tugging stopped and I felt warmth on my left as Jack leaned over me, and then his warm breath on my ear. "We're not leaving. I want this to work as much as you, but we need to get you outside and calmed down."

"Fine," I huffed, and didn't resist this time as Jack took my free hand and started leading me forward.

I heard people murmuring to each other. I probably looked like an unbalanced person, my eyes closed and a hand over my mouth. Hopefully they'd just think I was having a panic attack or something.

"You dropped these," a man said, pressing two bottles into my chest.

"Kevin?" I said, almost dropping my hand from my mouth in surprise when I recognized the voice.

"Hey, Everett," Kevin said.

"It's Evan now," I said, cupping my hand so my voice wasn't quite so muffled.

"Cool." Kevin laughed.

"I'll come back for the drinks once I get him outside," Jack said.

"Naw, I got it," Kevin said from behind me. "Can I ask about um, whatever this is going on here?" he asked as we slowly wound our way through the house.

"I'm struggling a little with my latest adolescence," I said, hoping Kevin would get it. I didn't exactly want to wave the words "vampire fangs" around.

Kevin chuckled knowingly, so I thought maybe he did.

Back outside, we passed through the cloud of cigarette smoke around the front door. "Leaving so soon?" Eric said, sounding disappointed.

"Three steps here, Ev," Jack said, then to Eric, "No, not leaving yet. Evan just had a panic attack and I'm getting him some fresh air."

"Shit. Here, I'll clear you out a place to sit." Eric's voice was quickly followed by the sound of tennis shoes squeaking on wooden steps.

As Jack, Kevin, and I slowly made our way down the steps, I could hear Eric shooing people out of some of the chairs on the lawn.

Stumbling a bit as we moved off the walk and onto the grass, I clung harder to Jack's hand. I sank gratefully down into the canvas camping chair, both Kevin and Jack's hands on my arms guiding me. It was getting old keeping my hand over my mouth, but my fangs just would not go up. As soon as I was seated, I doubled over and put my head in my knees, lacing my hands over my head.

Jack sat in a chair on my other side, a full plate of food now balanced in his lap. I risked a quick glance around, and quickly ducked my head back down when I saw Eric still stood next to Jack's chair.

"Anything I can do to help?" Eric asked.

"No, he'll be fine. Just give him a minute to calm down." I heard Jack shifting in his chair.

"All right. I'll be on the porch if you need anything," Eric said, and then the rustle of clothing moved off.

"Kevin, was it?" Jack said abruptly. "Don't think I didn't recognize you. Now tell me why shouldn't punch you out right here."

"Hey now," I said, sitting up and glancing between them.

They both ignored me.

Kevin said, "I'm sorry for what happened that night. If it makes you feel better, I lost my job over everything that happened." Kevin settled down to sit next to me, leaning back on his arms and stretching his legs out in front of him.

"Jack," I said, leaning over to put a hand on Jack's arm. "Be nice. Without his help I think neither of us would've survived that night."

Jack did not look mollified by this. In fact, his frown deepened. "You never should have been a cop in the first place. Cops like you that only want power and respect give us all a bad name." He stopped glaring at Kevin long enough to look at me. His voice lowered. "And your fangs are still down. Any idea what set you off?"

I sighed and opened my mouth to prod a fang with one finger. Finally, I dropped my hand and shook my head. "No."

"You probably just need to eat," Kevin said.

Both Jack and I turned to look at him. Jack said, "What do you know about vampires?"

Kevin shrugged, looking uncomfortable. He glanced up at me and then down at the ground at his side, fiddling with a piece of grass with one hand. "Since Everett—"

"Evan," I reminded him.

Kevin bobbed his head. "Right, Evan. Well, since he bit me, all I could think about was being bitten again. So Stacy hooked me up with this other vampire in town, Reggie. It's helped a little, but I really want you." He looked up at me now, his eyes boring into mine. "Does this mean you're back in town? Can I come live with you?"

I recoiled a little bit at the intensity of this gaze, shifting as much as I could in the camping chair away from him. "I'm only here for tonight."

Kevin's expression fell and he pulled his knees to his chest.

"Evan, is Kevin here the reason your fangs won't go down?" Jack bobbed his head at Kevin.

I shrugged, feeling helpless. "I don't know. Maybe." I didn't want to, but I leaned towards Kevin and closed my eyes, taking a deep breath. The rich flavor I'd caught before clung to Kevin's skin like a perfume. My jaw tightened and ached with longing. "Probably," I amended, settling back into the chair.

Jack looked expectantly at Kevin who shook his head. "I wish I could feed him." Kevin tilted his head back and to the side to show me his neck. Two red, partially healed puncture wounds marred the side of his neck. "Reggie bit me yesterday or I would."

I licked my lips and swallowed. Although I wouldn't say no to biting someone, I actually wasn't thirsty anymore. Frowning, I reached up to touch one fang, trying to figure out why that was.

Jack leaned sideways to me and ruffled my hair, misreading my puzzlement for disappointment. "You're cute, but that doesn't always mean you get what you want."

I stuck out my tongue at him and grinned.

Jack chuckled, but his expression quickly turned more serious. "Kevin, you'll have to go now."

Kevin looked unhappy at this, his eyebrows knitting together as he glared at Jack.

"Come on, it'll help Evan out. He can't go back to the party until he calms down," Jack said.

"You're here," Kevin said, pointing an accusing finger at Jack.

"He doesn't like my blood," Jack growled back.

I sighed. Jack was probably right. Kevin looked up at me, looking for all the world like a hurt puppy dog. "Please, Kevin?" I asked him.

"Fine, for you." Kevin stood up, but he didn't leave. Instead, he crossed his arms and loomed over me. "But I want you to promise to call me next time you're in town."

"I don't have a phone—"

"Promise!"

"All right, all right. Give Jack your number then. I'll call you next time as soon as I know I'm coming."

Kevin grinned and gave his number to Jack, who dutifully put it into his phone and sent Kevin a quick text. Kevin's phone chimed. He checked it, gave a thumbs up, then nodded to me and headed back into the house.

While Jack finished eating, I drank my water and then practiced calming exercises until my fangs went back up, which I was able to do about five minutes after Kevin left.

When Jack was done, he put his plate aside on the grass and then scooted his camping chair around face mine. "How you doing?" he asked me.

I gave him an open mouth grin to show my lack of fangs. "All better."

"Good." He patted his lap and I eagerly jumped up and moved over to sit across him, my legs slung over one of the camping chairs arms. As I sunk onto his warm chest, my fangs immediately came back down. I groaned and buried my face in his shoulder.

"Damn things." I mumbled. I'd noticed when I played with the toys Jack had sent me that my fangs always came down and stayed down. They liked strong emotions, and I began to wonder if that was why Stacy and Lin, the two oldest vampires I'd met so far, both seemed so emotionless and composed.

Jack laughed and rubbed my back in slow circles with one hand, resting his other hand on my knees. His hand began to run up and down my leg. I squirmed in his lap, and felt him getting hard underneath me.

"Maybe we should ditch this party," I whispered to Jack, trailing my fingers up his neck until my hand rested on his cheek, rubbing his beard.

"I thought you were still hungry," Jack growled, and then leaned down to kiss me. It was a bit awkward at first with my fangs, but we managed.

"A little, but I want this more," I said when we broke apart. Jack was breathing hard underneath me, and his erection ground into the side of my butt where I sat on him.

"Alright, get up, you win," Jack laughed, swatting my ass until I stood.

Grinning and giggling I hopped to my feet, twirled around, and came face to face with Eric.

His eyes went wide as he looked into my red eyes and at my fangs, still down from kissing Jack.

"A vampire?" Eric scrambled back away from me, going pale and lowering his voice to a growl. "You invited it into my house, Jack!"

"Sorry," I whispered, covering my mouth and backing away. "I didn't hear him coming... And I'm not an 'it'."

"It's fine. It would have come out eventually." Jack stood up and rubbed my shoulder, then to Eric he said, "Yes. Evan's a vampire. Is that a problem?"

"A problem? Yes that's a problem!" Eric's voice rose, and some of the smokers on the porch started looking our way. "Did you feed any of my guests to it?"

Jack held up his hands in a gesture of placation. "Eric, peace. I didn't know it would bother you so much."

Eric glanced over his shoulder, noticed the stares and whispers, and took a deep breath, lowering his voice. "Well now you do. If you ever bring that thing here again, I'll kill it."

"My boyfriend is not an 'it', Eric. And he's not evil." Jack's voice was steady, but his hand on my shoulder trembled. "I work with vampires every day at the PCA. Most of them just want to live and let live, just like us."

I wondered if he knew Reggie was a vampire, but held my tongue. As a trans guy I knew how awful it was to have someone else out me without consent, and figured outing another vampire was just as taboo.

Eric shook his head in disgust. "It's not the same. They chose to be that way. We didn't, but the humans persecute us both equally."

"Exactly. They persecute us both, and we need to help each other to thrive." Jack glared at Eric.

"That doesn't mean you have to date them!" Eric snapped back.

I appreciated him trying to defend me, but I'd learned when I transitioned that there was no use arguing with some people.

"Jack, stop," I said, stepping between them, putting back to Eric and holding up my hands. "It's fine. Drop it. We were leaving anyway."

Eric's fist struck me in the back of the head, knocking me off balance. I stumbled and almost fell face first into Jack, who caught me by my elbows. It didn't really hurt, but I still cried out in surprise. Without thinking I sped up and whirled on Eric, hitting him in the chest with my shoulder. We both went down in a tangle, smashing the camping chair I'd been sitting in as we fell. I landed on top and sunk my fangs into Eric's throat.

I regretted what I'd done almost immediately, even as I gulped down Eric's blood. If anything, Eric's blood tasted even worse than Jack's, but I set my jaw and held on as he yelled and thrashed under me. He convulsed, and I recognized it from Jack's transformations. I let go and scrambled away as tan fur sprouted along Eric's neck.

"What's going on?" one of the smokers yelled. They were all crowded along the porch railing, squinting to see past the glare of the porch light. "Is that a cougar?"

I looked back to see Eric had completely changed, and was rolling around on the ground fighting to claw his way out of his shirt and pants. "I'll kill you," he growled, shredding his shirt with a few kicks of his back paws to his chest.

"Time to go." Jack grabbed me. I took his hand in mine and we ran.

CHAPTER 9

A NIGHT OF BLISS

I FINISHED LICKING THE last of Eric's blood from my lips as I climbed into the passenger seat of the van. Eric's blood had tasted like Jack's: earthy and a bit gamy. I vastly preferred vampire, or even human blood—not that Eric would probably care to hear that he didn't taste good to vampires. I buckled up, rubbing my hands along my pants and studiously avoiding looking at Jack.

We drove in silence for a bit. Suddenly, Jack said, "I'm not mad at you for biting Eric."

I sighed in relief and slumped in the seat.

"Pro tip in the future though: don't turn your back on an angry shapeshifter. Especially a feline one."

"I was trying to defuse the situation." I finally looked over at Jack. "I didn't mean to bite him, I just reacted."

"I know, Evan." Jack glanced at me and reached across the gap between the seats to pat my knee before turning his attention back to the road. "That's why I'm not mad. Eric will say you provoked him by turning your back on him, but he's been a shifter long enough to be able to control himself."

I bit back a sigh. "Could you call me Everett in private? I appreciate you picking a name that's close, but..."

"Sure." Jack gave me a slight smile and a glance as he drove.

I had a hard time reconciling the momentary bloodlust that had overcome me with my own self-image. "Where are we going?" I asked, not just to change the subject. I felt the amulet getting farther away, yet we weren't going in the direction of Jack's apartment either.

"It's a surprise." Jack's tone was light and playful. Not to the vampire house then.

I sat up, intrigued, and began looking for landmarks. I didn't recognize anything, even as Jack pulled into the driveway of a small bungalow and turned off the engine.

"Here we are," he said.

"Wow, this is really cute," I said as I undid my seatbelt. It was, too. The house was the brick seventies style with raised flower beds along the front. Two large picture windows looked out over the tiny front yard and street. There wasn't a garage, just a carport on the side of the house, but the van was too tall to fit under the awning, so Jack had parked in the driveway. "Renting?" I guessed.

"Nope. Emily helped me find it. I closed on it last week and just moved in, so ignore the boxes." Jack opened his door and climbed out.

The living room had the couch, chair, and coffee table from his apartment, the green furniture and action movie posters clashing with the pink walls and carpet. A kitchen counter and table were visible through the doorway directly opposite the front door, and a second door, this one closed, was directly to the left. A pile of moving boxes sat in the corner of the living room, waiting to be unpacked.

Jack must have seen my grimace. "Yeah, I don't have the money to redecorate right now."

"It's cute." I grinned at Jack and winked. "Matches its owner."

Jack's eyes twinkled. "Does it now?"

"Do I get to see the bedroom?" I asked, looking through my lashes.

Jack went over and opened the closed door that led off the living room and flipped on the light.

The bedroom was neat and clean. A king size bed made of dark wood with a quilted green and white patchwork bedspread dominated the room. The dresser and nightstand were the same dark color. The walls in here were painted a more neutral shade of cream, except for one wall that was inexplicably painted bright red. Thick blackout curtains covered the two picture windows. The same shirtless men movie posters I recognized from his bedroom were hung here, with the extra-large Detective Pikachu poster in the place of honor above the headboard on the red wall. Another door to the right opened up into the bathroom.

Growling, Jack scooped me up and tossed me onto the bed on my back. I laughed as I landed and Jack jumped on top of me, landing with his hands and knees on either side of me. He leaned down and kissed me on the lips while I ran my hands along his shirt. Jack reached down and grabbed me between the thighs, squeezing my packer. I moaned into his mouth, spreading my legs wider until they hit Jack's thighs on either side of me.

Jack bit at my lower lip as he pulled away to get a breath of air. He squeezed the packer again, and I groaned in pleasure, my fangs coming down and my hands clenching the cloth of his shirt. Three buttons popped off with low pings, pelting me and the bed.

"Sorry," I reflexively gasped, pricking my lip with my fangs.

Laughing, Jack sat up, resting his weight on his knees as he straddled my hips, and looked down at his shirt where it now gaped open in the middle. "Do you know how many shirts I ruined with my claws my first month as a shapeshifter? At least buttons can be sewn back on."

He undid the top button and pulled it off over his head, tossing it carelessly aside. I took the opportunity to do the same with my shirt.

"Very nice." Jack put his hands lightly on my stomach and ran them up my chest, brushing my nipples as he leaned down to kiss the hollow of my breastbone. I threw my head back as he got higher, giving him access to my neck. He nipped at my throat and growled, sounding very feral. "Pants off, now."

He slipped back off me, off the bed, and started stripping down. I raced him, lifting my butt and wiggling my jeans off, but he beat me. I stood up, throwing my jeans and shirt away, to better admire Jack's body. My packer bounced out of my jeans, but I ignored it, eyes fixed on Jack. He was hard and throbbing with need.

I dropped to my knees and grabbed his cock in my hand. I wanted to suck it, but... I looked up at Jack as I stroked it with one hand. "I have no idea what I'm doing." I giggled.

Jack put a hand on my head and mussed my hair. "It's a dick, Ev, not rocket science. Just put your mouth on it and I'll enjoy it."

I opened my mouth and licked it from the tip down to the balls. Jack yelped and twisted his hand in my hair.

"Fangs, shit. I forgot." Jack eased back away, pushing at my head.

"Sorry," I said, sitting on the edge of the bed.

"I told you not to apologize for what you are." He leaned over and cupped my chin to raise my head, then gave me a deep kiss, tongue running along my fangs. He pulled away and crouched next to me, fingers resting on my face. "

"Can I take you from behind?" he whispered after pulling away. I bit my lip. I'd fantasized about exactly that happening to me one day, but now that the time was here, I was suddenly nervous. "I'll be gentle and go slow," he promised, kissing me again briefly. Too briefly. "And you can tell me to stop at any time."

"Alright." Jack kissed me on the forehead, and then reached around me to pull off the cute patchwork bedspread. "Get on the bed on your hands and knees, with your butt near the edge, while I get the lube."

I did as he said, jumping a bit when Jack returned and ran a greasy finger on my butt. I jumped, twisting around to look at him.

"Too cold for a vampire?" Jack asked, amusement dancing in his eyes as I squirmed.

"No," I admitted. "Just not used to the feeling... And... I'd be more comfortable if I could see you."

"Roll over then," Jack said, waiting while I shifted. When I was done, he pushed one of my bent legs down and to the side to rest on the bed.

I jumped as something warm gently pressed inside me, but I could still see and feel his erection pressing on the inside of my thigh. "What?"

"My finger." To illustrate, Jack wiggled his finger around in my ass.

"That feels odd, but also good," I said, groaning and bucking against Jack's hands.

Jack set his cock between my legs and rubbed it on me. I cried out at the feeling of his slick flesh rubbing me and Jack paused, eyes wide. "Don't stop, don't stop!" I yelled until Jack started moving again.

He was so warm against me, rubbing along me. I reached down and put my hand over his. Jack pulled his hand away and took my fingers, placing them where his had been. "Like this," he said, rocking his hips while he pressed on my hand until I got the movement right.

I tried to rock my hip too, but I messed up the timing, and pulled away when Jack pushed, causing him to lose the rhythm and fall forward onto me. He landed on my chest, almost face to face with me, and in the fall his finger came out of my ass.

"What was that?" He laughed, swatting at my chest.

I bared my fangs and pretended to growl at him, but it turned into a giggle at the end. "It felt good, I just reacted."

Jack pecked a kiss on the end of my nose and stood back up. "Do you like this, or want to try something else?"

"I like it." I wiggled my hips. "But what else did you have in mind?"

Jack winked. "I'll save that for next time. Are you relaxed enough for another finger?"

I nodded, grinning. I'd been expecting it, but I still gasped as Jack's fingers slid inside me. It felt strange, like I was being pushed open, but I enjoyed it. Jack started rocking back and forth again, rubbing himself along my clit and stomach. I stroked the top of his cock with my hand as he moved, pushing him down onto me. Jack started slowly pushing his fingers in and out of me in time with his thrusts.

"Yes!" I yelled, shuddering. "Harder."

Jack sped up the thrusts of his fingers and his hips, bouncing me on the bed. Warmth spread out over me, and I twitched, coming hard on Jack. I could feel myself clenching down on his fingers. Jack kept rubbing himself on me and, arching his back, came all over my stomach and hips a few moments later.

Panting, Jack stopped moving and smiled down at me. I grinned back and used the corner of the sheet to wipe myself off. Jack pulled his hand free and disappeared around the bed into the bathroom. Water ran and he came back a moment later with cold, clean hands. He climbed into bed with me and snuggled up to my back.

I relaxed into him, enjoying the feel of his warm skin against mine. My fangs were still being stubborn, and the points pricked my lower lip.

We lay there until Jack's phone began ringing, a cheerful pop song that Jack liked. I found it annoying and had told him so, and that's when he changed it to his ringtone.

Jack groaned and pulled me closer, snuggling against my back and side like a warm blanket.

"I hate to cut this short," Jack said into my hair, "but I have to have you back before sun-up."

I sighed and rolled over as Jack got up, resting my chin in my arm to watch him. I loved looking at Jack naked—especially from behind as he bent over to pull his phone out of the pocket of his discarded pants.

I whistled. Jack glanced over at me as he straightened, doing a shimmy of his hips and grinning at me. Then he put the phone to his ear.

"Hello?"

Jack listened for a moment, and then his face fell slack and he went a bit pale. He staggered over and sat down on the edge of the bed.

"What's wrong?" I sat up and slid across the sheets over to him. "Who is it?"

Jack shook his head at me. "No, I'll take him. Be there as soon as we can. Yes, see you there. Bye." He hung up and dropped the phone on the bed before turning to me.

"Ev, that was Stacy. Trevor is dead. Lin thinks you killed him."

CHAPTER 10

VAMPIRE MUMMY

THE RIDE BACK TO Estacada was quiet. I was lost in thought with a sinking feeling that I knew what had killed Trevor.

As we got closer, the call of the amulet grew louder. I had to clench my teeth and ball my hands into my lap to keep from crying out. It was definitely more powerful than it had been.

I swallowed hard, a wave of guilt crashing down on me. I'd known that younger vampires were drawn to it, and I'd known that it had been acting differently lately. I felt a tear leak out and roll down my cheek, but I wiped it away before Jack could see it.

The voice grew in strength. I bent over, resting my head in my hands. I could barely think over the sound of the amulet screaming in my head.

Why was it silent when I held it? I'd never wondered that before.

"Everett, don't worry. It wasn't you," Jack said as we turned on the road to the house. "But I am worried it might be your maker back in town."

I shook my head, making an effort to sit up. "God, I hope not."

Jack leaned across the seats to hug me. "Is that what's worrying you? Don't. We'll do our best to protect you."

I hugged Jack back, nodding into his neck. After a moment he let me go and sat back up.

"Don't forget your pajamas and tiger from the back," Jack said as he undid his seatbelt and got out.

Right, those. I staggered into the back of the van, my head splitting, and gathered up my things with shaking hands before getting out. Jack had disappeared inside already. My steps sounded very loud to me as I walked up the front steps and into the house.

The house smelled strongly of something musty and old, overlaid by a faint scent of smoke. Under all that was the tang that I associated with vampires. I seemed to be hyper aware of it without the amulet to blunt things. At least I was able to keep my fangs up, mostly because I didn't feel thirsty at all. Almost over-full, even though I'd only had a few drops from Eric and barely a sip from Jack.

"Upstairs, Ev," Jack called from above as I shut the door behind me.

I stopped in the foyer next to the stairs, gathering my courage, and then trudged up the stairs. As I reached the second floor, I heard the crunch of gravel as another car approached the house.

The door to Lin and Trevor's rooms were closed and dark, and my stomach dropped further when I saw the light was on in my room and the door open. Had he died in my room? My stomach twisted.

"Stacy is here," I called from the hall.

"Come in here," Lin ordered. I sighed and walked to my door.

Lin stood near the end of my bed. Jack knelt behind it, near the outside wall on the side with my nightstand. I could just see the top of his head and back. The nightstand drawer where I'd had the amulet was open and empty. Shit...

The musty-burning smell was much stronger in here, making me gag until I concentrated on not breathing. I wondered how Jack was handling it. I dumped my pajamas in my hamper next to the door and set the plush tiger on the floor, then crossed my arms. My room was feeling crowded already with the three of us in here. The amulet had calmed with me so close to it, and as long as no one tried to pick it up, I felt I'd be alright.

Jack stood up and moved over to the end of the bed, turning to face Lin and me with his arms crossed, frowning. "Ev, why is Trevor holding your amulet?"

Lin whipped her head around towards Jack, her eyes going wide. "He's what?" She pushed past Jack and dropped to her knees behind the bed.

"Don't touch it." Jack grabbed her arm and pulled her back up and away.

Both of them looked towards me.

I ducked my head and hunched over, crossing my arms. "I might have...accidentally...left it here when Jack picked me up."

"You what?" Stacy's voice from behind me was icy and low.

I jumped to the side, putting a hand to my throat. I gulped, turning to look at her. "I didn't hear you come in."

Her curly red hair was down loose around her shoulders. She wore a dark navy suit jacket and tight skirt that wouldn't have looked out of place in a board room, except that her feet were bare and the top two buttons of her shirt were undone. Even without her heels she stood several inches taller than me. She put her hands on her hips and stared down at me, her mouth a hard line. I squirmed under her examination.

After a long moment of silence as I squirmed under her gaze, she said, "It was entrusted it to you for safekeeping because last time we separated you from it you went into a frenzy. So how is it that it 'accidentally' got left behind?"

I bit my lower lip and glanced over at Lin and Jack. "Lin told me it makes her and Trevor uncomfortable..." I paused. "Made, I guess. And so I'd been practicing taking it off for short periods—"

"Yes. Lin told me about your attack on Trevor the other day." Stacy's lips got even thinner, if possible.

Lin cut in here, glaring at me as she spoke. "I warned him not to leave his room without it again."

Even Jack was frowning at me now.

"I know." I swallowed. "I'm sorry. I was still practicing removing it in my room, and I fell asleep while I had it off, and Jack..."

Jack came over and put his arms around me, pulling me forward against his chest. I didn't move, keeping my arms crossed between us, but I appreciated the gesture.

"I didn't know he wasn't wearing it," Jack said to them over his shoulder. "He didn't wake up when I got here, so I carried him out to the car."

I pushed Jack away from me and sidled a step away, bumping into the side of my bed. "I should have had you go back for it, but I didn't want to miss out on a night out with you. I'm sorry." I dropped my head, staring at my bed so I didn't have to look at any of them. "Why was he even in my room? Why would he have picked it up? I thought you said it repulsed you." I looked at Lin and then Stacy.

Lin grimaced, but it was Stacy that answered me. "It's repulsive, and yet draws you to it." Stacy shuddered.

I wrinkled my nose and nodded, remembering the three vampires that had accosted me for the thing on one of my first nights as a vampire had said something similar. Even I felt the call, though apparently more keenly than others. My eyes caught on the tangle of sheets and my Vita lying there on the bed. I reached over to pick it up and turned it over. "He must have come in to borrow this, and felt it in the drawer..."

Downstairs, the phone in the kitchen began to ring.

"Ignore it," Lin snapped when I took a step towards the bedroom door. "It's been ringing all night since I got home, but if it's important, whoever it is will call my cell."

I shrugged, letting the phone continue to ring while we talked.

"This is why I didn't want anyone else handling the amulet." Stacy's eyes glinted.

Lin turned to Stacy. "And why I don't want him here anymore."

"Maybe I can move in with Jack?" I glanced over at him hopefully.

Jack frowned and scratched his beard. "Look, I'm sorry, Everett. I like you and all, but I don't think our relationship is to that level yet." The ringing of the phone finally stopped.

My stomach twisted, and I nodded. I didn't trust myself to speak.

"Out of the question anyway," Stacy said. "On the drive up I arranged for a meeting with the head of the council tomorrow night. It will be his decision."

Lin scowled, but nodded.

"In the meantime, Evan, get your amulet back." Stacy nodded at the body. "Once you do, you are not to take it off your person again. This is an order."

I stiffened. I'd avoided looking at the body until now. "Understood," I managed to stutter out. I took a deep breath to steady myself, and that was a mistake. Stacy's scent mixed with the musty burned smell of Trevor's body, making me gag. I held my breath as I went the rest of the way around the bed past Stacy.

At first I couldn't see anything but his socks and jeans, and then I rounded the bed the rest of the way and stopped in shock. Trevor's skin was dried out and his cheeks hollow. His eyes were closed and he lay on his back, hands clasping the amulet to his chest, looking for all the world like a mummy except for his modern clothing— jeans and the leather jacket covered in band patches that he'd worn to the bar.

I stepped over his legs and crouched down. I wrinkled my nose as I reached down and pried his hands apart. They were stiff as rocks. There was an audible crack, and one of the wrists flopped as if boneless. I winced, but kept going. Now that I'd gotten this close, the amulet wasn't going to let me back off. I ended up having to snap almost all of his fingers to get the amulet loose from his grasp.

As soon as touched it, a wave of calm washed over me. The scents around me seemed to dull in their intensity. Hands shaking both with terror and relief, I hung the chain back around my neck and tucked it into the collar of my shirt to rest against my skin.

Downstairs, the house phone began to ring again. I scrambled to my feet and Stacy ushered us all out.

"Lin, Jack, I brought a body bag. Put the body in the basement." She pointed to a crumpled black bag lying in the hallway outside my door. "Then get it ready for Evan. He's going to be locked up until the head of the council arrives tomorrow."

73

My stomach twisted at her words. I opened my mouth to protest, and Stacy cut me off with a glare.

"Evan, you come with me. We need to talk." Stacy strode off without waiting for acknowledgment.

Stacy went into the living room, but I paused in the foyer, glancing into the kitchen where the phone was still ringing.

"Can I get that?" I asked.

"After, if they're still calling." Stacy sat on the couch and patted the seat next to her.

Nibbling my lip, I sat next to her.

"What happened with Jack?" Stacy asked quietly.

I blinked. I wasn't sure what she'd wanted to talk about, but that hadn't been what I expected. "I got in a fight with his friend, Eric, so we didn't stay at the party long. Then we went back to his house, and—"

"Not that." Stacy slashed a hand as she cut me off, but her lips were twitching. "Did anything unusual happen?"

"You mean besides the fight I had with the were-cougar?" The ringing of the phone continued in the background.

Stacy nodded, a smile appearing then disappearing just as fast. "Besides that."

"I had a seizure and fell over. And after I wasn't as thirsty anymore." I twisted my fingers together in my lap.

"And you were able to function without the amulet?"

"Only because we were so far away. I could still feel it trying to pull me in, but I could ignore it." I licked my lips. "I did struggle a little with bloodlust. I think the amulet masks it. I could feel the difference today when I put it back on."

Stacy nodded, eyes going distant. "I see."

The stairs creaked and I leaned forward to see Jack and Lin, the body bag hanging between them, coming down the stairs. Jack was in the lead, walking slowly backwards so he could hold the bag. They had to lift the bag over the balustrade to get it around the ninety degree turn at the bottom of the stairs into the foyer. We were silent as they made their way past the living room into the kitchen.

The phone was still ringing. "Don't we have an answering machine or something?" I asked as Lin disappeared from view.

"No, just let it ring." Stacy waved a hand. "Tell me about this seizure. That shouldn't happen to a vampire."

"I don't know. It was like..." I stared blankly at the living room drapes as I tried to put my swirling feelings into words. "...euphoria washed over me. It reminded me of when I feed, especially because my thirst went away too."

74

"But you didn't taste anything?" Stacy was perfectly still as she stared at me.

I shook my head in a blatant lie. "Can I get the phone now?" It was still ringing, the shrill sound making me wince.

"Fine." She waved a hand.

I dashed into the kitchen and grabbed the handset. "Hello?"

"Finally!" the man on the other end said, punctuating it with a sob of relief. "Is Evan there?"

"That's me." I twisted the springy cord running off the handset with a finger. I was a bit delighted of the novelty of having not only a landline, but a phone so old that it didn't even have a wireless handset. "Can I help you?"

"It's Gregory, from the bar," he said in a rush.

"The bar?" I blinked, trying to remember.

"You found me in the bathroom? I asked the bartender, he said you were the one. You are, right?" His tone was pleading.

"Oh, right. Yeah, that was me." I did remember now biting him in the stall. I'd left the house phone number and my name with the bartender, just in case. "What can I do for you?"

"What..." Gregory stopped and took a shuddering breath. "I don't remember what happened, it's fuzzy. What did you give me?"

"Give?" I looked at the ceiling, wrapping the cord around my hand, trying to follow Gregory's halting sentences.

"The drugs!" Another sob. "I need another hit of whatever it was... Please."

Shit. I closed my eyes and thumped my head back into the wall. He'd gotten it bad, just like Kevin. "That's not..." I didn't know what to tell him.

"Please. You gotta help me," Gregory sobbed into the phone. "Soon. I'm desperate."

"Alright, hold on." I put the phone to my chest and went into the foyer as far as the cord could reach, and gestured to Stacy.

She raised one eyebrow but stood and came over to me.

"It's a guy I bit last week," I whispered. "He's addicted. I need to go meet him—"

"Evan, it'll be dawn soon. No time." She crossed her arms.

"He can come over here." She was shaking her head before I'd even finished talking.

"No, not with this..." She gestured towards the ceiling. "...mess."

I sighed, but saw her point. I put the phone back to my ear. "Gregory, now's not a good time—"

"Please!"

"Look, give me your phone number and I'll call you back this evening." I went into the kitchen and rummaged in the junk drawer for a pen and pad of paper.

"Alright." Gregory gave me his number, which I wrote down before hanging up.

Lin and Jack came out of the pantry.

"Stacy, it's all set." Lin grabbed my arm. "But I'll need help chaining him up."

"What!" I froze, feeling sick as I remembered the chains hanging from the basement walls. Last time she'd just locked me in the room.

"Can I say goodnight first?" Jack glanced back and forth between Stacy and Lin.

Lin scowled but Stacy shrugged. "Make it fast. Lin, let him go."

Jack opened his arms, and I let him sweep me into a hug. "Everett, I wish you would have trusted me enough to tell me," Jack said, snuggling me close.

"I'm sorry." I buried my face in his chest. "You're right."

He leaned down and kissed the top of my head. "And about moving in together—"

"It's alright." I sighed and snuggled against him. "I shouldn't have suggested it like that without talking to you first."

"Call me after you get out, alright?" Jack held me out at arm's length.

I nodded. "I will. I promise." I made an X across my chest.

He hesitated, and he pulled me into another hug and leaned down to whisper into my ear, "I'm sorry about the basement. But you're strong. You'll be fine. Just remember there are people who care about you and trying to keep you safe."

I nodded, tears pricking my eyes. "I don't want to spend the night in the basement with Trevor's body," I whispered.

Jack chuckled softly. "I thought you were the big tough archaeologist. I've seen every Indiana Jones movie. That man dealt with a lot of skeletons."

"First, Jones is a horrible archaeologist. Don't even get me started." I laughed a little despite myself. "Second, I'm more of an art history major who does painting restoration."

"Noted." Jack laughed again. "Look, Ev. Think about it this way. Vampires are the top of the supernatural food chain. A ghost would be no match for you, if they even exist."

I giggled a little, despite myself. "If they even exist? You're saying you, a were-jackal who's dating a vampire, don't believe in ghosts?"

"Dead vampires never leave ghosts," Stacy added, hands on her hips as she stared at us, impatiently tapping her foot.

Jack shrugged. "Now, can I get one last kiss before I go?"

I happily obliged him. But my high quickly faded when Lin grabbed my arm, yanking me away and marching down the stairs. Unlike last time, she went into the room with me.

Trevor's body, still in the black nylon body bag, was laid out on the floor near the door. I averted my eyes as Stacy locked one of the metal cuffs around my ankle. It was attached to a long chain that ended at the wall near the mattress. She and Lin left without another word, slamming the door behind them and leaving me in total darkness, alone with a corpse.

Chapter 11

Chained Up

The dark surrounded me like a living being when I woke up the next night. Even with my vampire vision, I couldn't even see my hand when I waved it in front of my eyes. I rolled over on the thin mattress and closed my eyes, to no avail. I'd lost my ability to nap. My sleep was now like a switch for on/off with no in between, so I started singing to myself to pass the time.

Eventually the door clanged and swung open. I scrambled to my feet as light flooded in from the hall.

A vampire strode in. He had a long face that matched his stick-thin build, bleach-blonde hair that came down to his shoulders, and a thick unibrow. He looked early forties. With the hair and how lanky he was, he reminded me of a borzoi dog.

His face was impassive as he scanned me from head to toe. I crossed my arms and tried not to shrink under the weight of his gaze. I hadn't fed yet, and smell of him swirled around me. My fangs ached to come down, but I managed to keep them up for now with a combination of willpower and holding my breath.

Stacy came in and stood next to the man. "Lord Pembroke, I'd like to introduce you to Evan, formerly Everett."

Pembroke inclined his head to me. "Well met, Evan, formerly Everett."

"Nice to meet you," I said, trying not to shake. I could feel an aura swirling around Pembroke, like nothing I'd ever felt before.

"Where is the body?" Pembroke said.

"Here, Lord." Stacy went around behind him and dragged the bag into the middle of the floor, in reach of my chains. I could tell because the fingernail marks on the concrete reached to a little past where she'd put the bag. She knelt next to the body and unzipped the bag from head to toe and flipped it open. The musty smell came out strong, but quickly faded.

Pembroke slowly walked the length of the body, bending at the waist like a stork to get a closer look at the hands.

"What happened here?" Pembroke flicked one of Trevor's broken fingers. It flopped back, revealing bone sticking out through the paper-like cracked skin.

"He was all stiff. I had to break them to get the amulet out of his grip," I said, trying not to look at the way Trevor's peeled back lips looked like a smile.

"Interesting," Pembroke muttered. He knelt and turned over Trevor's hand to examine the palm. "You, Evan, come over here," Pembroke said.

The chains rattled as I walked over and knelt next to Pembroke. Two jagged holes marred the skin in the center of Trevor's right palm.

"Did you notice these?" His voice was bland and without inflection, but I shivered.

I swallowed down my disgust. "I didn't, but I was trying to look at it as little as possible."

"Is this the hand he had the amulet in?" Pembroke asked.

"Yes, Lin sent me pictures." Stacy shifted to sit back on her heels and got out her phone, then leaned across the mummy to show him the pictures, zoomed in on his hands clasped around the amulet.

"Speaking of the amulet," Pembroke said, "show it to me."

I hooked a finger through the chain, tugging it free of my T-shirt and holding it up.

Pembroke narrowed his eyes and leaned forward to study it as it swung, twisting around at the end of the chain. My fangs came down, and I couldn't hold back a growl at how close he was. Pembroke ignored me, but Stacy hissed at me.

"Knock it off, Evan. Show some respect," she whispered.

"Those holes in his palm look to be about the same distance as the vampire's fangs on the decoration. What direction was it facing when you retrieved it?" he asked.

"I don't remember," I said. I didn't. I'd been so focused on holding it again that I hadn't paid much attention. "Here." I pressed the face of the amulet against Trevor's palm and then tilted it away. The puncture wounds lined up perfectly, just as he'd suspected. That was disturbing. I dropped Trevor's hand and wiped my fingers on my shirt.

"That's what killed him?" Pembroke asked, getting to his feet.

I shrugged and glanced at Stacy. "I don't know that for sure."

"Lin thought Evan did it, but he has an alibi. Jack was with him the whole night," Stacy said with a sigh. "Could the amulet really do this, though?"

"Jack said he thought it could be my maker," I said.

"Another excellent possibility," Stacy admitted.

"How about we find out for sure." Pembroke snapped his fingers. "Isabella?"

A woman popped in from the hall and strolled over to join us. She had her long auburn hair up in a ponytail, and wore a peasant-style blouse and long skirt. A utility belt lined with pouches and bottles encircled her waist, and made her clink when she moved.

"I need to know what killed him." Pembroke gestured to Trevor's body.

"Of course." She nodded to Pembroke and began fiddling with the pouches on her belt. She got a green powder out, tossing it over the body as she began to intone a chant in a low voice.

I fell back on my hands and crawled away backwards as magic filled the room, making my skin crawl. Her hand began to glow with a blue light. I looked around the room to see the others' reactions, but no one else seemed as bothered by it. Stacy had stood and brushed off her skirt, moving to the side of the room. Pembroke stood next to Isabella, his arms crossed, staring at Trevor's body with interest.

The light on Isabella's hands winked out, and the feel of the magic brushing my senses faded. She dropped her arms and turned to Pembroke. "His blood was magically drained, through here." She put squatted and hovered her hand over Trevor's palm. "And the magical signature matches that." She pointed to the amulet on my chest. "There is something else, but there are layers of spells, and I'm having trouble untangling them all."

"What do you need to do that?" Pembroke asked, both of them staring at the amulet. I scrambled back father until my back hit the stone wall and put a hand over the amulet.

"Time to examine it properly." Isabella put her hands on her hips and stared at me. "What kind of vampire is he?" she said, pointing at me. "He felt different when I used my magic."

"An old one, we suspect," Pembroke said.

"Old one?" I asked, curious despite myself.

Pembroke shrugged. "Before my time even, and I have been around a very long time. Old ones are tales told to scare new vampires. But they seem to be legends no more." Pembroke looked at me like I was a bug about to be pinned. His gaze slid down to my chest and my hands clasped over the amulet, much like Trevor's had been. "I've had vampires combing the archives since you were found, and the time of that amulet was the last verified sighting of them."

"What happened to them?" My love of history was quickly overcoming my earlier fear, and I stared at Pembroke in wide-eyed fascination. My imagination gave me dazzling images of the kinds of lost texts that could be found in the archives of immortal beings. I suspected the amulet was from the Middle Kingdom of ancient Egyptian history, the peak of the Pharaoh's rule, although with my banishment to the house I hadn't been able to do any research to be sure.

"According to the archives, they were hunted." Pembroke gave me a nasty smile. "To extinction."

He was trying to scare me, but I refused to be intimidated. "Apparently not, because I'm here. And so is my maker."

"Your maker, yes..." Pembroke frowned, turning to Isabella. "Could this be communicating with his maker?"

"Possibly? I'd need to examine it closer. And if I seal it in a barrier, it will block both the compulsion that draws vampires to it as well as any connection to his maker that may exist."

"Wait, the mages said it's tied to my life force. That was why they didn't do any intrusive magics on it. Doing that might kill me." My instinct was to bolt. The door to the room was open but I knew from trying last night that I couldn't break the chain that locked me to the wall.

Pembroke gave me a long, silent look. "Is that true?" he asked Isabella.

"It's a possibility, yes."

"That's a risk I'm willing to take." Pembroke shrugged. "Do it."

I kicked away from them, scrambling across the mattress to wedge myself in the corner of the room. My head pounded as the voice screamed at me to protect the amulet.

"Wait," Stacy said. I sagged in relief, sure she was going to stand up for me against this insanity. "Last time we tried to take the amulet he frenzied, and four of us could barely hold him down."

I froze and stared at Stacy in shock, my mouth dropping open.

"Good point." Pembroke tapped his chin and glanced to the side, at the other restraints bolted along the wall. "Actually, in case this does kill him, I'd like to see something first."

"What's that?" Stacy asked.

"I want to see him feed from a vampire," Pembroke said. "The very idea is fascinating and repulsive."

"No one will volunteer for that," Isabella said with a laugh.

"I will," Stacy said.

Pembroke frowned. "Are you sure? I was going to order one of my underlings to do it."

"I know you wanted a demonstration, and I've already been bitten by him before." Stacy put a hand on my shoulder.

I perked up and looked at Stacy, my fangs coming down before I could stop myself, but held off and looked at Pembroke. He shrugged, so I took that as ascent.

"Yes, here." She held out her arm, offering me her wrist.

Didn't have to tell me twice. I lunged and grabbed her arm with both hands, burying my fangs into her wrist. I greedily gulped down her lukewarm blood.

After a few moments Stacy said, "That's enough, Everett—I mean Evan."

"No, keep going," Pembroke said as I started to retract my fangs.

I sunk my fangs back in, rebreaking skin that had already healed, and drank deeply. I hadn't had this much vampire blood since the first time, and I felt more than a little tipsy. My head spun and I couldn't think. I retracted my fangs and stumbled back. I took a few steps, wobbling on legs that felt like jelly and tripped over my own foot. I landed on my face, rolled over onto my back, and then lay there groaning as the world spun around me. An urge came over me, and it felt like my body moved on its own. I got up, pulling off my necklace as I did. My body held it out in front of me and charged at Stacy.

Suddenly my arm that held the amulet was flying away from me, unconnected to my body. I gasped, in control of myself again, and stumbled to a stop, grabbing the stump of my right arm with my left hand. I stared in shock at my arm lying on the floor next to Stacy, the amulet still clasped firmly in its hand.

Pembroke stood between me and Stacy, a small short sword held at the ready. Blood dripped from the edge. Mine, I assumed. Where had he been keeping that sword anyway?

"What the hell, Evan!" Stacy yelled.

Pembroke took out a cloth from his pocket and started cleaning the blade while looking at me

"It wasn't me," I gasped, eyes drawn back to my stump. It wasn't bleeding; in fact, it barely hurt. "I wasn't moving. It was like my body moved on its own." I took a step towards my arm, intending to pick it up to put it back on.

"Freeze," Pembroke snarled. I froze. Pembroke sheathed the sword behind his head before walking over and grabbing my remaining arm.

Stacy flopped down onto the mattress and put her head between her knees.

"What's wrong with her?" Pembroke asked me, shaking my arm.

"My venom," I slurred, dizzy from the aftereffects of the vampire blood. "It affects vampires too."

Pembroke grabbed my chin with his other hand and pulled my head up to look me in the eyes. "Interesting... It affected you almost as much as her."

I nodded.

"Isabella, get the amulet. By the chain, be careful not to touch it." He dragged me to my feet, then turned to Stacy. "Stacy, get his arm then follow."

I snarled and pulled against Pembroke's grip as Isabella knelt down next to the amulet still clasped in my severed hand, but his grip was even stronger that Stacy's, and he lifted me by the neck into the air.

After Stacy reattached my arm, they locked me into one of the sets of manacles, my arms pulled tight over my head so that my toes barely touched the floor. The floor restraints had only a few links attaching them, so that I could only move my feet a few inches in any direction. Not that I could have moved far anyway, with my arms stretched up like they were.

Time passed in a haze as I fought against the restraints. Isabella had gone out to get supplies for her spell, and Pembroke and Stacy had gone upstairs to talk, leaving me hanging, screaming and raving, in the basement. The amulet demanded I pick it up. It still lay on the floor where Isabella had dropped it after taking it from my cut off hand.

An eternity passed before the door creaked open again. I snarled and growled at the three as they filed back in.

Isabella pulled out a handful of what looked like table salt from one of the pouches on her belt. She walked in a slow circle around the amulet, chanting under her breath and letting salt trickle out of her fist onto the concrete. When she was done, her hand was empty. She took the knife and pointed the tip at the ground. She spat out a word I didn't recognize, and the little hairs on my arms stood on end. I shivered at the abrupt change of atmosphere. Although I couldn't tell what had changed, I felt...something.

The charge in the air grew as she paced around the circle, stopping at each corner turn to point with her knife in a different direction and saying a different word each time. By the time she got back to her starting point, my skin was crawling and my teeth ached with the magic crackling in the air.

The vampires watched silently as Isabella raised the knife and began screaming a spell into the air.

An empty feeling began in the pit of my stomach and slowly grew with the spell. I felt like someone was hollowing me out piece by piece with a spoon. I tried to scream, but couldn't find air in my lungs. Gone with the rest of my insides. The chains stopped me from moving, but if I could have, I would have curled up in a ball on the floor. Instead my knees buckled and I hung from my wrists on the chains, desperately gasping for air I suddenly needed very badly but couldn't get.

Isabella ended the spell by tossing a handful of things in the air that she pulled from another pouch on her belt. They clattered to the floor in the sudden silence.

That done, Isabella sheathed her knife and came over, leaning over me to examine me more closely. I felt like I'd been split in half. The two sides of me felt disconnected, and I didn't think I could have moved if I'd wanted to. My chin rested on my chest and my shoulders and wrists hurt from hanging. I tried to move my hand and wasn't even sure if a finger had twitched. Isabella reached for me, but Stacy was suddenly there, stopping her.

"Let me. I've already been bitten."

Isabella nodded and stepped to the side. Stacy took my chin and lifted my head. It lolled in her hand, despite me trying to move. My eyelids fluttered with fatigue at the effort, but I managed to keep them open. Just barely.

"Are you alright?" Stacy asked.

I tried to answer "no", but all that came out was a low moan.

Stacy frowned and dropped my head back to my chest, but Isabella nodded with satisfaction.

"Well, he's still alive," Isabella said. "So he isn't being animated by the thing." She put a finger on my forehead and pushed my head up to look me in the eyes, then used her other hand to push one of my eyelids up. I moaned again in protest, but couldn't do much more than hang there.

The empty spot in my chest began filling back up. At first it was just a trickle, but it was enough to let me lift my head, drop my fangs, and hiss at Isabella. She yanked her hand back with a frown and twisted to look at her circle.

Then the dam broke, and it was like the empty hole in my middle filled back up, knitting me back together. I got my feet back under me and stood on my tiptoes, trying to give my arms some relief. It didn't really hurt my shoulders, but being stretched so far was very uncomfortable.

"The seal..." Isabella murmured to herself, eyes widening. She ran a hand through her hair, shaking her head as she spun back towards her circle and my amulet.

"What happened?" Stacy asked.

"I've just sucked one year of your life away. How do you feel?" I groaned out. I felt a bit better, but my head was swimming and my whole body ached.

Stacy laughed. "I guess you're feeling better if you can make jokes like that."

Pembroke—and surprisingly, Isabella—just stared at me blankly.

"The seal I put over the item failed..." Isabella paced around her circle, frowning, her chin in her hand. "That's never happened to me before." I held my tongue on that one, as hard as it was.

"What does it mean? It may not have been animating him, but it clearly affected him deeply when your spell was working," Pembroke asked, walking over to touch Isabella's shoulder to stop her pacing.

"If you're done, can you let me down now?" My jaw clenched with thirst as I tried to keep my fangs up. I'd had so much from Stacy, but somehow I was thirsty again. Whatever she'd done to my amulet had drained me.

They all ignored me. The only sign anyone heard me was Stacy briefly flicking her eyes my direction.

Isabella pursed her lips and put her hands on her arms, her brow furrowing. "He's tied deeply to it. Soul deep. I'm not sure of the spell. Or its purpose."

"Any hypothesis?" Pembroke probed.

"I'd need to study it further." Isabella squatted down and stared at the amulet, resting her elbows on her knees.

"Anything you need," Pembroke said to Isabella before turning to Stacy. "In the meantime, what are your thoughts on this one?" He gestured at me.

Stacy glanced at me and sighed. "He's trying. I think he needs a new house mentor in order to thrive. He and Lin have been butting heads."

"Irrelevant. Is he dangerous?" Pembroke asked.

"No." Her voice was firm. "He has more self-control than any vampire I've ever seen, given his age. Trevor knew better than to touch that amulet. I think he'd be safe to stay here. Without the amulet."

Pembroke crossed his arms and clicked his tongue as he examined me but didn't say anything.

Isabella scowled and looked up from her examination. "I'm not certain about freeing him. He tried to bite me as the spell failed."

"He was in pain and scared," Stacy said. "He can control himself now." She put her arm up in front of my mouth, but kept her attention on Isabella. I clenched my jaw and held my breath, trying not to show how much effort it was taking me to not bite her.

"He recently fed," Pembroke waved a hand. "That tells us nothing."

"So what do you suggest?" Stacy's heels clicked on the concrete in the silence as she went over to Pembroke.

"Isabella will take the amulet with her for further study. Meanwhile, he'll stay here for a few days for observation," Pembroke said finally. "I'd also like to get the opinion of a few more of the council members."

"Very well." Stacy inclined her head to Pembroke and left the room.

Isabella took a metal box from one of the pockets of her skirt and used the chain to scoop the amulet into it. She and Pembroke left together, the metal door clanging shut behind them, leaving me alone.

"No, no! Mine! Bring it back!" I screamed as the amulet moved away from me, rattling my chains as much as I could, fighting without success to get free. Then the lights shut off, leaving me in darkness again.

Chapter 12

OMAHA

The land here was so flat. I'd never been to Nebraska before. I scanned the horizon on the cab ride in from the airport in between reading the report about the latest dead vampire. Another woman and man missing. It helped me keep my mind off of Everett, but I was still worried about him, and how his meeting with the council had gone.

In a stroke of luck, two passing vampires had witnessed the body being dumped in the early hours of the morning and managed to grab one of the culprits after seeing the corpse's fangs. They'd taken him and the body to the Omaha PCA office, who'd then called me. That had been last night.

I checked my phone again as I waited in the lobby for my guide; it was after dark in Portland, but Everett still hadn't called me. I guessed it was still too early in the evening for me to really worry. Maybe he was out getting something to eat?

A girl skipped out of the hallway and up to me. Her red-brown skin glowed in the harsh overhead lights and her curly black hair came to the middle of her back. Her silk shirt and pants belonged in another century and country. "You must be Jack," she said, spinning to a stop in front of me. "Pleased to meet you." I stood and offered her my hand with a grin.

"Varija." Her mouth quirked as we shook. "Where are you from?"

"Maryland, originally, but now I'm at the Portland office." Her hand was ice cold; she hadn't fed yet. "You got here fast." Varija took her hand back and gestured at me to follow her.

"Well, this is at least the fourth vampire death by draining in the last six months." I shouldered my bag and stood to trail her farther into the office. "I've been assigned to investigate. I'm playing catch up here, and I'm hoping your prisoner can give me some answers."

Varija grimaced. "Don't be so sure. I tried to talk with him last night, and well, I couldn't even get a name from him. Just nonsense." She stopped in front of a metal door. "I'll be coming in with you, to keep watch."

I shrugged. Vampires seemed to think shapeshifters were helpless against them, but in this case I welcomed the company. The vampire bar in New York had been creepy.

I nodded and we went in together, me dropping my bag by the door in the hall. With a start, I realized I recognized the vampire chained to the opposite wall. He was short and pale, with short brown hair, generic enough. But he still wore the outfit I'd seen in the security footage from the bodega, now the worse for wear. He was slumped over, and didn't look up as we came into the room.

"Dolf," I said, kneeling in front of him. "I'm Jack."

Dolf flicked his eyes up to look at me but otherwise didn't respond.

Varija sat down cross-legged next to me. "You know him?"

"Recognize him." I flipped through my notebook until I found the print-out I'd made of the security still, zoomed in on the three vampires and the old woman. I pulled it out and showed it to Varija before flipping it around and holding it up in front of Dolf. "I need to know what happened in New York."

Dolf glanced away from the picture. "Goddess," he whispered.

"I'm sorry to tell you this, but your wife is dead. We need your help to find her killer." I kept my voice low and compassionate, although I stayed carefully out of range, I did move a little closer.

Dolf narrowed his eyes at me and sat up, but didn't say anything. I frowned. This wasn't working.

"Don't you want justice for your wife, Dolf?" I pointed to Ada in the picture. "To find her killer?"

His eyes went red, and he bared his fangs at me and lunged. I didn't even twitch as the chains pulled him to a stop a few inches from me. That had not been the answer I'd expected.

"Has he eaten yet?" I glanced at Varija.

"Yeah." Varija pursed her lips and took the picture from me to examine it. "This is, was, his wife?"

"Ada, the third dead we know of. Haley, the bar owner in New York, said that they'd been married for hundreds of years."

Varija's eyes widened and she put a hand to her mouth, tears forming.

"Exactly, but yet he doesn't seem to care." I tapped on my notebook. "Is there another tact we can try maybe?"

"Dolf, are you thirsty?" Varija asked him.

"Not thirsty," Dolf said, licking his lips. He shook, the chains rattling.

"Is there something else I can get you?" I asked him.

"Nothing you can do for me. I need her." He got to his feet and struggled against his chains. "Let me go back to Goddess!" I exchanged a baffled look with Varija.

"Goddess?" she asked me.

I shrugged, as clueless as her.

"I need her! Please." Dolf wept openly now, still fighting the chains.

"I'd love to help you get back to the goddess, but I don't know where to find her." I offered him a friendly smile. "Sit, tell me about her."

Dolf stopped struggling. He didn't sit, but it was an improvement. "Goddess is wonderful." He clasped his hands and looked up at the ceiling. "She takes all the bad away."

I fought down a shiver. "That sounds nice." Keep it calm, Jack. "I'd like to meet her. What does she look like?"

"Everyone knows Goddess in their hearts." Dolf closed his eyes.

I asked a few more questions, but he didn't respond. Eventually Varija got up and left, and I followed her.

"See what I mean?" Varija said as she locked the door behind her. "He's been attacking anyone who comes close, and all he talks about is this goddess. Useless."

I shook my head. "On the contrary. I learned a lot."

"What do you mean?" Varija took me down the hall to her office. It looked a lot like mine: old computer, broken down and rattling desk, and threadbare chair. Only difference was her office was decorated with paintings and colorful tapestries of traditional Indian designs. Mine I'd put up soothing landscape paintings from Maine and the PNW, to try to help calm down the stressed-out new shapeshifters who were my most frequent visitors. She sat down behind her desk and I took the guest chair.

"I now know that we're looking for a woman, this goddess that Dolf referred to. It would help if we knew what she looked like, but we do know at least one person she's traveling with." I slid Kurt's photo out of my notebook and held it up for her.

"How many are missing?"

I put Kurt's photo back in my notebook. "Just the one now for sure. But you know how vampires are. She could have twenty more like Dolf with her already. It's not like we track vampires. Dolf and Kurt we know were missing only because she killed their partners. We found the dead bodies and looked into it..." I leaned back in my chair to look at the ceiling in thought.

Speaking of caring for someone, I pulled out my phone and checked it. No new messages. I sighed.

"You seem anxious about something." Varija leaned back into her chair and flipped a coin in her hand, running it along her fingers.

"Just my boyfriend. He had to go see the local vampire council last night and he said he'd message me when he got back..." I stuffed it back in my pocket. "But still haven't heard from him."

"Why would your boyfriend need to see the vampire council?"

"He's a vampire," I admitted. "That's part of why they put me on this assignment. I can fly at a moment's notice, and I don't mind working with vampires on this."

"Why not have a vampire investigate?" Varija cocked her head and flashed her fangs at me.

"You've seen what she does to them." I flapped my hand back the way we'd come, to Dolf. "Safer for a shapeshifter to investigate."

Varija snorted. "You're not telling me the whole truth."

"You're good." I raised my eyebrows. I thought I was pretty good at keeping a neutral face.

"You don't get to be hundreds of years old without learning a few tricks." Varija laughed.

"The truth is, my boyfriend was turned against his will, and we're trying to find his maker. We think it could be the same person who's draining these vampires." I ran a hand along my chin, scratching my beard in frustration.

"Do tell." Varija relaxed back in her chair and gave me an encouraging smile. "What's the connection?"

"The drained vampire," I said. "One was found in Portland around the same time he was changed."

"Loose connection." Varija tapped the arm of her chair. "There's got to be something more."

"There is, but I can't say any more." I thought back to Stacy stumbling around near-drunk the night Zoe had died, when he'd bitten her. And Lin saying Everett had attacked Trevor, craving vampire blood. Shit. "I figured out the pattern." I closed my eyes and massaged my temple.

"Pattern?"

"The disappearances. The drained vampires. I'd wondered why they were so few dead." I felt sick as it hit me what Dolf wanted from the goddess: the same thing Kevin had wanted from Everett. The same thing Stacy had wanted from him. I'd seen her withdrawals the last few days. Although she'd hidden it well, I'd been around her for a year and was observant. I'd seen the shake in her hands, and the way she'd snap her head around at any mention I made of Everett.

"You'll have to spell it out for me." Varija leaned over her desk.

"She couldn't stand having someone else these men cared for, so she killed their partners." I pounded the desk. Shit. Everett was in trouble. And so was I.

Chapter 13

THE TEST OF CONTROL

In the dark and unable to move, the amulet pulsing in the distance took up all my focus. I don't know how long I hung there, thirsty and cold.

The door creaked open and the lights clicked on. I blinked against the glare.

Pembroke slouched in, followed by Lin, Stacy, and a line of three more vampires I didn't recognize. They pulsed a dark red that was almost black.

I growled and showed them my fangs.

"Thirsty," I hissed at them, straining against my chains.

"Evan," Stacy said, coming up to me. "These are a few more members of the council. Put your fangs away."

I closed my eyes, holding my breath until I could get my fangs to go up. I concentrated on not breathing as I opened my eyes again and gave Stacy a toothy smile.

"Much better." She turned to the council members and presented me like a game show host. "As you can see, he's still in control despite not having anything to eat for three days."

I jerked my head around to stare at her. I'd been here three days? I groaned and gently hit my head on the wall behind me. "Three days?" I had to take a breath, and the scent of vampires almost brought my fangs down. "I promised Jack I'd call him."

"I sent him a message, don't worry," Stacy said quietly to me.

Pembroke waved a hand at me. "Stacy, unlock him."

"Be on your best behavior," she said after freeing me.

I stepped free of the chains and clasped my hands in front of me. I didn't know the proper etiquette, so I kept an eye on Stacy out of the corner of my eye. "Nice to meet you all," I said, keeping my head down.

Lin put a hand on her hip and glared at me. I did my best to ignore her.

"Let's hear from Stacy first," Pembroke said.

"Thank you, Lord Pembroke." Stacy put a hand on my shoulder. "I really don't have much to say. He's in control. His first night as a vampire, he was walking around downtown Portland. I recommend letting him stay here with supervision. Trevor was killed by the amulet, not Evan."

"He attacked Trevor! Tried to bite him. He's not in control." Lin scowled at me.

I bit my lip and turned my head away so I didn't have to look at her.

"Evan, do you have a response to that?" Pembroke asked.

"That was my fault. I left the amulet in my room. He unknowingly moved between me and it, and I lost it." I hugged myself tighter, but made myself look up and meet Pembroke's eyes. "But with the amulet so far away from me, that won't happen anymore."

Lin stamped a foot and pointed her finger at me. "Not true. You didn't have the amulet the night you went out with Jack, but I heard you attacked a shifter there and bit him."

I straightened, balling my fists up at my side. "He sucker-punched me in the back of the head first."

"Calm, Evan." Stacy strolled between me and the council members. She stopped with her back to me, facing the members. "Who among us hasn't made a few mistakes in their first few years as a vampire?"

She paused. Pembroke and the others council members were nodding thoughtfully and exchanging glances with each other. Even Lin looked embarrassed, blushing and rubbing her arm.

Stacy continued. "But we didn't have the PCA looking over our shoulders. Evan is still learning, and he should be given another chance."

Lin stomped on the ground and pointed an accusing finger at me. "But why should I be the one forced to stay here and teach him, just because I had been the one next in line to make a new vampire? I never even got to change my boyfriend."

Pembroke nodded, hand moving to his chin. "She makes a good point."

"I—" Lin stopped her rant and blinked up at Pembroke. "Well, yes, of course I do. But I see why. I can't take care of two new vampires at once."

Pembroke made a humming noise, then snapped his fingers. Two more vampires came in, dragging a human man who had his hands tied behind his back and a blindfold tied tight over his eyes.

I froze, grabbing my arms with my hands and clenching my jaw to keep my fangs up. I liked the smell of vampires, but the warmth of the human called to me in a different way.

The vampires dragged the human in, kicking aside Trevor's corpse which still sat near the center of the room. They forced him to his knees, and one of them grabbed his short hair, forcing his head back to expose his neck. I couldn't take my eyes off the pulse of blood flowing right under the skin.

"Evan," Pembroke said, his voice so hard I managed to tear my eyes away for a second to look at him. "This is your test. You are to bite this man, but not drink any of his blood."

"What?" I said at the same time as the human, making me look back at him in shock.

"You said he'd give me what I wanted!" the human yelled, struggling against the two vampires that held him. But their hands remained firm, keeping his head pulled back.

The voice from the phone. Gregory.

"Biting will give you what you want," Pembroke said with a chuckle. "But it won't give Evan what he wants, which is the point."

"You can do it," Stacy whispered to me, moving out of the way.

I didn't even know it was possible to bite someone but not drink from them. My feet dragged as I shuffled over to Gregory. As I knelt down next to him and let my fangs come down, Pembroke spoke again.

"Keep your fangs in until I say so. If I see you swallow, there will be consequences." Finished, Pembroke put his hands behind his back, now making me think of a stork.

I inclined my head to him before going for Gregory's throat. I sunk my fangs in. Gregory moaned as blood filled my mouth. I shook with the effort of not swallowing, and letting all the delicious blood run out of my mouth and down my throat.

"Enough, I'm impressed," Pembroke called. "Retract your fangs, and let go. You may swallow what you still have in your mouth."

I concentrated, finally getting my fangs to go away, and stood up, swallowing and licking the last of the blood from my lips. Blood streaked my shirt and pants. I used my palm to rub the worst of it off my chin, then wondered if it would be bad manners to lick it off my hand. Probably, but I was still tempted. I shivered. Being that close to Gregory, warmth filling my mouth, had accented the cold I was feeling in comparison.

Gregory looked like he was in heaven as the two vampires dragged his limp body back out into the hall.

I clasped my hands behind my back to cut down on my temptation. "What now?" I said softly, trying not to glance at the chains on the wall behind me. My stomach twisted at the thought of being locked back into them.

"The others and I will need to confer," Pembroke said. They filed out, leaving me alone with Lin and Stacy. The door clanged shut behind them.

Lin crossed her arms and glared at me, her eyebrows pulled so low they almost hid her eyes. I shuffled closer to Stacy. I wanted to ask what was happening, but I didn't want to be the first to break the silence. I'd passed the test, what did they have to confer about?

Stacy gave me an encouraging smile.

So thirsty. I grabbed my dirty hand with my clean one to stop myself from trying to lick it.

The door creaked open and Pembroke came back in alone.

"The council has made a decision." He paused, looking at the three of us.

I held my breath.

"Evan will stay at the house with Lin," Pembroke said, back ramrod straight.

"No!" Lin yelled, her fangs coming out. Her expression made me shiver.

Pembroke silenced her with a glare. "Silence. I am not finished. My progeny, William, will also be staying at the house to assist."

Lin huffed and crossed her arms, but her fangs stayed out.

"Evan clearly has the control of a much older vampire, as Stacy claimed, but yet he's so young that he still needs to learn. To this end, Lin, you have permission to change Stephen. William will help you contain him, and Evan can learn along with Stephen."

"Oh!" Lin grinned and her fangs popped back out of sight. "Thank you, Lord Pembroke."

"Help contain him?" I repeated with disbelief. I'd been hoping to go out and live on my own, but I guess this was much better than the vague consequences that Pembroke had hinted at.

"This will be a good experience, Evan." Stacy held her hands in front of her, eyes shining.

CHAPTER 14

MEETING THE PACK

SUNSET PINKS STREAKED THE sky overhead. The sun was already hidden behind the trees on the horizon, which meant it was safe for me to be out, albeit far too bright. I wore thick, wraparound polarized shades, but even with those I had to squint against the brightness.

Trevor's car was a tiny little hatchback that struggled to go over fifty on the freeway, but it got me to the park where I was meeting Jack. I had a few nights of near-freedom before Stephen was going to be changed.

I still had to spend the days at the house, and wasn't allowed a cellphone yet—they still wanted to monitor my calls just in case—but I could go out unattended.

William would be moving in tonight while I was out. He'd been with Pembroke last night and had introduced himself after I'd been released. Nice enough guy, I guessed, especially compared to Pembroke. William had an English accent and dressed like he'd stepped out of an old movie: vest, cravat, tight pants, and hose.

The sky in the west was still the purples and pinks of sunset when I parked in the lot, but I took off my sunglasses as I made my way over to the pavilion. No human would still be wearing them this late into the evening.

Crowds of people were gathered around the pavilion, the brick BBQ, and the surrounding picnic tables. There were quite a few families with kids as young as toddler age running around.

I paused at the edge of the parking lot and scanned the faces, looking for Jack. A waving hand caught my attention and I waved back, then wended my way through the crowd towards him.

He sat at a table with just one other person sitting across from him, a woman that looked to be in her late twenties with short curly hair and a friendly grin.

I sat down next to him and he slung an arm around my shoulders. He had a half-eaten hamburger on a plate in front of him.

"There you are. Glad you could make it. Vanessa, I'd like you to meet my boyfriend, Evan."

I blushed and lifted a hand to give a halfhearted wave to her. "Nice to meet you."

"Ohh, boyfriend? Finally." Vanessa looked me up and down then shot Jack a sly, lopsided grin. "Very cute. No wonder you've been keeping him all to yourself." She leaned across the table over her plate and held out her hand to me. "I'm Vanessa."

"Nice to meet you, Vanessa," I said, taking her hand.

Her grip was strong enough to make me wince, the muscles on her arms visible with her sleeveless shirt.

The smile slid off her face as she held my hand. "Your skin is like ice, Evan."

I took my hand back and crossed my arms, shooting Jack a glare. He'd assured me I'd be fine to come to a shapeshifter event; no one would even know I was a vampire. Yeah, right.

Vanessa just stared at me, her grin slowly coming back. "You're a vampire. Jack, you're dating a vampire!" She turned to him and put her head on her palms. "That's so cool. Why didn't you tell me?"

I groaned and put my arms on the table, then laid my head in it facedown. "I'm the worst vampire ever. I didn't even pass for five minutes."

"Vanessa's very observant." Jack rubbed my back in a circle. "Don't worry about it."

"Pro-tip," Vanessa said, and I raised my head enough to look at her. "Next time, eat before you come. Not only will you be flush from feeding, but you'll be warm enough that you won't have to avoid handshakes. Also, your mentor really did you a disservice if they didn't even teach you that much."

"My mentor really doesn't like me, that's what happened," I said, briefly raising my head.

"I should have figured you'd understand, Vanessa, but I was afraid after your breakup..." He shook his head and gave me a side hug before pulling his hand back and picking up the rest of his hamburger.

"Breakup?" I asked, cocking my head. "Were you dating a vampire too?"

Jack popped the last bite of his hamburger in his mouth and swallowed it.

"Yeah, I was, but as Jack mentioned, she and I aren't together anymore." Vanessa laughed. "I'm afraid we don't have anything for you to eat. If Jack had warned me..."

I elbowed him gently, and he winced and let out a rueful laugh, saying, "I was hoping to keep the vampire part to myself. I'm a little paranoid after what happened at Eric's party."

"That was you?" Vanessa laughed louder and harder until tears seeped out the corners of her eyes and she wiped them away. "Damn."

"I'm going to get another burger," he said, grabbing his now empty plate. "You want anything, Evan, Vanessa?"

"I'm good," Vanessa said, munching on one of the pile of chips left in front of her.

"Gatorade for me, or a water," I said.

Jack nodded and got up to head towards the smoking grill.

"I can't believe Jack introduced you to Eric first," Vanessa said a few minutes later after eating a few more chips. "What did he think would happen, honestly?"

"He thought they were friends." I shrugged.

"That boy's been hung up on Jack for a while. Not the smartest move on his part." Vanessa brandished a chip at me.

A couple of kids ran behind me, brushing my back and bare arms near my elbows. The shock of the warmth of their skin on mine almost made my fangs come down, and I had to close my eyes and clench my jaw until the feeling passed.

"You alright? You look a bit pale. When was the last time you ate?" Vanessa leaned towards me and gave me a critical look.

"Last night." I rubbed my legs and licked my lips. "I'll be fine till the run starts. I'll find someone after."

I glanced up at the full moon rising overhead, making the night bright enough that it would have hurt my eyes if I hadn't been out earlier. Still, it was bright enough to make me squint. "Can I ask you something?"

"Sure."

"Shifters don't need the full moon to change, so why schedule your runs on the night of the full moon?"

Vanessa chuckled. "I thought for sure you were going to ask what animal I turn into." She shook her head. "The full moon thing is tradition, mostly."

A plate landed on the table next to me, followed by a bottle of Gatorade, and then Jack plopped down back into his spot. "Plus, not everyone's animals are naturally nocturnal. This way it's bright enough that we all can play."

I sat back up straight and tried to ignore the smell of the freshly cooked burger from next to me. It was making me a bit nauseated. I scooted away from Jack as discreetly as I could.

Jack slid the bottle of Gatorade down to me. I twisted the top off and took a swig, puckering my face at the taste, but it really did help with the thirst. I lowered it and looked at Vanessa to keep from having to watch Jack eat his burger.

"Who was this vampire you dated?" I asked. "If you don't mind me asking."

"I don't kiss and tell." Vanessa blew me a kiss.

I laughed. "So, why'd you two break up? Because of the vampire thing?"

"What?" Vanessa wrinkled her nose. "Of course not. The sex was incredible." At this she sighed and pretend to fan herself. "And she was super cute. But she broke it off with me. Decided it was time to move on. Didn't want to fall into a rut. You know how it is." Vanessa sighed again, deeper this time, and nibbled on another chip.

I shifted uncomfortably. "Not really. I'm pretty new."

"No kidding." Vanessa sat forward, propping her elbows on the table and resting her chin on top of her palms, "I thought I knew all the vampires in town. Where'd you move from?"

I shook my head. "No, like new at being a vampire." I paused, her statement sinking in. "Wait, you know ALL the vampires in Portland?"

"Yeah, I mean, not well, but I met them all at the newest Portland vampire's—Trevor's—party. Why weren't you there?"

"Party?" I frowned. The mention of Trevor made my stomach twist, and combined with the smells of BBQ permeating the air were making me nauseated.

"You know, his party." She looked at me expectantly.

I glanced at Jack, who shrugged and shook his head. He swallowed. "No idea, sorry, Ev."

"I don't know what that is," I admitted, turning back to Vanessa.

Vanessa's eyes widened. "You're kidding, right? Every new vampire gets a party after they're turned. Usually a year or two later, when they've got the bloodlust under control. Clearly you do." She waved at the party around us. "So, didn't you get one?"

I'd tensed as Vanessa mentioned the party, upset that I hadn't gotten one, but relaxed as she finished. "A year or two after turning?" I shook my head. "I'll probably get one eventually, but I see why Stacy hasn't organized one yet. Maybe I'll get a dual party with Stephen. Two-for-one."

Vanessa's eyebrows raised as I spoke. "Wait, when were you turned?"

I drummed my fingers on the table, thinking. "A few months ago?" I craned to look at Jack for confirmation.

"About right." Jack nodded.

Vanessa's eyes widened. "What!" Her voice was high-pitched, close to a scream, but at a whisper volume. She leaned back away from me, giving me a wary look. "Why are you here?"

"It's fine, Vanessa."

"I met with the whole council last night." I twisted my Gatorade bottle on the table. "I was cleared to be going out."

"A month..." Vanessa whispered, staring at me with fear in her eyes. Her voice shook. "He's dangerous, Jack, you shouldn't have brought him."

Tears pricked my eyes. I thought Vanessa would understand.

Jack growled and put down his burger, but I held up my hand.

"Stop. Jack, I don't want to make you miss the run. I'll go." I didn't want to be here anymore. I climbed out of the seat and ran.

"Ev, wait!" Jack called out after me, but I ignored him as I jogged away. My fangs were pressing on my lips anyway, so I would have needed to leave soon regardless. I didn't want to eat any of the shapeshifters. Not only would it cause them pain as I'd seen with Jack, since my venom didn't work on them, but I actually didn't like how they tasted.

The park officially closed after dark, but I found a family still packing up at the far end. While the wife carried the kids to the car, I ambushed the husband from behind a pillar, latching onto the back of his neck. He spun, flailing at his back trying to get me off, but he couldn't get a good grip on me from that angle. A moment after my fangs pierced his skin, he fell to his knees, his arms slack at his side. I sucked hard, trying to take as much as I could before his wife came looking for him. When I was done I pushed him over in his side, snagged an unopened bottle of beer, and dumped a little into his mouth and the rest over his clothing. Not that she'd really believe he got so drunk in the few minutes since she left him, but it gave enough plausible deniability of the supernatural.

Feeling a lot better now, I ran off, using a little bit of speed to get to the cover of the trees. A howl went up in the distance, followed by a roar and a screeching cry of an animal I didn't recognize. The run must have started.

I stopped in the trees and stared up at the night sky, feeling hollow. I missed Jack, and I'd been looking forward to spending time with him. Lin had left to go set things up with Stephen, so I definitely didn't want to go back to the house, dark and empty and potentially filled with ghosts.

This park was near Estacada, out in the wilderness away from Portland's light pollution, and the stars were bright overhead. Calming.

I strolled through the woods, kicking at the pine needles, until I found an empty picnic table out in the open, that wasn't covered by one of the pavilions, and lay down on it on my back to watch the stars.

I wasn't there long before the howling and yipping cries seemed to get closer to me. I sat up just as a wave of animals broke out of the trees. I jumped to my feet and spun, but more animals came out from behind me. I froze in place, feeling a bit trapped as the animals circled around the picnic table and stopped.

A jackal trotted out of the crowd and hopped up onto the table next to me. The jackal wagged its fluffy tail and plopped down next to me, looking up at me with an open-mouthed grin.

"Uh, hi Jack." I gulped and hugged myself, looking around. It was like all the animals in the zoo had escaped. Wolves were predominant, making up about a fourth of the crowd. Mixed in among them were foxes, coyotes, skunks, raccoons, hyenas, wild African dogs, badgers, lynxes, panthers, and even a giant brown bear that towered above everyone else.

A cougar prowled out of the crowd and put its front paws up on the bench of the picnic table. Jack's huge ears went back.

I put my fangs down and bared my teeth at the cougar. "Eric, stay away. Don't think I won't bite you again."

The cougar lashed his tail and started —for want of a better word—getting bigger. Muscles bulged on his legs and arms as he staggered to his feet. His muzzle grew longer, growing more teeth. I widened my eyes and stepped back, careful of the edge of the picnic table. Eric stood tall on two legs, but he wasn't human; he was something between human and cougar, a strange fusion of the two.

"What the hell is that?" I gasped.

Snarling, Jack moved between me and the biped cougar man. "Eric, what do you think you're doing?"

"I'm killing that thing to free you," Eric rasped, barely understandable between the malformed jaw. He reminded me of the werewolves from the movies, bipedal and furry with big claws and even bigger teeth, except for the feline tail and the tawny cougar fur.

"I'm not under a compulsion," Jack barked. "You know vampire tricks don't work on us."

The other animals were shifting restlessly. A large black wolf stepped from the crowd, ears pricked high. "Eric, Jack's right. You may not understand it, but that doesn't mean the vampire did any sort of trick."

"Well, he still deserves to die," the creature growled as it lunged at me.

Jack jumped up to intercept him, but he was less than half Eric's size and Eric swatted him aside with one swipe, sending Jack flying away. I stepped back, forgetting that I was already standing on the edge of the table. I tumbled backwards off the table, landing painfully on my back on the bench seat as Eric's monster form flew over me.

Somewhere nearby, Jack landed with a pained yelp. I rolled sideways under the table as Eric flipped around midair and landed, his claws tearing long furrows in the grass. He snarled at me and charged, spittle flying from his jaws. I screamed and scrambled backwards until I hit the bench seat on the other side.

Jack howled and charged under the table between me and Eric. The rest of the shapeshifters had their ears back, but none of them moved to help me or Jack.

Eric hit the bench, snarling and swiping at me under the table, but his muscled torso was too big to fit in the space between them. I screamed louder and curled up into a ball, hands over my head. His claws raked down my arm, leaving four long gashes. They didn't heal instantly like I'd expected they would, but continued to ooze blood.

Jack snarled and bit at Eric's arm.

"Jack, change like him, fight him off!" I yelled as Eric's claws got my side, ripping my shirt and tearing at my side.

"I can't," Jack was panting, blood staining his teeth. "Don't know how."

"Eric, that's enough!" the wolf snarled. "The rest of you go, enjoy your run. I'll take care of this."

Sounds of lots of feet pounding on the grass overlapped with a wolf's howl. Then there was a snarl and then a loud yelp. Eric's swiping arm withdrew. More snarling, along with the sound of tearing and shredding.

I risked a peek out, lowering my arms and pushing up to one elbow.

A black-furred wolf creature rolled on the grass with Eric's large form.

The rest of the animals were gone.

"You two go!" the wolf snarled at us.

Shaking, I crawled out from under the table, Jack's furry body brushing my legs. I ran through the dark woods, letting Jack nudge me in a direction.

"Are we at least going away from the other shifters?" I asked after a few minutes.

Honestly, except for the circumstances, running through the woods at night with Jack was pretty fun. The stars shone overhead, and the woods buzzed with nightlife. Pine needles crunched under my feet and the cool breeze rushed past my face.

"Yeah, they ran the other direction," Jack barked, running at my side.

"Won't Eric be able to track us by scent?" I vaulted over a fallen log with an excited whoop.

"He would, yeah," Jack said, "but Felicia won't let him."

"What?" I slid a little on the pine needles and fell, rolling to a stop in the dirt. I sat up, and Jack came up and licked my face. "Felicia? That big black wolf is a woman? The alpha's a woman?" I asked.

Jack sat between my legs. "That alpha thing is a load of crap, Everett. All she has to do is hold him off for a few minutes. I've been told it takes a lot of energy to hold the warrior form. After that he'll be too tired to come after us."

"That's good then." I pulled my knees up to my chest. The gashes on my arm had almost healed. "Why'd you lead them all over to me, though?"

Jack whined and his ears went back. "I wanted to introduce you to everyone. I thought if they just met you..."

I picked up a pine needle, twirling it front of my face before dropping it and letting out a long sigh. "It's fine."

Jack leaned against my leg, his wagging tail thumping the back of my thighs, and I unthinkingly reached out with my free hand to rub the top of his furry head.

"I'm not a dog, Ev," Jack said, but he sounded more amused than angry. Still, I moved my hand down to rest on the thick ruff of fur around his neck.

"I'm sorry I made you miss the run." I flopped back into the pine needles. I'd fallen in a clearing, and the sky spread out above me, bordered by treetops.

Jack lay down next to me and rolled over onto his back. He nosed the side of my face. "That's alright, I'd rather spend time with you." He turned his head, one ear flopping to the side, and gave me a sideways smile, flashing teeth. His tail wagged.

I smiled and put a hand on his tummy to rub it while looking up at the stars. "It's a beautiful night, and I had a lot of fun running with you." It was, too. Only a few small clouds floated by, dark blots briefly obscuring the stars as they floated past.

"I did too."

We lay like that, watching the stars wheeling overhead in silence for a while. Eventually, Jack flopped over to put his front paws on me.

"You know, I don't have to have you back till dawn, and I saw a motel just off the highway on the way here."

I giggled. "We could just go back to the house. Lin is gone. She went to see Stephen to plan for his change. And William won't be moving in until close to dawn." Jack cocked his head at me. "William is my new babysitter," I explained.

One of Jack's ears went back and he gave me a playful smile. "You only have a twin bed, Ev."

"What, you not up for the challenge?" I tugged on one of his large eartips.

Jack nipped at my hand. "Fine, challenge accepted. Race you back to the cars." With that, he launched over my stomach and raced off into the woods.

Laughing, I chased after him. I teased him a few times, letting him get ahead of me briefly before putting on a burst of superhuman speed that even a jackal running on all fours couldn't keep up with.

We burst out of the trees behind the picnic tables the BBQ had started at. Discarded clothing was scattered everywhere. I followed Jack over to the picnic table he'd been sitting at before.

Jack's clothes sat on the top of the table, neatly folded up. His keys, wallet, and cellphone piled on top.

"Aren't you afraid of these getting stolen?" I said, plopping down on the end of the bench and leaning back against the table on my elbows.

The jackal crouched and leapt up onto the tabletop next to me. "Naw, someone always stays behind to watch the stuff." He nodded to the pavilion behind me. "There."

I twisted around and frowned, scanning the area. "I don't see anyone," I said finally.

"That's the point," a growly voice said from under the table. "Thanks for giving away my position, Jack."

I jumped, scrambling up the rest of the way onto the table as a black shape squeezed out from under the bench where I'd been sitting. It stood and stretched up to full height, putting its eyes level with the table. It had dark gray fur with darker black stripes on its front and back legs, and a mane of black hair that went from its hunched head all the way down its back. It looked like a hyena with its hunched body and muscled chest.

"What is that?" I asked Jack, staring at the animal. "And who?"

"Vanessa," the creature said, lips pulling back in a facsimile of a human smile. "And I'm an aardwolf." She turned her attention to Jack. "I take it introductions didn't go well. I hate to say I told you so, but..."

Jack snarled, the ruff of hair on his neck puffing out and his ears going back flat to his head. "Don't start, Vanessa. At least I tried. You didn't even have the guts to tell anyone in the pack you were dating a vampire."

"Whatever." The aardwolf snorted and padded away, disappearing into the shadows of the pavilion.

Her black and gray coat blended into the shifting shadows almost perfectly. Even knowing she was there, I could barely make her out until I let my fangs come down. Then her warmth blossomed to life in my view as a bright red blot against the cooler background. I put my fangs back up and shook my head, sitting back down where I'd been.

Next to me Jack's form stretched and grew, his fur and tail receding back into his skin. He grunted softly in what sounded like pain, and then a fully human and naked Jack was crouched next to me on the table.

I tucked my legs up under me and rested my head in my hand, enjoying the view as he got dressed.

"Meet me at the house?" I said as he sat down next to me to put on his shoes.

"Yeah, I'll be right behind you." Jack rested his foot on his knee and bent down to give me a brief kiss on the lips.

The parking lot had been pretty full when I arrived, so I was parked at the very end of the lot, out of sight of the pavilion. Everything was peaceful, the only sounds the hooting of owls and the chirping of crickets.

As I got behind the wheel of Trevor's car, I heard another car door slam. Jack sure had put his shoes on fast. Must be motivated. I grinned in anticipation.

My headlights came on and I backed out of my spot. Closer to the pavilion, a set of headlights turned on. The second car, a light-colored sedan like Jack's, trailed me out of the lot and onto the highway, but I lost track of it once I was on the freeway with all the cars. I got off the highway, wending my way back to Estacada. A light-colored car followed me off the exit, matching me turn for turn. I was starting to get worried, but when I turned onto the gravel driveway that led to the house, the car kept going up the paved road. I relaxed. They must live nearby, and it was just a coincidence.

The house was dark as I pulled up and parked in the roundabout driveway in front. Even the porch light was off.

I should have asked Lin when she was coming back, but knowing her and Stephen, I counted on her not being back until dawn. It occurred to me that I didn't know if it was against the rules to bring a date back to the house. Then again, it wasn't like Jack didn't already know where the house was.

I went inside, turning on all the lights on the first floor and the porch light in an attempt to make the house feel a bit more welcoming, and then paced restlessly while I waited for Jack to arrive. Fifteen minutes later I heard the crunch of tires on gravel and ran out onto the porch to see Jack pulling up in his white sedan.

"What took you?" I joked as he got out. "Hit every red light after you got off the freeway?"

"Actually, I made great time. You're just impatient." Jack swept me into a hug.

I laughed. "True, but I thought you followed me out of the lot. Guess it must have been another shifter who decided to leave early."

"Must have been," Jack agreed as I snuggled him closer. "I didn't leave until about ten minutes after you. I had to finish getting my shoes on, and then Vanessa wanted to chat for a minute."

"Enough talk," I said with a breathy laugh, grabbing his shirt and pulling his head down to meet mine as I pushed up to my tiptoes. Jack grabbed my ass with both hands, cupping my cheeks and lifting me up into the air as we explored each other's mouths with our tongues. He carried me into the house and up the stairs, where we fell breathlessly into my bed.

CHAPTER 15

SALT LAKE CITY

ANOTHER VAMPIRE DEATH, ANOTHER plane trip for me. This latest one was just hop over from Portland, only a few-hour flight away, in the Salt Lake valley.

A wall of heat hit me when I left the air-conditioned interior of the airport. I was sweating through my shirt before I even made it ten steps to the street.

I called Varija in Ohio for an update on Dolf while I waited in line for a cab. This news about another death had reminded me to check in with her. The phone rang twice before she picked up. "Varija."

"Hey, it's Jack. Have you gotten anything from Dolf yet?"

Varija sighed. "No, and I have even worse news. We lost him."

"What?" I groaned. "When was this?"

"Day after you left." Varija paused. Probably she heard me grinding my teeth.

"Why didn't anyone tell me?"

"Look, it's not a big deal." I heard sounds of typing on the other end of the line. "He didn't do anything wrong, so we let him go. I did send an agent to tail him, to see if we could follow him to this goddess he mentioned."

I massaged my forehead. "What about the..." I paused, glancing around at all the normal folk waiting for their cabs around me. "The problem he was found with?"

"Even if he did help kill her, it's not a crime for a vampire to kill another vampire," Varija said.

"What?" I almost dropped the phone. "Then why am I in this hot hellhole investigating another one?"

"Hey! Don't swear. There are kids around," the woman behind me in line yelled.

"Sorry," I said to her, covering up the mouthpiece of the phone for a moment.

"I think I gave you the wrong impression," Varija said. "We live for a very long time."

I sighed. "Elaborate then."

"We do take killing seriously, and investigate any vampire deaths, but we really only do more than a slap on the wrist if the vampire makes a habit out of it."

I sighed again and rubbed the bridge of my nose. "You're kidding me. Alright. So you let Dolf off with a warning. Then what happened?"

"My fault, you warned me." The typing stopped, and this time it was Varija's turn to sigh. "The vampire I sent to follow him stopped checking in, and worse, we tracked her phone and found it in a dumpster."

"Send me her information. I'll keep an eye out for her," I said.

"Just did," Varija said.

"Thanks. I'm on my way to see another one, so I'll update you after that." I hung up as I'd gotten to the front of the line for a cab.

The ride over to the address was short. The driver insisted, after I let it slip that I hadn't been here before, that I just had to see the temple.

I had to admit, it was a pretty building, but a bit stark for my taste. White marble and gold. Severe Gothic architecture. Where was all the color, the life? Still, I told the cabbie it was impressive, because it was.

The driver dropped me off at the PCA office for the area. I was getting quite the tour of them.

While I waited for my guide, I checked my email on my phone; the ride had been short enough that even with the detour, I hadn't had a chance to check it. Sure enough, I found an email from Varija with the file on her missing agent along with a photo attachment.

My guide, a girl who couldn't have been more than eighteen with curly blond hair and a bubbly smile, took me back to the morgue to show me the dead vampire.

"Have you identified who it is yet?" I asked her as she pulled out the body. It was totally covered by a white sheet.

She shrugged. "How should I know?"

I sighed and pulled the sheet off. Another mummified corpse. Sunken eye-sockets and a mouth that seemed to scream at me.

"Ew." The girl wrinkled her nose. "That's gross."

I glanced at her, hiding a smile. "Punishment duty, I'm guessing? You don't have to stay."

"Thanks." She ran to the door and paused there. "Uh, knock when you're done." Then she was gone, the door swinging shut behind her.

They'd left the clothes on the body, which was helpful. A woman, wearing a low-cut blouse and tight jeans.

I checked her pockets, but no ID or any else that would identify her. I noted the hair color, brown and long, at least to her shoulder. I measured her height, five foot eight. I wrote it in my notebook, but was getting a sinking feeling.

I'd just read about a brown-haired vampire woman of that height. I undressed her and laid out the clothing on an empty autopsy table, then took a photo of the outfit.

I emailed it to Varija. "Do you recognize these?"

I folded up the clothing and set it on the body, putting it back into the drawer. I was about ready to knock for the girl when my phone rang.

"Varija?" I answered without looking at the screen.

"No, sorry to disappoint you," Eric replied, sounding amused. "Who is this Varija you're breathlessly waiting on a call from, hmm?" He chuckled. "Cheating on your boyfriend?"

"Eric." I rolled my eyes. "No, she's a coworker. What do you want?"

"I'm giving you one more warning to dump that vampire."

I put my head in my hand. "Eric, I'm not going to date you, even if Everett and I do break up."

"Everett? Before you called him Evan."

I winced. Damn Everett for asking me to call him that in private, I forgot to use his new name. "Ah, yeah, he changed his name. But that's not important now. Why did you call?"

"That name sounds familiar..." Eric mused.

"Eric, focus." I ground my teeth, turning to stare down at the mummy on the autopsy table in front of me. "I'm at work right now, and I haven't slept yet. This should have been my day off but I got an emergency call on my way home from the run, and now I'm in Salt Lake and I have a very short fuse. Why. Did. You. Call?"

"I'm trying to warn you. Your boyfriend is hanging around a vampire named Lord Pembroke. I asked around about him, and he's bad news."

I suppressed a sigh. "Thank you for telling me." A beep drowned out my next words. "Look, Eric. I need to go, I have another call coming. Probably Varija. I'll talk to you later." I had no idea who this Pembroke was, but I'd have to worry about that later.

I hung up on Eric without waiting and immediately clicked over to the other call.

"Where did you find those?" Varija demanded as soon as I picked up. She had a slight lisp in her voice that told me her fangs were down. Much more subtle than Everett's pronounced one, but listening to him had tuned me in to it.

"The dead vampire in Salt Lake City was wearing them."

The blond girl poked her head in. "Jack? Was that a phone ringing?"

"Yeah, give me a sec." I held up my hand to her. "Varija, so I take it this is her?"

"Shit, yes." Varija sounded defeated.

"Sorry, I really am. This dead vampire is your lost agent." I sighed. "I'll arrange to have her body sent back to Omaha."

Chapter 16

Brand New Vampire

Without Trevor, the house was quiet. I'd had so much fun with Jack the night before that I missed him already. I got on my Vita and messaged him. A half hour or so later he replied back that he'd call me. I would have called him myself, but I didn't know his phone number; I couldn't remember it, and it wasn't on the list of numbers posted on the refrigerator. I'd remedy that today.

A few minutes later the house phone rang. I used vampire speed to dash into the kitchen to answer it.

"Hello?" I answered in a rush before the first ring had even finished. I slid on the laminate floor, my socks not finding any traction until I crashed into the counter and almost dropped the phone.

"Geez, Ev," Jack laughed. "I'm guessing you're excited to hear from me. Where are your babysitters?"

"William went out to hunt, and Lin's out with Stephan. One last human hurrah or something." I walked, more slowly this time, back through the kitchen. I wanted to sit on the couch, but the stupid cord wouldn't reach that far. The phone's novelty had already worn off. Instead I sat at one of the stools at the bar.

"Maybe a little of that." Jack's voice turned more serious. "But they'll also be setting up Stephan's fake death. Probably a car accident."

"That sounds serious." I spun on the stool and flopped back, draping an arm across my face. "So then after they'll come back to the house and..." I shuddered. "I wonder if Stephan is still having second thoughts?" I hoped that the extra time had been what he needed.

"When did he tell you that?" Jack asked quietly. "Heck, when did you even meet him?"

"Stephan and his friend, Lance, met us at the bar one night."

"He told you this with Lin right there?"

"Well..." I squirmed. I didn't really want to get Lin in trouble, but I guess if he told then he'd have to admit where I got internet access. "Don't tell Lin I told you this."

Another laugh. "My lips are sealed."

"Lin snuck him over one day after dawn." I sat up to rest on my elbow.

"Lin seems smarter than that. Wouldn't she wait till you were asleep?"

I hadn't told anyone this yet, and the undertones were more sinister now that Trevor was dead. "I guess I slept-walked or something? Stephen woke me up in the hall... I had my hand on Trevor's doorknob."

"What? Ev, vampires don't sleepwalk." I could practically hear him shaking his head. "You probably haven't seen it, but it's not sleep like you think of it. Vampires are effectively dead during the day. You aren't walking anywhere."

I frowned, remembering how it had been the other times, like I hadn't been in control. I wondered...

"Ev? You still with me?" Jack's voice broke me out of my musing.

"Yeah, anyway, I went downstairs and hung out with him and Lance for a few hours. He's the one that got me the Wi-Fi password from Lin's room."

"Ev, that living room isn't light-proofed."

"I'm fine, obviously," I said. Jack was being so dramatic.

"You're playing with fire, you just don't realize it."

Jack was exaggerating about the sunlight, he had to be. I sighed and ran a hand through my hair. I had been so busy I'd forgotten to get it cut.

"Hey, Everett." Jack's voice cut through my thoughts. "Who's Lord Pembroke?"

"Huh?" I sat up blinking, swapping the phone to my other ear. "Oh, he's the head of the vampire council. Why?"

"Eric called me. Just..." Jack huffed. "I looked him up in the system. He's, well, just be careful around him."

Weird. Where would Eric have gotten his name from? I couldn't see him socializing with vampires. "I will, Jack. Honestly he creeped me out."

"Good." Jack sighed. "I'm glad you messaged, but I've got to go. My flight just got in and I'm exhausted. Heading home to bed. I'll talk to you later."

"Flight?" I asked, but Jack had already hung up. I wondered where he'd gone and why.

I PLAYED ON THE vita until I heard a car on the gravel outside. I rushed upstairs to put it away before going down to wait in the living room. A key rattled in the lock, and then Stacy opened the door.

"Evan." She nodded to me and went to the living room to sit on the couch. "Jack asked me to show this to you. Come." She patted the couch next to her as she pulled out a tablet out of her bag.

"Jack called me earlier. He said he had just flown somewhere. Do you know where he went? Is something wrong?" I asked her as I sat down.

"Just an emergency work trip, no big deal." Stacy gave me an easy smile that didn't reach her eyes.

She wasn't telling me everything, but I didn't want to confront her; she'd done too much to help me out. "Alright. So what's this video?"

"Just watch." She opened a video and pressed play. It looked like a home video shot on a cellphone, vertically, of a sunny garden shot from inside through an open door. Two people were talking in the background not visible in the camera shot, challenging each other.

"You first."

"No you."

"Look," the camera-holder said, and held out a hand, moving closer to the light, but not even in it. He held his hand there a few moments until smoke came up and his skin darkened to almost black. He pulled it back. "It's a bad idea, I told you."

The video got shakier, as if the cameraman was shoved. Then the cameraman pushed the other man away from him, into the camera shot. The man stumbled forward and smoke wafted from his exposed skin. He threw his hands in front of himself to catch himself. He managed to stop, but his outstretched hands went in the light.

Immediately the skin of his fingers burst into flame. He began screaming and hopped back from the sun. But it was too late. The flame spread fast; only a few seconds passed before he was engulfed. The person holding the camera backed up, but kept filming until the flaming vampire was nothing but ash and the video ended.

I sat back on the couch, blinking, and put my hands on my lap, turning them over and looking at them. I'd been closer to the sun than the cameraman the day I'd hung out with Stephan and Lance. It had itched a little in the moment, and it'd felt like I had a mild sunburn the next morning, but that was it.

"Why did I need to see that?" I asked, putting down my hands and looking over at Stacy who was looking at me with raised eyebrows.

"You tell me." Stacy deadpanned. "Why was Jack so insistent about you seeing this?"

I scowled and stood, then whirled back around to face Stacy again with my hands on my hips. "Sometimes I can't sleep and I wander around during the day. I'm careful. I told him that."

Stacy frowned deeply and put the tablet face down in her lap. "Jack's just worried about you. I am too. I know you and Lin aren't getting on, but you need to listen to her."

I threw up my hands and huffed.

"If you won't listen to her, listen to me. Evan, if you can't sleep, just stay in your room. We leave the first floor untouched so it's not suspicious to visitors. Yet, as you saw from the video, a small mistake with sunlight can be fatal."

I ran my hand through my hair and huffed again. "Fine. I'll be careful. When is Stephen getting here?"

"Soon. Are you nervous?" She relaxed back into the couch and watched me pace.

"Honestly, yes. I don't like that room, and..." I glanced at Stacy and fell silent, not wanting to drive a wedge between us.

"And?" Stacy prompted.

"I think it's wrong, turning someone into..." I gestured down myself. "... into this."

"So, you think it's better for them to not be given a choice?" Stacy crossed her legs and clasped her hands in front of her. "Like you and me? Forcefully changed? Stephen had a choice. Free will."

"You?" I stumbled to a stop to stare at Stacy.

She stared at me impassively.

"I guess I thought you hadn't been a vampire that long," I admitted. "You always get my dumb film references."

"A long, long time ago," Stacy said, standing and tossing the tablet aside on the couch. "It doesn't matter."

"But when—"

"Doesn't matter." Stacy gestured for me to follow her. "Come, I need some help carrying in supplies."

I helped her carry down a long metal box from her car into the secret room in the basement. It was heavy and awkwardly weighted; even with our increased vampire strength, Stacy and I struggled to get it down the stairs. We set it in the corner of the basement, far from the chains on the wall where I'd been held.

Lin showed up with Stephen and William an hour before dawn. Lin was grinning and hanging off Stephen's arm. Bruises mottled the right side of Stephen's face, and partially dried blood tracked down his forehead. William's jacket, folded over his arm, had blood on the sleeve.

"I'll wait up here," William said as all the rest of us trooped downstairs.

Stephen's face fell when he saw the basement, but when Lin cuddled up to him, he looked down at her and grinned. It seemed he'd gotten over his doubts.

I glanced away, feeling like I was spying on a private moment. He loved Lin, it was obvious in the way he looked at her. I was almost a little jealous. I hoped maybe Jack and I could be that close eventually.

"Does he have to be here?" Lin said, jerking a thumb at me as she led Stephen over to the mattress.

"Do I?" I asked, turning to Stacy. I didn't really want to watch.

"Lin, it's fine." Stephen pulled her close and bent to kiss her forehead. "I don't mind him observing."

"I do," I muttered.

Stacy smacked my chest with the back of her hand. "You need to see how it's done."

Lin had Stephen kneel down on the mattress and bit his neck, drinking deeply. Too deeply. She was going to kill him. I took a step towards them, but Stacy grabbed my arm and hauled me back to pin me to the wall. She leaned close to whisper in my ear. "Part of the process. Lin knows what she's doing. Now stay still and be quiet."

When Lin pulled back, fangs dripping blood, Stephen's head was lolling and he was incoherent, barely alive. Lin put her own wrist to her mouth and bit down, then shoved her bloody wrist into Stephen's mouth.

Lin repeated this process until Stephen took one last, shuddering breath, some of Lin's blood trickling out of his mouth. Lin gently laid Stephen on his side and curled up around his back as the big spoon, putting an arm around him and pulling him close.

"We can go now," Stacy whispered, leading me towards the door. After we went out, she bolted it from the outside on the top, bottom, and side with large sliding metal locks.

I raised my eyebrows. "Overkill much?"

"It's not. You'll see tomorrow evening." Stacy gestured for me to go ahead of her up the stairs out of the basement.

Stacy slept in Trevor's old room for the day.

I tossed and turned, unable to sleep, but the video Stacy had showed me kept me in my room. Finally I passed out.

That night, Stacy shook me awake.

"It's dark," she said as I sat up. "Time to go see if Stephen rose as a vampire."

"He might not?" I felt like I was going to throw up at the thought that we might get downstairs to find Lin sleeping with a corpse.

Stacy stopped on her way out of the room. "It's rare, but it does happen. I just wanted to prepare you for the possibility."

"Did—" I swallowed hard. "Did Stephen know that?"

"Yes, he was warned. He was fully aware when he made his choice. Now, get dressed." Stacy left.

I quickly threw on an outfit and then we went downstairs together. Everything was deathly quiet and still in the basement.

Stacy rapped strongly on the door and waited, but there was no answer. Frowning, she knocked again. After a few moments of no response, she shrugged and unlocked the deadbolts.

As the door swung open silently, a putrid smell rolled out. I gagged until I held my breath.

"What is that?" I said, risking another whiff of the foul scent, and wrinkling my nose to make it obvious what I was referring to.

"Death," Stacy replied tersely over her shoulder as she entered.

Oh, god, he hadn't turned after all? I hugged myself and counted to ten to psyche myself up before following her in.

Lin lay on the mattress curled around Stephen, both where I'd last seen them. Neither was moving or even breathing. It was a bit creepy how still they both were. The mattress under them was covered in brown stains that hadn't been there last night.

Stacy stopped and crossed her arms, staring down at Lin and Stephen with a deep frown.

"Did," I swallowed a gag, "did he not turn?"

"Can't tell yet. But I know how to find out." Her gaze settled on the long metal box we'd carried in from the van last night. Lin had been coy about the purpose of the box, so I was dying of curiosity about what was inside. She went over and knelt next to the box, then rapped on the lid.

I jumped when someone rapped back and a weak, "Oh thank god, help me!" came from inside the box.

"There's someone in there?" I yelled. Gah, that smell coated my mouth when I breathed.

"Yes," Stacy replied, twisting to give me a steady look as if it were obvious. "He's going to need something to eat when he wakes up."

"The bottled blood, upstairs—"

Stacy shook her head once, sharply. "Not for the first meal. Only fresh will do. On that note, shut the door and lock it before I open this." She tossed me a padlock.

My stomach twisted, but I did as she asked. There was a deadbolt on this side too, so I set it and then put the padlock through the bolt and clicked it into place.

When I was done I turned to face her, but stayed where I was and leaned against the door.

"Not long now," Stacy said, checking her phone.

Lin took a deep breath and sat up. Like watching a lifeless puppet suddenly come to life. I saw now why Jack said it was creepy seeing me sleep.

She blinked at us and then looked down at Stephen with a smile. "Wake up, honey."

Stephen's eyes popped open; they glowed red in the darkness of the room. I jumped back into the door with a start. Had he woken with his fangs out?

"Hungry, Stephen?" Stacy asked.

Stephen's head whipped around to look at her.

Stacy opened open the latch of the long metal box, flipped the lid up, and stood, moving to the side.

Stephen growled and ripped out of Lin's arms, jumping to his feet. He ran straight for the box, teeth bared and fangs fully down.

The man barely had time to do more than sit up before Stephen was on him, teeth ripping at his throat. The tang of blood in the air almost overpowered the stomach-churning smell of Stephen's death. Almost.

I covered my mouth in horror as Stephen messily fed, biting so hard he nearly tore the man's throat out.

Stephen's throat worked frantically to swallow it all. Blood trickled down his chin as the spray became too much for him to handle. The man went limp, his eyes going lifeless, but Stephen kept tearing at his throat.

"That's enough. He's dead," Stacy said, putting a hand on Stephen's back. "You don't want dead blood; it'll make you sick."

I hadn't heard that before. Why had no one thought to tell me? One of those things that was vampire common sense, something that everyone already knew.

When Stephen didn't respond, Stacy grabbed the back of his neck and yanked him backwards, pulling him off the corpse.

"I said stop," Stacy growled, her fangs coming down and her eyes glowing red. She was scary. I shivered and moved my arms from my face to hug my sides.

Stephen growled back at her and thrashed, fighting to get back to the dead man, but he couldn't break Stacy's iron grip.

No wonder everyone had been so worried about me at first, if this was the norm for new vampires. He wasn't even verbal, even after drinking enough to kill his victim. In fact, he still seemed thirsty; his fangs were down and his eyes still glowing.

"Stephen, darling, calm yourself." Lin stood and approached slowly, speaking in a low, soothing voice.

"Lin?" Stephen stopped fighting Stacy's grip and froze, eyes darting around. His chest heaved and his face was smeared with blood.

"That's right. You remember." Lin crouched down next to them Stacy and put a hand on Stephen's cheek.

"So thirsty," he slurred around his fangs.

Stacy relaxed and let go of his neck, dropping her arm, but otherwise didn't move.

"You'll get used to it." Lin smiled at him and caressed his cheek.

Stephen's eyes filled with tears and he dropped his hand from hers and held out his arms. Lin fell into them and he pulled her into a hug.

The padlock seemed like a bit of overkill, but I guess things had gone as well as they could have. If they hadn't, the padlock was a backup protection to keep a rabid new vampire from getting out.

Stacy shoved the man's body back in the metal coffin and closed the lid. "Glad you're back with us, Stephen."

"Thanks." Stephen shot her a smile over Lin's shoulder then pulled back from her to turn and look at me. "You too, Evan."

I gave him a nod. "Same. Also, your fangs are still down."

Stephen put a hand up to his mouth and probed a tip with one finger. "How do I..."

Lin shot me a glare. "Not something to worry about right now, darling."

I shrugged. I had the opposite problem, unable to figure out how to get them to come down, so it struck me as funny.

"We'll leave you to clean up." Stacy checked her watch. "Be back in an hour with some blood."

She pulled me along with her, popping out the padlock, and exiting the room. Once we were outside, she bolted it shut and locked it again.

I pulled at my shirt and sniffed it, then made a face. The smell had seeped in during our short time in there.

"Thoughts?" Stacy asked as we went upstairs.

"He was like an animal." I shuddered.

"That's why new vampires are so dangerous. The bloodlust is overwhelming to many at first."

I nodded. "Now I get why everyone freaked out when you and Jack found out I'd only been a vampire a few days."

Upstairs, Stacy rummaged in the freezer and pulled out four packets of the blood and tossed them in the microwave.

I made a face as I sat down in one of the barstools at the kitchen island. "Can't I go out to hunt? Those things are, quite frankly, disgusting, and I've had more than enough of them to last several lifetimes."

"No." Stacy crossed her arms and leaned back against the counter. "Until Lin can teach Stephen control, they'll be staying in the basement.

Your job is to help them, which means you need to stay nearby, short trips only. That's why there's always three at the house."

I groaned and slumped face-first down onto the counter top.

"Once Stephen is ready to come out, you serve as another mentor. Sometimes the older vampires like Lin are too far away from their human life to be able to really help the new ones."

I sighed and sat up. "How old is Lin anyway?"

Stacy quirked a smile at me. "You'll have to ask her that."

I stuck out my tongue at her. "And risk death? No thanks. But I do have another question. Why did you have to restrain him like that? Why didn't Lin just order him to stop? Wouldn't that be easier that this whole thing with the locked basement?"

Stacy frowned. "What do you mean?"

"She made Stephen, right? So doesn't he have to do what she says?" I hadn't heard a voice when I'd lost control, but I was still being controlled.

Stacy reached up to massage the bridge of her nose. "I'm sorry. I keep forgetting you don't know the basics. It doesn't work like those bad vampire movies, Evan."

"It doesn't?" My hands started to shake and I raised my head, lowering my hands and putting them under the bar, clasping them in my lap.

"God, Evan, were you worried that was going to happen if your maker showed up?" Stacy walked over to the island and sat next to me, twisting the barstool around to face me.

"Maybe," I whispered. But then, what was happening to me? Shit. I looked up and raised my voice. "Are you sure it isn't that way for my bloodline? I mean, that myth had to be started somehow."

"Honestly, I couldn't say. But I can tell you that I've never heard of it happening. And I've been around a long time."

CHAPTER 17

CATS ARE VINDICTIVE

THE NEXT FEW DAYS ran together in a blur of loneliness. William spent most of his time in the basement with Lin and Stephen, working on Stephen's control. William would come upstairs randomly to check on me, and the rest of the night I'd spend rattling around the house or taking rambling walks in the woods nearby.

I had permission to use the house phone to call Jack, but with the new vampire in the house, Stacey had said it was safer not to have any other non-vampires around for a while, which meant phone calls were all I got. Meanwhile, William was ferrying supplies back and forth from Eugene, leaving me to watch the house while he was out.

Tonight I got to get out of the house for at least an hour: the house mail needed to be retrieved from the post office box in town. I left right at dusk. By the time I drove out of the woods around the house, the sun was almost fully set, but I still had to squint against the glare of the headlights as I drove through town looking for the post office.

Lin had given me written directions, but I was unfamiliar with the town and must have missed a turn or something. I missed my phone's navigation app. I·drove around in circles for a few minutes until I saw something I recognized: the bar Lin had taken me to.

I parked in the next empty spot and walked back to the bar, figuring I'd ask the bartender or one of the patrons for directions.

"Evan!" The call came from behind me.

The call startled me so much I stopped walking and whipped my head around. Warm arms swept me into a hug.

"Hey," I said, gently pushing Gregory away. "Uh, nice to see again too." I looked him up and down, almost wincing at how awful he looked. His loud shirt was rumpled and stained, and all the jewelry he'd been wearing last time was absent. His cheeks were flushed and he was sweating, like he'd been running.

"I've missed you." He grabbed at my hand, but I easily evaded him and stepped back out of his reach. "When can I come over again?"

"Not for a while," I said, thinking of Stephen in the basement.

"I need another hit," he pleaded, his eyes rolling. He pulled the collar of his shirt to the side with one hand and made another grab for me with the other, stumbling a step towards me.

I made another hop-step back from him. I wasn't opposed to biting him; it'd been days of nothing but reheated dinner, and my fangs ached at having him this close. The problem was...

"Where's your girlfriend?" I asked, glancing around. Only a few other shoppers were visible, and none of them looked familiar.

"She broke up with me." Gregory pulled his collar further, and the top button of his shirt popped off. "Accused me of being a drug addict, can you believe it? I'd never do the hard stuff."

"Wild," I said, taking another look at him with fresh eyes. The flushed cheeks, the sweat, the lack of hygiene. He was having withdrawals. Just like Kevin, who'd lost his job.

"So, can you help me?" Gregory pleaded, pushing closer again.

"Sure, yeah, come with me." I took his hand and led him back to Trevor's car. "Get in the passenger seat. You're going to give me directions to the post office, then when we get there I'll help you out."

It turned out I was only a block away. I parked on the street, in the darkest spot I could find. Then I took Gregory's arm and bent it to bite his wrist. Before I bit, I looked up at him.

"I'll give you a call in a week for your next, um..." Ga, calling it biting sounded so barbaric. "...donation."

"A week?" His eyes pleaded with me. "That long?"

"It's safer to space it out." I bent towards him but he stopped me, putting his hand over his wrist. "Five days?" he countered.

I sighed. "Six, best I can do."

"Fine."

I gently bit him and drank as much as I felt safe taking. I left him blissed out in the passenger seat while I ran up to the post office and retrieved the mail from the box. When I got back, Gregory still had a goofy smile plastered on his face and had his head thrown back, eyes closed.

I got back in and then sat there, staring at him as guilt washed over me. I hated what my bite had done to him, yet I still had given in to my thirst and bit him again. From what I understood, the more a person was bit, the deeper that their addiction grew. I should have turned him down, but would that have really been better? At least now he was happy for a while. I had no easy answers.

THE RINGING OF THE doorbell woke me. I groaned and sat up to check the time on the clock on my nightstand, the doorbell ringing in the distance. Five PM. Who would be at the house? All package deliveries went to the PO box in town.

I wish I could check when the sun should be down, but without a cellphone the only way I'd know would be actually going out to check.

The doorbell kept ringing like the person was pressing down the button. Asshole.

I rolled out of bed and threw on some clothes from my floor. My hand was on the doorknob before I remembered Stacy's warning. I bit my lip, but the continued annoying ringing of the doorbell decided for me.

After one last deep breath I opened the door. The hallway was dark, but light brightened the area around the stairs.

I crept forward to the railing that looked down over the front door and foyer. I sat down on the top step and rested my cheeks against the bars. Orange, late-afternoon sunlight coming in through the front picture window made a bar of light across half the foyer.

The doorbell let up for half a moment and then rang again, the tone extending.

I judged the position of the strip of light. The doorway to the living room broke up the light before it reached the front door, leaving a patch of shadow directly in front of the door. If I was careful I could open the door without getting burned.

I went down the stairs, back against the wall, and edged around the bit of light that fell onto the stairs. I took a moment to smooth down my hair, trying to make it look a little less like I'd just rolled out of bed. I kept my body positioned behind the door and cracked it open.

The sun was slightly behind the person on the porch, backlighting them, but I recognized Eric by his height and lanky build. His index finger pressed firmly against the doorbell button.

"Knock it off. That ringing is drilling into my brain," I said, shading my eyes against the glare and wishing I hadn't left my sunglasses in the car. I wedged my foot firmly behind the door in case he rushed me.

"Got you up, didn't it?" Eric snorted and left his finger there for a moment more before letting go. The incessant ringing finally stopped.

"I don't think it works that way," I said with a little hesitation because I actually wasn't sure what it took to wake a sleeping vampire. I turned to look up at the landing, but it seemed the doorbell hadn't woken William. Or at least he hadn't stirred from Trevor's old room.

Eric rolled his eyes, so maybe I was wrong.

The light was making me squint and my eyes water. "Who visits a vampire in the middle of the day?"

"A smart person, that's who. And I'm here to give you a warning. I would have called, but I didn't know your number." Eric crossed his arms and widened his stance.

I shifted, gripping the door tighter. "How did you even know where I lived? No, wait." I held up a hand, feeling like a fool. "That was your car in the parking lot. You followed me here..." I sighed, and moved my hand back to shield my eyes again. "Tell me your damn warning and then get out of here."

I think Eric was sneering, but it was hard to see past the glare of the sun. "This is my warning to you. You are bad news, and I don't want you to drag Jack with you. You break it off with him, tonight, or there will be consequences."

He poked a finger at me and I jerked back, blinking at him. "What the hell does that mean?"

"It means what it means. I'm not going to spell it out for you." Eric stepped back away from the door. "I'm going to call Jack tomorrow morning and if he doesn't tell me you broke up with him, I'll be back. With the consequences I mentioned." With that he turned tail and jogged down the front steps.

His car crunched on the gravel as he left.

I went back upstairs, but needless to say I couldn't get back to sleep.

THAT EVENING, THE CALL of the amulet pulsed loudly at the edge of my awareness, feeling stronger than it had been. I didn't know if it was because I was upset about Eric's threat or something else. It was loud enough that I couldn't relax.

I was sure I heard it say "Come to me" in my head several times, and the tone of the calls grew increasingly irate as midnight approached.

I paced around the house, debating what to do about Eric's threat. I wasn't going to break up with Jack because of it, that's for sure. But there was the question of if I should tell anyone else about his threat. I didn't want to worry Jack with this; he was so busy at work with this mysterious project Stacy had him working on.

Stacy... I could go to her, but I had no proof; it was just my word against his. Did I want to make this accusation? Who knew what these consequences were? Nothing, probably. What could he do, anyway?

I paced, unsure of what to do. Maybe hearing Jack's voice would help. I went to the kitchen and called his cellphone. It rang seemingly forever before going to voicemail. I left a message asking for him to call me back. Jack was probably busy at work. I didn't even know if he was in town or not. Sighing, I hung the receiver back up then slid back down to the floor and buried my head in my knees.

The voice called in my head again, the loudest it had been, demanding me to come. I wrapped my arms around my legs and locked my fingers around my wrists, fighting the compulsion by imagining Jack standing over me, urging me to stay here for him.

After a while it faded, leaving me shaking and nauseated, but I didn't dare move away from the phone in case Jack called. Instead I focused on the steady tick of the kitchen clock as it counted the seconds, until I heard the jingling of the phone.

"Hello?" I answered.

"Hey Ev, it's Jack." I heard ice cubes clink into a glass over the line, then the sound of pouring liquid. "What's up?"

"You remember the sleepwalking thing I asked you about?"

"Yeah, what of it? Did it happen again?"

"Yes, but I was awake." I hugged my knees tighter with my free hand. My hands started shaking just remembering it, and I tightened my grip on the phone to stop it.

"It sounds to me like stress. You said yesterday when I called that you were lonely and feeling isolated, with Lin and William spending all their time in the basement."

"Maybe..." I didn't really buy that. "But it really felt more like someone was calling me to them."

"The amulet?"

I shrugged before remembering Jack couldn't see me. "I guess so." But when I concentrated I felt the amulet northwest of me, pulsing gently in my awareness. However, the voice in the fugue state had been having me go south, the direction of the highway.

"Everett, you need to find something to take your mind off things—" He was interrupted by someone in the background. There was a pause and the voices sounded muffled, like he had his hand over the receiver, then he came back on the line. "Sorry, something's come up. Emergency. I have to go. You stay safe, I'll try and call you before dawn. Love you, bye."

He talked in a rush and hung up before I could protest. I hadn't even had a chance to figure out how to bring up Eric's threat.

"I love you too," I said to the dial tone before hanging up the phone with a sigh.

CHAPTER 18

LATE NIGHT GUEST

I KNOCKED ON THE basement door with a little trepidation. I'd finally worked up the courage to take Jack's advice. "Lin, can I come in?"

A few moments later her voice came from the other side of the door. "Fine. Come in."

I unlocked the door and pushed it open. Lin and Stephen were sitting on one of the couches that we'd carried down from the living room. William was out getting supplies from Eugene; young vampires needed a lot of blood, and we'd already run low.

"Hey Lin," I said, just poking my head in. "Can I hang out down here with you for the rest of the night?"

Lin frowned at me. "Why?"

"I'm lonely, and Jack says I'm stressed out and need to relax." I sighed. "I'm sorry, this was a bad idea." I started to pull back, but Lin stopped me.

"No, it's a great idea." Lin stood, pulling Stephen up after her. "I'm tired of this basement too. I think Stephen's improved enough that he can come upstairs. So let's all go hang out there, instead."

"Really?" I grinned. "That's great."

The two of them followed me upstairs. Stephen couldn't get his fangs up, which I found both funny and creepy. Funny, because when I first was turned I couldn't get mine to come down. Creepy, because of his blood-red eyes. Still, I got used to it after a half hour or so.

Lin and Stephen took the love seat, which we pulled around to be where the couch had been facing the television. I sat on the floor on the other side of the coffee table. One of the benefits of being a vampire was that there really wasn't an uncomfortable way to sit. It was a bit awkward at first, but we eventually found things to talk about.

I had a few more episodes of feeling disconnected with my own body. My body didn't move, but I could tell I was no longer in control as I looked, smiling, at Lin and Stephen. The feeling would fade after a few minutes. Almost like it didn't want someone else to witness these moments, but that was madness.

Near dawn we were watching a movie together. I'd moved around to lean back against the love seat.

The doorbell ring startled all three of us. Stephen snarled and tensed. All of us looked over to the door.

"Were you expecting someone?" Lin sat forward to glare down at me.

I used the remote to pause the movie and shook my head. "Who would I be expecting?"

"Who else would be ringing our doorbell at," she checked her watch, "five thirty in the morning?"

I shrugged, but my stomach went tight. Had Eric come back?

The doorbell rang again, followed by a sharp series of knocks at the door.

"I'll get it." Lin stood up and pointed at me, then Stephen. "He even twitches towards the door, you stop him. But you bite him while I'm out of sight and I rip your head off."

I saluted her. Lin rolled her eyes as she stalked past me.

I craned in my seat to get a better view of the door, but Lin opened it only a crack, and the wall of the living room blocked my view of everything but Lin's back. That wall had protected me from the sunlight earlier, but now I cursed its existence.

"Can I help you?" Lin said. Her words were polite, but her tone and body language were stiff and antagonistic, her back ramrod straight.

"I'm here to see Evan." The voice sounded like a woman, low and sultry, with a slight accent I couldn't place.

I glanced at Stephen. He sat forward on his chair at the sound of the woman's voice, but he'd managed to stop himself from moving farther. The strain of not going after the woman showed in his tense expression and the clench of his fists digging into the cushions on either side of him.

"No, I'm sorry, he can't see you," Lin snapped.

"Look, Miss Lin, I just need to talk to him for a moment," the woman said in a low voice. "I understand your hesitation, but I'm a vampire, like you. You don't need to worry about me."

"I'm not." Lin shot back. "We have a new one here. Evan, I can hear him from here. Take Stephen to the basement, now," Lin snapped over her shoulder at me.

"Come on, Stephen." I grabbed his arm and hauled him off the couch.

"He isn't available right now. You need to go," Lin said to the woman as I led Stephen into the foyer.

"He's right there." The woman tittered. "And I think you'll find he wants to come with me."

I furrowed my brow at the words, and risked a glance over my shoulder at the woman at the door. She had dark skin and straight black hair that went down past her shoulders, paired with severe bangs that almost covered her eyes. She had winged eyeliner, bright red lipstick, and a matching tight red sleeveless dress. I most definitely did not know her. I would have remembered someone as striking as her.

I wanted to respond, but when I'd paused, Stephen had also turned and gotten a good look at her. He lunged, and it took all my strength to hold him back. He was much bigger than me, a vampire now with that strength, and set on getting to the woman at the door. I pushed at him like a linebacker, but my shoes slid on the tile. I couldn't hold him off long.

"Lin, help!" I yelped over Stephen's snarls.

Lin slammed the door in the woman's face. As soon as the door closed, Stephen relaxed and I slammed against his chest, still pushing against a force that was no longer there.

"Stephen," Lin said softly, walking up behind me. "You good?" He put a hand to his head as I stepped back away from him.

"Yes, no." Stephen put his hands over his face and crouched. "I don't know."

"Let's go back to the basement." Lin crouched next to him and rubbed his back.

"Okay." Stephen stood.

"You, come with us," Lin said, pointing to me as she took Stephen's arm.

Scowling, I trailed after them back down to the basement. Lin and Stephen sat back down on the couch I'd found them on.

"Shut the door for a moment, Evan," Lin said.

It clanged behind me, and I leaned against it, crossing my arms.

"So, who is she?"

"I don't know." I threw up my hands at her suspicious glare. "I'm telling the truth."

Lin started to say something else, but I didn't hear her. Another episode swept over me. My body turned, pulling the metal door open with a squeal.

"Where do you think you're going?" Lin flew across the room with vampire speed, slamming into the half-open door and smashing it shut again. She kept one hand against the door, keeping it closed, and grabbed my arm with her other hand.

"Out," my body said in my voice, turning to look at her. Inside I was screaming, but as far as I could tell it didn't show. "I need to talk to her."

Lin gave me a flat look, her fingers tightening on my arm. "I thought you didn't know her."

"I do, and I have something very important to discuss with her," I heard myself say.

I tried to pull away from Lin, but she swung me away from the door and tossed me across the room.

My fangs came down and I hissed at Lin as I twisted to bounce back to my feet. I fought to stop myself from rushing at her with my fangs bared, but without success. It was like my body was doing its own thing and I was just along for the ride.

Lin's own fangs dropped down and her eyes blazed red. She dropped into a crouch, grabbed my arm, and spun me around. I landed face-first on the concrete, Lin's knee in my back, and one arm twisted around behind my back at a painful angle. My body struggled against her, using my free hand to try to push myself up. Stephen shot up from the couch, snarling and circling us in a sideways walk.

"Evan, stop." Lin shifted her weight to drive her knee deeper into my back.

Her gaze shifted to follow Stephen. "And you, sit back down. I can handle this."

I wanted to stop, but that force was still controlling me. Lin jerked my arm harder and I felt my elbow and shoulder pop. Stephen growled but huffed and went back over to the couch as ordered.

The force faded out of me, or maybe the pain drove it away. Either way I was back to myself, and I froze, gritting my teeth against the pain.

"Lin, I'm—" I closed my eyes and steadied myself against the pain. "I'm sorry. Can you let me up please?"

"You tried to bite me," Lin growled, not letting up the pressure in the least. "And leave against my direct orders."

"I didn't..." I didn't know how to explain it to her, so I tried to come at it in a roundabout-way. "I don't want to leave the house. Please don't let me leave. I feel like I'm not totally in control."

"I won't let you leave." Lin didn't get off me but she did relax her grip on my arm, enough that my shoulder and elbowed popped back into place and the pain faded.

What I was worried about was when Lin let me up again. Would that feeling come over me again, walk me out of my house against my will? "Can you lock me up with you in the basement for today?"

Lin leaned over me to look me in the eyes on the floor. From my point of view it looked like she was upside down. Her eyebrows were drawn together and her eyes were back to their dark brown. "I'm so confused. Is this reverse psychology?"

"No." I remained as still as possible. No need to make her think I was trying to escape from her. "I'm serious."

"Tell me what happened there. Why did you say a moment ago that you were leaving?" Lin moved off me and sat cross-legged on the concrete next to my head. I moved my hand off my back and placed it next to my chest but stayed face down. "You can sit up," Lin said.

I rolled over and sat up, mirroring Lin's pose. "I swear I don't know the person at the door. And I've been having these... episodes where, I don't know, it's like I'm not in control." I cocked my head. "Like when you gave me blood and I put the amulet in the cup."

Lin frowned. "So you had one of those episodes just now?"

I nodded.

"Look, Evan, I need you to help me with Stephen. I can't have you being unreliable."

"I don't know what's causing them or how to get them to stop." I pulled my knees to my chest and put my head down. "They're starting to really scare me."

"They could have to do with your bloodline. It's odd that you've only manifested very minor powers so far, increased strength and speed." She cocked her head as she regarded me, her eyes narrowing.

"Minor?" I raised my head and narrowed my eyes at her. "I can move so fast humans can't even see me."

"Minor." Lin flipped her long hair back. "As in, lots of vampires of different bloodlines can do that. But each bloodline, or clan, has a trait that defines them. Something only they can do. Maybe these episodes have something to do with yours."

"Worst power ever." I waved my hand over my head. "My body tries to go places without me," I muttered and dropped my face back to my knees. "A power that, what, might be leading me to my doom?"

"It's never benefited you, one of these periods of loss of control?" Stephen said from the couch. I rolled my head to eye him.

I pursed my lips as I considered. "It guess it has, actually. When Jack was about to be sacrificed, that feeling came over me, and helped me fight. I wouldn't have been able to save Jack otherwise. But I assumed it was the amulet doing it. And it only controlled my body to help me fight. I still felt like I was in control. But not lately."

"But the amulet isn't here." Lin crossed her arms and leaned back against Stephen's legs.

Without looking, I lifted my hand and pointed. With my eyes closed, if I concentrated, I could feel it there in the distance, pulsing, calling to me, but far enough away that I could ignore its siren call. I opened my eyes and looked at Lin.

"What are you pointing at?" Stephen and Lin both twisted to look at the basement wall where I was pointing.

"The amulet. It's there. I can still feel it."

Lin turned back, shaking her head. "I can see it wanting you to give it more blood, but I can't see it helping you fight or wanting you to go with a woman you don't know. Is there anything else it could be?"

I blew out a breath and ran a hand through my hair. "Maybe... Maybe I know her from a memory I picked up from the blood."

Lin and Stephen both stared at me with blank look.

"You know," I felt like I needed to elaborate. "Like, how you live random memories from the people you feed from? Maybe someone I ate knew her..." I trailed off when I saw that the confusion in their faces deepening.

"Memories?" Lin asked. "Explain."

"When I go to sleep, I dream. No, more like I live memories from the person I ate."

"Why didn't you tell this to anyone?" Lin's tone was like ice and her expression was blank.

I blinked. "I told Jack."

"He doesn't count. Why didn't you tell another vampire?"

"You don't really make it easy to talk to you, Lin! Besides, I guess I assumed it was something that everyone, every vampire, had happen. Why would I bring up something everyone knows and have you yell at me like I'm an idiot?" I threw up my hands and tried to keep the tears from my eyes. I wasn't successful. I wiped at my cheeks with my sleeve.

Lin sighed. "You're right, I'm sorry. I admit I haven't been the easiest to work with. I've been trying. For the record, that does not happen to anyone else. It's not a power I've heard of before." Lin put a hand to her chin and lowered her head, thinking. "That could be one of your bloodline's major powers."

"Major?" I scoffed and rolled my eyes. "How? By reliving birthday parties and office day jobs? I mean the only good part of it is that I get to see the sun regularly." There were other good parts, but those were for my own enjoyment.

"Of course it seems useless, but you're untrained. For instance, our clan," Lin leaned back and rubbed Steven's leg, "is known for being able to read things by touching them. An untrained vampire, like Stephen—" He grinned at her and leaned over to kiss the top of her head. "—only will get vague impressions or glimpses. But someone trained in the art can get much more than that. Like knowing the last person to touch the item, or see things that happened nearby, that kind of thing."

I furrowed my brow, considering how that applied to me. "So, you're saying I'm getting the vague impressions. But if I knew what I were doing..."

"You could find out things that person knows, things that they wouldn't tell anyone otherwise. Or maybe even more than that. Much more." She shrugged, then scowled. "I would not have fed you my blood if I'd known that."

I bit my lip. "Sorry."

"I'm going to have to call Stacy about this, give her a heads up," Lin said, pulling her cellphone out of her pocket.

"Can I stay in the basement tonight?" I perked up.

"Absolutely not." Lin gave me a small smile. "William will be upstairs with you. You'll be fine with him around. He's an old vampire, powerful."

I sighed. "I don't know if that'll be enough."

"Look Evan, your fugue states, they've only happened at night, right?"

Fugue state. I liked that term for my periods of loss of control. I rolled my eyes at Stephen, who raised his eyebrows at me. I wasn't sure if he'd realized yet or not that when he'd caught me in the hallway, I'd been in one of those states. "Not every time," I finally hedged.

"Well, I still trust it won't lead you into danger, like going out into sunlight." Lin waved a hand like she was swatting a fly as she put her phone to her ear with her other hand. "You should be fine alone during the day today. It's too close to dawn for anyone, even from the local PCA office, to get here before light. Just to be safe, wake William or call the emergency number if anything happens during the day today."

Lin gave me a smile as I got to my feet. "Evan, don't worry."

Chapter 19

Vampire Hunters

WILLIAM GOT BACK A bit before dawn. I told him what happened with the woman, but he didn't seem too worried, brushing off Lin and my concerns. "Evan, even if she does come back during the day, this house is a fortress. The windows are laminated safety glass, virtually unbreakable, and the front and back doors are both reinforced. Thieves have tried to break in during the day before and failed." With that he went into his room and shut the door.

I laid down and tried to sleep, but I was too freaked out. Finally about ten AM I gave up and went downstairs, turning on the TV to fill the house with noise and light. It made me feel a little less alone as I sat on the couch, fiddling with my Vita.

I debated opening the curtains to let in some of the midday sun, but it wasn't just Stacy's fiery video that stopped me. If Eric came by during the day today, I didn't want him to be able to see into the house. I decided not to rat him out to Stacy or Jack. He was bluffing, he had to be.

Gravel crunched in the driveway, and I sat up on the couch in alarm, muting the television. With it off I could hear the roar of an engine. Sounded like a large truck, nothing like the small car I'd heard Eric driving earlier.

Enough sunlight came through the cracks in the drapes that I didn't feel safe looking out the window. Gravel crackled in front of the house and the roar of the engine cut off.

I turned off the television and sat in silence, listening. Car doors slammed and then the front steps creaked as multiple people came up the front steps. More than one set of feet. I tensed. Not a good sign. The front doorknob rattled like someone was trying the knob.

More footsteps. It sounded like someone was walking around the wraparound deck in front of the living room where I sat. The window rattled, and then I jumped as something smashed into it. It didn't break, but the sound was loud enough that I jumped to my feet. Someone was trying to break in. I ran up the stairs to the second floor and quietly knocked on Trevor's door—well, now William's, but I couldn't stop thinking of it as Trevor's.

"William?" I knocked again, but no answer. I remembered how he hadn't woken up yesterday to the doorbell. There was another bang from downstairs. I'd need to be more forceful. I knocked again and then tried the door. Locked. Shit. I knocked again, harder, and raised my voice a little louder. "William!" Still no answer.

Downstairs the noise had ceased, which I found even more suspicious.

I gave up trying to get William up and went back downstairs. At the bottom of the stairs I put my ear against the door and listened. I heard muted voices in conversation, but I couldn't make out what they were saying. William had mentioned thieves. Maybe that's all it was, and they'd go away after realizing that they couldn't get in.

Just to be safe, I went around the house and made sure the back door and the door to the garage were firmly bolted shut. That done, I set my Vita on the kitchen island and then went over to stand next to the phone on the wall just in case. I wish they'd let me have a cellphone or even that this phone had a wireless handset so I could retreat up to my room—or the basement on the other side of the secret door—but I was stuck here if I wanted to call for help.

The longer I waited without hearing a car door or engine to tell me the visitors had left, the more the uneasy feeling in the pit of my stomach grew. Chewing my lip, I pulled down the list of emergency numbers that was posted next to the phone. Scanning the list, I settled on the emergency line to the local PCA office in nearby Eugene, which had "24 hours" written after it in parenthesis, but I didn't dial yet. I craned my head around to look at the front door, debating what to do. If I called and it turned out to be nothing...

Suddenly, the house shook and the front door bowed in. A crack formed in the middle of the door. I jumped and mashed myself against the wall, accidentally crushing the phone list in my fist. Guess it was something after all. My fingers shook as I dialed. In my ear, the phone rang once.

"Again!" someone shouted outside, then the house shook again.

Eyes wide, I clutched the phone, and tilted my head to peak down the hall. The front door's crack had grown and the hinges were buckled. Light came in on the edges of the door. Another hit would bring it down. The phone was still ringing, but I took a glance at the secret door. Maybe I should abandon the phone and take refuge there.

There was third boom and a huge crash. Shards of wood flew all the way into the kitchen. Shit, too late. Even if I used my vampire speed to get to the secret door, they'd see me and I'd end up leading them right to the basement and the helpless Lin and Stephen.

Booted feet crunched on debris in the hall, and I heard a man yell, "Living room, clear!"

A moment later two other men came into the kitchen, sweeping their assault rifles to either side. Both were dressed in fatigues with Kevlar vests and ski masks. They had small hand axes strapped to their belts, but the axe heads gleamed too bright for steel. Silver?

I dropped the phone, which was still ringing, and backed up from the two men. "There's one here!" They both trained their guns on me. "I thought you said they'd all be asleep!"

"What the hell?" I spat out, putting my hands in the air.

A third man, tall and dressed like the other two came in from the living room, his gun pointed at the floor. "I said probably."

The voice sounded familiar. So did the height and build.

"Eric?" I squinted against the glare of the sunlight coming in through the open front door, lowering my hands.

"Dang it," Eric spat and pulled off his ski mask. He threw the mask on the ground and lifted his gun to point it at me. "At least the one awake is the one we're after. Get those hands back up," he snarled at me. "I told you there'd be consequences."

Swallowing hard, I lifted my hands back over my head.

"You mean the one you're after," one of the still-masked gunmen said. "We're still taking down this whole nest."

I widened my eyes and almost glanced at the pantry and the secret entrance, but managed to keep my focus on Eric. Shit. I had to lead them away from the kitchen and then figure out a way to get out of here alive. The guns probably wouldn't kill me, but enough shots would leave me weakened and unable to defend myself from their hatchets.

"Gregory? You want in on this?" Eric called over his shoulder towards the front door, then moved aside to make room.

My mouth dropped open as Gregory came into the kitchen. His short hair was mussed. He had a shotgun held in both hands, but they shook so badly he could barely hold the gun. His jacket left his neck exposed, and my fang marks stood out bright on his pale skin.

The four of them were arranged in a semi-circle around the door leading to the front door and living room. The back door behind me was unguarded, but it was half past noon and the sun would fry me before I got ten feet. That was if I even got outside with four gunmen shooting at my exposed back.

But maybe there was another way to get out of this. I focused on Gregory, looking him in the eyes. I'd bit him multiple times. Lin wasn't a great teacher, but she did try. She'd told me the more times a vampire bit a person, the more they'd be devoted to their vampire. And Gregory had been desperate for a second and third bite.

"Gregory, you don't want to hurt me," I said slowly in a steady calm voice.

"I do!" Tears running down his face, Gregory raised his gun. "This is for what you did to me! I hate how much I want you to bite me again. These men are going to help me get back to myself."

"Gregory, it doesn't work like that," I said, but he kept his gun trained on me.

Not good. This wasn't working. The phone's handset still lay on the ground. I hoped someone at the PCA had picked up and was listening in, sending help. I had to survive until that help arrived, and then meant getting away from these gunmen.

Gregory stood right in the doorway; I'd have to get past him somehow. His legs were spread for balance as he psyched himself up to fire on me. Gregory wasn't very tall, but I was short and small. They wouldn't shoot at each other. That was my way out.

I tensed, readying to run and took a big breath out of habit. Then I concentrated on speeding up. I lunged to the side, sweeping out my hand to run it along the island counter to grab the Vita as I ran towards Gregory. His eyes widened in slow motion. Eric yelled something, and so did one of the still ski-masked men. I blocked them from my mind and focused on my goal: getting upstairs. I'd figure out the next step once I got there.

I tucked the game system under my arm like a football and dropped into a slide, aiming for the space between Gregory's legs. My feet clipped one of his thighs as I slid underneath him.

Gregory teetered and started falling backwards, but I was moving fast enough that I was already out of the way before he landed. Sun came in through where the front door had been, falling over the bottom of the stairs leading up to the second floor.

I skidded to a stop and took a risk to look back over my shoulder. Eric and the armed men with him were all yelling. Their guns were pointed in my direction, but as I hoped they held off on firing, not willing to risk hitting Gregory on the floor between us.

My legs shook with fatigue; I only had a few more seconds of speed. I'd mostly been surviving on the bottled stuff, except for the bite from Gregory a few days ago, and I could tell it didn't give me as much energy.

So where to go? Three choices. To my left was the living room, but someone had opened the drapes and now it was filled with sunlight. To my right was the short hallway that led to the downstairs bathroom and the garage. Neither good choices. The garage had Lin's car but not much else, and the bathroom was a dead end.

That left the third option: the second floor. Sunlight covered the bottom of the steps, but my eyes snagged on the stair railing and I followed it with my eyes up to the second-floor hallway that looked down over the foyer. If I'd been still human I couldn't have made the jump, but I was a vampire now, with vampire strength.

I crouched and pushed off, jumping as high as I could. I tossed the Vita over and then grabbed the railing with both hands, feet slipping on the edge of the carpet where it met the overhang. Bullets roared below me, biting into the wood where I'd been standing a moment before. One of the bullets whizzed by my leg, taking out a chunk of skin and ripping my pajama pants.

I was shaking and cold, and felt really tired. I'd already been fighting off sleep when I'd heard the truck, and the extra exertion had pushed me to the edge.

I flipped myself over the railing, landing on my back on the carpet. My legs shook when I tried to stand, so I crawled the few feet over to the door to my bedroom, picking up the Vita on the way. As I went by I yelled, "William, emergency!" and banged his door with one fist before bolting into my room. I slammed the door behind me, locking it with a shaking hand.

Booted feet pounded down the hallway below me.

"I heard a door! Check all the rooms up here!" a man yelled.

Just in case my phone call hadn't gotten through, I tapped the Vita on and sent a quick voice message to Jack. "Help." Then I stuffed it down the back of my pants and crawled away from the door.

There was a bang of a door slamming into drywall. It sounded like it came from down the hall. The master bedroom, Lin's room. At the same time, the door handle of my room jiggled as someone tried the doorknob.

I couldn't stay here, it wasn't safe. Yet I couldn't take all four of them, even if I hadn't been dead tired. Biting an opponent would take them out— except Eric, who was immune—but it would take time to take effect and while I was feeding I was vulnerable.

Running was my best option, but to where? The only safe space in the house was the basement, but I just couldn't risk leading them right to Lin and Stephen.

Outside was certain death. And what about William?

Someone yelled, and a gun boomed right outside my door. I yelped and curled into fetal position on the floor as a bullet came through the door above my head.

Inside was certain death too. I couldn't protect them and myself. If all this noise hadn't woken William, I wasn't sure what I could do for him.

Protection. I needed protection from the sunlight if I were going to run. I risked putting my head up to glance around the room. My plush tiger. The wardrobe. My closet door and clothing. My bed. The bedspread. That might be thick enough to protect me, at least long enough for me to make it to the tree cover.

I felt like a coward for considering leaving Lin and Stephen alone with what were looking to be more and more likely to be vampire hunters. But what else could I do?

There was another crack of gunshot, and chunks of wood showered me. I glanced back at the door. The holes were all around the handle and lock.

"Any sign of any of them?" someone yelled in the distance.

"No, check the closets and under the beds. I'm still trying to get through this door." I didn't recognize the voice. They'd split up to search for me. I could use that to my advantage.

I got up on my knees, slowly unlocked the door so it wouldn't click, and concentrated on going fast again. It was like swimming through mud, and I knew it wouldn't last long. I opened the door and reached through, grabbing the front of the man's flak jacket to yank him into the room with me. I slammed and locked the door before the speed faded entirely.

He barely had time to let out a cry of protest before I pulled up the ski mask far enough to give me access to his neck. His blood was warm on my throat and I eagerly gulped it down, knowing I wouldn't have much time before the others missed him. I pulled away, still thirsty, but I didn't want to risk killing him. At least I felt well enough now to have a chance of getting away. I left the hunter on the floor moaning.

Feeling better, I stood up and ripped the covers off my bed. Pretty thick. Now I just needed a way out of the house.

I went over to the fake wall built over the bedroom's window and gave it an experimental shove. It was pretty solid, barely rattling ever when I used all my strength.

It'd take too much time and effort to get out this way. I'd just have to hope the way to the front door was unguarded—a fair bet since they didn't think I'd risk the sun. But just in case, a human shield would do the trick.

Escape route set, I wrapped the blanket around my shoulders and knotted it like a cape, then I leaned over and threaded my arms under the shoulders of the man I'd bit and hoisted him up. His head lolled, too drunk on vampire venom to resist. He was taller than me, so his bent knees dragged on the ground.

"Where'd Bill go?" Eric's voice came from the other side of my bedroom door. This must be Bill. Now or never.

"Back up, or Bill gets it!" I raised my voice as loud as I could.

"Shit!" Eric swore, then lower he said, "Back up, back up."

I kicked my door the rest of the way down and barged out. Eric and the other armed man had backed up to stand against the door to Lin's room, conveniently blocking the stairs down as well. That was alright. I just needed to get to the landing, and I'd get down the way I came up.

I didn't see Gregory. He might've been in one of the rooms, or still downstairs, but I wasn't worried. He didn't seem as committed as the other three, despite his strong words to me.

Bill was heavy, and I was already getting thirsty again with the effort of holding him up. I needed to get out of here now. In the back of my pants, the Vita chimed. Really? Now? I scowled and hefted Bill higher so I could shuffle forward into the hall.

"Don't hurt him." Eric scowled.

"Fuck, he's been bit," the remaining ski-masked man spat.

I frowned. "He's still alive. He's fine."

"Bit is not fine." Eric's scowl deepened.

I shrugged. I wasn't going to argue semantics with vampire-hunters. I moved closer. Eric and the man both had their guns pointed at me. I didn't think they'd shoot, not with Bill between us, but with the way that they were looking at him now, I wasn't so sure. Better not press my luck.

A few more steps and the railing would be in reach. I wanted to get closer, but the hunter's finger moved towards his trigger and I couldn't risk waiting.

"Catch."

Bill had at least a foot of height and a hundred pounds on me, so it wasn't a good throw, or a far throw, but it was a good distraction. Bill flew a few feet down the hall and landed on his stomach, sprawled out.

Meanwhile I dashed forward, grabbed the railing, and jumped off, my bedspread cape fluttering behind me.

My socks slipped on the hardwood as I landed, and my knee cracked painfully into the ground. Gunshots sounded above me, and I caught movement out of the corner of my eye on the steps.

The sun was bright in my eyes, and I had to take a moment to steel myself before charging towards it. As I ran, I untied the cape knot and pulled the covers over my head and down over my face.

With the cover over me, all I could see was the ground directly in front of my feet. As I got into the sunlight, the skin of my leg started to itch and burn where the bullet had torn my pajama pants, leaving my skin exposed.

I ran down the steps and then veered when I got to bottom to break line-of-sight from the house. The gravel on the driveway dug into the souls of my feet, tearing through my socks, but I didn't dare slow down. Vampires might heal instantly, but it still hurt. I cursed as I hopped across the driveway. When I got to the edge of the garage I turned, following the line of the house, running a few feet parallel before breaking away towards the trees.

Behind me I heard yelling and more gunfire. I hoped Lin and Stephen would be safe. The basement entrance was well-hidden, but with unlimited access to the house to search, they might find them. Once I got to a hiding place I'd check the message waiting for me on my Vita.

Smoke came up from my feet where the gravel had shredded my socks away, leaving my feet exposed. I couldn't help but see them as I ran, and they were turning black on the tops. Cursing, I sped up, but I was too tired and drained to do more than stumble by the time I reached the trees.

Low-hanging branches tore at the bed cover, impeding my flight and tearing the bedspread from my grasp. Sunlight, pain. I couldn't remember why I was running, only that I was in pain and needed to get away.

Sunlight filtering through the trees burned my face, driving me further into the forest, instinct driving me to the deepest shadows. I found a fallen log and crawled underneath it. Dark and safe, I let the exhaustion pull me under.

CHAPTER 20

FIRE

I FLOORED IT ALL the way to Estacada, only stopping once to get a huge to-go cup of coffee. I'd only just gotten back from work and had been getting ready to go to bed when I got Everett's message. I had been more puzzled than worried at first, until he didn't reply. My worry changed to panic when I'd tried to call the house and the line had been busy.

During the drive down I kept trying the house, but the phone stayed busy. Something was very wrong there.

Afternoon traffic slowed me down, and it took almost an hour before I turned onto the gravel drive that led up to the house. The house couldn't be seen from the road.

When I took the last curve and the house came into view, I saw a dark, oversized truck parked in the round-about behind Trevor's sedan. The front door and living room blinds were both wide open. Shapes moved in the living room; they had to be intruders, as none of the vampires would be up and about with the blinds open at two in the afternoon on a sunny day.

My car skidded to a stop behind the truck and I threw open my door before the engine had even cut out. The car dinged helpfully at me about the open door, but I ignored it as I sprinted across the grass.

A man came running out of the house. An assault rifle was slung over one shoulder and he was dressed like a cosplayer's idea of a soldier in camo with a too-small Kevlar vest.

"Hey!" I yelled at him. "Stop!" I changed course to run towards the man.

"Hurry up," another man called from the truck. A third man glanced at me from the back seat, his pale face streaked with tears.

Smoke came pouring out of the front door behind him, and a moment later the living room windows shattered. Flames licked the curtains and more black smoke rolled from the broken windows.

Shit. I let the man run past me and turned to the front door. A car door slammed, and the truck started up with a roar. The tires spun, throwing gravel everywhere before the treads got traction and the truck tore off, spraying gravel all over my car. I wanted to go after them, stop them, but more smoke belched from the house. Saving Everett was the first priority.

I repeated the license plate number to myself to fix the memory in my head as I took the front steps two at a time. The couch was upside down, the cushions were on the floor in the foyer. Bullet holes had chipped the tiles in the foyer and peppered the walls. Past that, in the kitchen, the contents of the cupboards were all over the floor.

"Everett!" I called, then doubled over coughing and choking on the smoke.

The living room was on fire; flames crawled on the walls and had already engulfed the curtains. Two bodies lay in a puddle of blood on the living room carpet. Eric's blank eyes stared up at me. His lower half was already on fire, and the flames were slowly surrounding the rest of him. The second body was so burned I couldn't tell who it had been, but the vampire fangs sticking from the burned corpse gave me a clue. I couldn't tell who it was, other than not Everett; the burned vampire was far too tall to be him or Lin.

The stink of gasoline permeated the house. I had to find Everett quickly.

"Everett!" I screamed again, pulling off my jacket. I wrapped it around my face, holding it tight over my mouth and nose with one hand.

The house was deadly silent except for the crackle of flames.

Upstairs. Maybe he was still asleep up there. I went up the stairs, eyes watering from the smoke. It couldn't be because I was worried I was too late.

Lin's room had been tossed, the dressers and closet emptied, the mattress on the floor. I staggered on. The smoke was much worse up here, curling and gathering at the ceiling. So far only the living room was on fire, but if they'd stoked it with gasoline—and judging by the explosion they had—the rest of the house wouldn't be standing for long.

The lock on Everett's door was surrounded by holes from a shotgun blast. His door was open and his room had been tossed as well. There was no sign of him.

"Everett!" I called again, digging with one hand through some of the mess on the floor to make sure he wasn't underneath. I spotted the tiger I'd given him. Tears sprung to my eyes. I grabbed it and stuffed it into the straps of my underarm gun holster.

I glanced in Trevor's old room, now William's, but didn't see any sign of anyone there. I wondered if that was William downstairs. No more time to search; smoke was filling the upstairs, choking me even through the cloth of my jacket.

Hopefully Everett had made it to safety. Maybe he'd made it to safety in the basement. Hopefully.

I dropped to my knees and crawled back down the hall then down the stairs. The flames had spread to the foyer, blocking the way to the kitchen and completely engulfing Eric's body. Coughing, I staggered out of the house. I could get into the kitchen by way of the back door and check the basement for the three vampires.

Once I crawled out of the front door I stood, and started around the house by the garage.

Why had Eric even been here? His car wasn't here, so had he come with the three men in the truck? I had no answers, but thinking about those questions kept me from thinking about what might have happened to Everett.

An explosion rocked the house as I got part of the way around the garage. I sped up to a jog, ignoring the burn in my throat and chest from the smoke inhalation.

When I rounded the corner, I found the back of the house had been blown out. Debris scattered out from where the kitchen had been. I ran to the back door, but a wall of heat forced me back. The hair on my upper arms had been burned off and my face felt blistered.

I had no idea if the hunters had found the basement or not, but I couldn't find out until this fire was put out. I pulled out my cellphone—no signal.

Black smoke plumed up from the roof. I'd have to go drive to call the fire department, but then I'd be back.

CHAPTER 21

AFTERMATH

THE FIRST THING THAT hit me when I woke up was the smell of smoke. I pushed aside the dirt and peered out through the gap between the ground and the downed tree I was lying under.

The sun was still up, but barely. The tree cover provided enough shadow that it was safe enough for me to get out of hiding, at least. I wiggled out of my hiding place, wincing as the bark on the tree scratched my burned feet.

So thirsty. I couldn't think of anything but finding something to drink. I didn't remember what I was doing out here. Something pressed painfully into my back. I reached behind me and found a plastic thing stuck in the waistband of my pajama bottoms. I turned it over in my hands, struggling to remember what it was past the burning ache in my throat. A large crack bisected the screen, but it still flashed on as I randomly hit the buttons on it. Something told me not to drop it. I hugged it to my chest.

For want of a better direction to go, I limped towards the smoke smell. Red and blue flashing lights became visible as I neared the house. I dropped down and crawled into the bushes bordering the driveway so I could see what was going on. I was so thirsty, but there was enough sunlight still that I didn't want to leave the shadow of the trees.

Several firetrucks were there, their hoses snaking towards the house through the mud that was all that was left of the yard.

The house was gone. All that remained were a few blackened beams sticking up where the wraparound first-floor porch had been, and burned up outlines of the inside walls. The roof had collapsed into the first floor, obscuring and crushing everything.

The fire on the house was out; the smoke I'd smelled was wafting up from the still-smoldering remains. My heart went into my throat. I put my hands over my mouth, staring at the remains of the house.

What had happened to Lin, Stephen, and William?

As the last of the sunlight faded, one by one the firefighters in their outfits with the light-reflecting stripes rolled up their hoses and left.

Watching them, I played with the cracked plastic thing. Eventually I remembered what it was: my Vita. But I was too thirsty to think coherently enough to use it.

By now it was full dark, but I no longer could see any people around. I crawled out from under the bush and stalked towards the remains of the house. The warmth drew me to it, but I also hoped that I might be able to salvage something from the wreckage. Yet as I got closer, I could see everything inside was a total loss.

I hugged myself and stared at the devastation. What had happened here? Where was the PCA? Had they not even come?

Shaking, I turned my back on the house and determined to come up with a plan. First thing was first, I needed to eat. I also had nothing but my torn pajamas and a cracked Vita that was useless without an internet connection.

Trevor's car was still where I'd left it parked it. I walked around it. It was wet from the hoses and splashed with mud, but otherwise looked driveable. The problem was the keys had been in my room.

My fangs were down, and I didn't see any people left around. I was burned, in pain, and in my pajamas. I didn't know where to go or even where the nearest neighbor was. It was a twenty-minute drive into town, and I had no idea if I could even make it on foot in the condition I was in.

Headlights shone as a car drove up towards the house. I ran behind Trevor's car and crouched down by the front tire to watch as the dark hatchback parked in the driveway. A second car followed the first, this one a light sedan. It parked behind the first car.

Four people got out of the two cars, and as a group started walking up towards the house, flashlights played over the trees and down to the still smoking ruins of the house. I squinted against the light of the flashlights, trying to make out the faces of the people there.

"God, there's nothing left," a woman in the group said, horror in her voice.

"Were they all in the basement?" a man asked.

"I don't know," Jack said, cutting off with a sob. "I don't even know if those hunters found the basement or not. The house exploded before I could check."

God, Jack.

I stood up from behind the car. I tried to say his name, but I couldn't get it out from my dry lips. "There!" the man said.

Both the flashlights jerked and settled on me. I winced and put up my hand to protect my eyes. The Vita I'd been clutching dropped to the gravel.

"Everett!" Jack yelled. He started towards me, but one of the people with him grabbed his arm, yanking him to a stop. One of the lights on me bobbed away, playing up over the sky and trees. "Let go, let me go to him!" Jack yelled, dropping the flashlight.

I tried to say Jack's name, but coughed around a lump in my throat. I couldn't get the words out. The world bled to nothing but red on black. Red veins pulsed on faceless shapes of people. So thirsty. My eyes locked on the four people in front of me. Three of them pulsed red with life. I shuffled down the car, so focused on the people that I kept bumping into it, trying to walk through it.

"Everyone, watch out. He's gone feral," the man said. He was a vampire, the only one of the three that wasn't bright red in my vision. "Looks like he got badly burned in the fire."

"Shit," Jack said, stripping out of his shirt and dropping it on the ground. "But I didn't see any sign of him in the house."

"You said yourself you didn't get a chance to check the first floor." This was a woman's voice. She dropped her flashlight and began pulling her shirt over her head.

Jack already had his pants off and was down on all fours, his form stretching and changing as I stumbled past the end of the car. Nothing stood between me and my meal now. I sped up, headed for Jack, but as fur sprouted off him, my attention shifted to the people around him.

The second woman didn't bother trying to remove her clothing, instead dropping to all fours and starting to grow, her expanding muscles shredding her shirt and pants like paper.

The vampire had moved between the changing shapeshifters and me, so I shifted my course to aim at him. I was more drawn to the warmth of the shifters, but the power pulsing in his blood had its own appeal.

My lips drew back from my fangs and I snarled as I charged him. He looked surprised, his eyes widening as I lunged at him with snapping teeth. He managed to grab my shoulders, holding me at arm's length while I fought to get to him.

"Why's he going after me?" the vampire yelled, wrestling with me to keep me from biting his arms.

A jackal jumped up between me and the vampire, yapping wildly and clawing at my face with his front paws. I didn't see the jackal as food, and the teeth and claws didn't scare me in my crazed state. But if I used a hand to swat at the thing, the vampire would get the upper hand. I was already having trouble, since he was larger and stronger.

I brought up a knee and kicked at the jackal the next time it jumped at me. It fell away with a high-pitched yelp, which caused the vampire to glance away from me for a moment. I took advantage of the distraction, ducking low and twisting to take advantage of my smaller size to break his grip on my shoulders, and then hit at his chest with my shoulder.

The vampire stumbled back and fell, and we landed on the grass, me on top. I reared back my head and bit his arm at the elbow through the shirt, the closest part of him I could reach that pulsed red with blood flow.

The shock of blood hitting my throat was almost as good as any orgasm I'd ever had. I closed my eyes in ecstasy and sucked hard.

"Fuck!" the vampire swore. "What the hell?" He grabbed my hair at the back of my head and jerked me away. My fangs were still buried in his arm, and I took a good bit of flesh with me when he pulled me off.

I spit out the skin, and then arched my back and clawed at his hands on my head, screaming out for more. The angle was too awkward and I couldn't get a grip on his hands.

"Evan," the jackal barked as it ran in a circle around my feet. "Everett. Stop, it's me. We're here to help you."

I licked my lips, savoring the taste of the vampire blood on my lips. The world swam into focus again.

"Jack?" I asked. I froze, blinking at him.

The prowling jackal was joined by a massive black wolf and a lynx. The wolf looked a lot like the one that had saved me from Eric.

Pain shot through my hands and feet, and I felt a bit woozy and drunk from the vampire blood. The vampire holding me took advantage of my distraction to throw me face-down on the gravel and jumped on my back, crushing my face into the rocks and putting all his weight on me. I'd gotten enough of my sense of self back that I stopped fighting. The menagerie of creatures prowled around me in a circle.

"Why are only the tops of his feet and the back of his hands burned?" the wolf asked with a growl?

The vampire put more weight on my head, driving my mouth into the gravel of the driveway. "I don't know, but more importantly we need to make him throw up, or that much of my blood will kill him."

"No, no. He'll be fine. He can eat vampire blood. Probably why he went after you." Jack dropped to his belly and crawled up to my face wagging his tail. "Ev, I'm so happy you're alive." He licked my forehead.

I snarled at him and tried to move my hand, but then froze. I swallowed, hard. "Sorry. Thirsty. Hurts." I closed my eyes and enjoyed the scrape of Jack's tongue on my skin, but I couldn't stop a small tear from coming out. "Lin? Stephen? William?"

"I have some restraints in the car strong enough to hold a vampire," the vampire said from on top of me.

"William is dead, I'm sorry. The other two, we don't know," Jack whispered, gently bopping me with his nose. "Weren't they with you?"

"Colton, I'll get the restraints," The lynx yapped, then bounded away back towards the cars.

"I won't fight you," I said, slurring a little around my fangs. "The amount I got from you brought me out of it." My hands shaking, I reached over to pet Jack, but at the last moment I remembered how he'd snapped at me last time I'd pet his ears, and instead I dropped my hand back to the gravel.

"I came in to look for you, but the fire spread and I had to get out." Jack licked my cheek again.

"I wasn't in there." I swallowed, closing my eyes. "What happened?"

"How'd you get burned then?" Colton, the vampire, asked, shifting his grip on me.

"Sunlight. I ran outside to get away from them," I said. "Are Lin and Stephen alright? They were in the basement."

"Sunlight?" Colton snorted under his breath. "That's impossible. If that's true you'd be dead."

"We were waiting until the fire was out to check the basement," Jack said, shifting closer to me. His tail brushed my side.

The large black wolf padded into my sight. Even in my vampire sight I had a hard time seeing her against the black backdrop of the night. "Basement stairs are blocked by debris. We'll need to come back with tools to get to it."

I closed my eyes and blew out a breath, counting to ten calm myself down. Panicking wouldn't help them.

The lynx came bounding back, a little black duffel bag dangling from its mouth. It dropped it next to my side, out of my side.

I flinched and jerked against Colton's hands. "I told you I'm fine now. You don't need to restrain me."

"Stop moving," Colton growled, driving his knee into my back. I had flashbacks to last night, with Lin and me in the same position, and I burst into tears as he snapped a cuff around my wrist.

"Stop, you're hurting him!" Jack barked.

"He's fine." Colton grabbed my other elbow and jerked it back, snapping the other cuff around that hand, securing them behind my back. They didn't feel like normal cuffs. No give at all in them, and thicker than normal on my wrists.

Jack pressed his nose to mine. "It's alright, Ev. We're here to help."

"I know," I said, struggling against Colton. "But I want to go help dig Lin and Stephen out, to make sure they're okay."

"No," Colton growled, pushing a metal bar against my lips. "You're going back to the Eugene office with me. The shifters can dig for your friends."

I clamped my mouth shut, shaking my head and twisting my body as much as I could under Colton's weight on my back.

The wolf growled low. "What if they're frenzied, like this one? It'd be better for vampires to do it."

"Plus, Everett's freaked out enough already. He should go to somewhere familiar." Jack nuzzled my cheek again, and I gave him a tightlipped smile.

Colton sat up on me, letting up on pressing the thing against my mouth. He sighed. "Like where?" he said, gesturing at the house with the metal muzzle thing. "His house was destroyed."

"My house." Jack sat up on his back legs, his wagging tail brushing the gravel around. "I'm his boyfriend. He's obviously hurt, but he's not trying to bite anyone anymore."

"Because you're a jackal right now," Colton growled.

"No, I'll show you." Jack's fur started to pull back in. His ears shrunk and moved down, and his black beard sprouted. A few moments later, a panting and sweating, naked Jack was on his hands and knees on the gravel.

"That was a bad idea," Colton said, grabbing my bound hands.

"No, it's to prove a point," Jack said, brushing gravel off his hands as he sat back on his heels. "Let him up."

"Jack—" the wolf began.

"Felicia," Jack said, holding up one hand. "I know what I'm doing. He won't hurt me. Let him up." The last he directed at Colton.

"Fine, but only because he doesn't seem to be frenzied anymore. And I won't be saying I told you so when he bites you." Shrugging, Colton climbed off me and let go of my arms.

I had to wiggle a bit to sit up without using my arms. I looked at Colton over my shoulder once I was kneeling. "Can you take these off?"

"Not yet. Prove you don't need them first." Colton crouched, resting his arms on his knees.

I gave him a bared smile, then wiggled, sliding my knees across the gravel, pushing towards Jack. When I got close Jack wrapped me in a hug. I relaxed against him, resting my cheek on his bare chest. "Jack, thank you," I said softly.

Jack gently kissed the top of my head, then looked over at Colton. "See, he's fine."

I leaned back from Jack and twisted to smile at Colton, to show him there was no blood.

"Jack's right. We'll help dig, but it safest if a vampire is here to assist," Felicia the wolf growled.

The lynx who'd been quietly watching meowed. "I agree, Colton. Even changed we're no match for a vampire out of their mind in pain."

Colton let his fangs drop for a moment. "Fine, I see I'm outnumbered."

CHAPTER 22

SWORD OF DAMOCLES

EVERETT CURLED UP IN my passenger seat, bare feet resting on the upholstery. His arms were wrapped around his legs and he stared morosely out the window at the passing trees.

We'd been riding in silence since we left the house. Felicia had ridden down with me, but had offered to stay behind to help Colton and his partner dig out the staircase to the basement to see if Lin and Stephen were still alive. Someone from the Eugene office would give her a ride back later.

I'd gone through a drive-through and gotten three hamburgers; changing always made me ravenous.

"Did you really run out into the sun?" I finally asked to break the silence after I swallowed the last bite of my final burger. I tossed the wrapper in the back seat with the rest of the trash. I hated eating in the car, but I needed to get Everett home. "That was really dangerous, Ev. You could have died."

He glanced at me, then went back to staring out the window. He hugged his legs tighter. "I would have died if I stayed," he whispered. "They had assault rifles and silver axes, Jack. And—" He glanced at me again, and his voice dropped so low I barely heard him over the roar of the road. "Eric was helping them."

I sighed. "I know. I found his body in the living room before the fire spread."

Now Everett turned fully in his seat to face me, putting his feet back on the floor. "Oh, Jack. I'm sorry." He reached across the console to touch my arm before shrinking back into himself. "I think they were vampire hunters. Do you," he swallowed, "do you think they killed Lin and Stephen?"

"I'm not sure." I sighed. "I should have checked the secret door first, but I was just so worried about you that I went to your room instead."

"It's my fault," Everett said.

"It's not." I risked a glance at him. "Eric messed up, not you."

"No." Everett put his hands over his face. "Eric came over yesterday a little before dark, threatened me. He said if I didn't break up with you that there would be consequences."

"That would explain the odd phone call I got from him this morning." He'd been almost babbling, and then asked me out on a date. He'd taken my rejection, where I'd reminded him that I still had a boyfriend, silently. I glanced at Ev again. "He made a choice when he hooked up with vampire hunters."

"Gregory was with them too." Everett twisted his hands in the bottom of his pajama top.

"Who is he?" I asked him.

"A human I've been feeding from." His reply was tense and clipped. "He was angry that he craved being bitten again. I don't blame him for being mad." He started crying and hugged himself again. "I ruined his life, just like I ruined Kevin's."

I passed a dark, empty parking lot on the right. I slowed and turned into the lot, parking the car, then turned to face Everett in the passenger seat. "You didn't ruin their lives." I opened my arms and leaned across the console. Everett didn't move, so I wrapped my arms around him, pulling him to me sideways.

"But Kevin lost his job, and Gregory lost his girlfriend and his apartment because of me." Everett turned his head away from me, curling tighter. "And then I got Lin and Stephen possibly killed, and I did get William killed."

I pulled him up over the center console and into my lap. It was a tight squeeze, but he fit. "Well, I haven't met this Gregory, but Kevin didn't seem unhappy. And jobs come and go, as do girl and boyfriends." I kissed the top of his head.

Everett wiggled an arm free of my embrace and wiped his eyes with his sleeve. "I don't know what happened. He seemed so excited to see me when I ran into him a few days ago. Practically begged me to bite him. But then at the house today he was so angry..."

"The vampire hunters had been working on him..." I sighed, and scrubbed my face with one hand. "Them and Eric."

"If I hadn't bit him—"

I cut Everett off with a growl. "You'd starve, that's what."

He closed his eyes and hung his head. "But Gregory was acting like a junkie looking for a fix. Kevin too, in a way. I think my bite is really addictive. It's evil."

"I don't pretend to understand your dilemma, Ev." I kissed the top of his head then snuggled him close. "But you aren't evil. Powers, even addiction, aren't good or evil. You didn't force Gregory—or Eric—to help those hunters. In fact, Kevin turned his life around because you bit him. Try to see the good in it."

Everett was silent for a moment. "Shapeshifting is different than being a vampire. You just don't understand."

"I know I don't, but I also know you. You're misguided sometimes, and too reluctant to ask for help, but you are not evil. Tell me, does Stacy seem evil to you? Lin?"

He shook his head, giving me a small glancing smile. "No. But what should I do then?" His face fell.

"I can't tell you that. But you should follow your heart. Maybe start by only biting people who want to be bitten." I waved a hand. "And don't eat any babies, for example."

Everett let out a little laugh at that and I ruffled his hair. "Kind of an extreme example, Jack," he said, swatting my hand away as he wiggled out of my hug.

"I was trying to make a point. Did it work?" I let him crawl back into the passenger seat.

"Yes, thank you."

I started the car back up. "And put your seatbelt on this time, Ev."

He glanced at me. "Why? A car crash won't kill me."

"Because I asked, please. I'd rather not see you hurt if I don't have to." I was pleased to see him pull the seatbelt out and click it into place. "Thank you."

"What do other vampires do for food?" Everett asked, eyes thoughtful.

I checked for traffic before pulling back out onto the highway. "That would be a good question to ask other vampires. You and Lin never talked about it?"

Everett bit his lip and shook his head. "Not really."

"Alright then, what are your thoughts?" I asked. "Really that's the most important."

He blew out a breath, and was silent for a while as trees and dark houses and business flashed by on the sides of the road. Good, it seemed he really was thinking about this. Finally he spoke again. "So far I've only bitten adults, but I have taken some people against their will. I think that's what's been bothering me. But, how do you ask for permission when no one believes in vampires?"

"Your first bite might have to be forced," I admitted. "So the trick might be deciding who to bite in the first place."

"I feel like I'm becoming a drug dealer," Everett muttered. "First taste is free." He dropped his fangs for a moment and giggled.

I'D SPENT A LOT of time thinking on the drive to Portland after my talk with Jack. He'd been right; Kevin had looked much happier than he'd been when I first met him. He hadn't been angry, just excited to see me. Same with Gregory. The only difference was that at some point he must have met Eric and the hunters, who convinced him to help them.

So the trick, as Jack had pointed out, was being careful about who I bit. Some trick. I was a Sword of Damocles; it was a matter of when, not if, I'd cut some poor person's life to shreds.

When we got to Jack's house I hopped into the shower. The hot water helped, washing away the grime and warming me up at the same time. I hadn't been entirely truthful back at the house; those few gulps I'd taken from that vampire had not really been enough, but I wanted to go back with Jack. Surprisingly, my hands and feet didn't really hurt anymore, although they were still blackened and charred.

I got out of the shower, feeling a lot better. The bottom of Jack's shower was brown with gunk. I threw away my ruined pajamas and put on one of Jack's T-shirts that he'd lent me. He told me he'd go shopping for me today while I slept and pick me up a few things.

I'd lost everything. Again. This was becoming a pattern, one that I didn't like.

The T-shirt was so large it went almost down to my knees. Yawning, I shuffled out into the bedroom.

Jack stood on a stepstool, where he was using duct tape to seal up any gaps where light might get through the foil he'd plastered over the glass. His cellphone lay on the bed set on speakerphone, and Stacy was walking him through making sure the room was lightproof enough for me to stay the day here.

"You should also hang a foil blanket over the doorway, or else tape up the gaps around the bedroom door too," she was saying. Sounded a bit extreme to me, but what did I know?

"Hi Stacy," I said, flopping across the bed near the phone.

"Everett." Her tone was flat. "I told Jack when he called that I'd much preferred if you'd have stayed the day at the Eugene office, or even the Portland office."

I groaned and pulled a pillow over my head. The thought of staying in the room there, plain concrete with a drain in the center, nothing but a camping cot to sleep on, was too much to even think about.

"There is no way I was going to leave him there alone." There was a thump as Jack stepped back down from the stool. Quieter, he said, "You didn't see his face, Stacy."

"He's dangerous, Jack, and the fact that he is isn't getting through to you. Colton said he was totally feral when you found him at the house."

I lifted up the pillow to scowl at the phone. "I'd never bite Jack." I paused. "Without his permission."

Jack grinned at me and bent down to kiss me on my forehead before scooping up his phone. He tapped the screen and then brought it to his ear. "Thanks for the help with the lightproofing, Stacy. Bye." Jack hung up the phone as sat down on the bed next to me.

Rolling over, I stuffed the pillow under my head and tried to relax.

"I have something for you," Jack said.

I pried my eyes open and lifted the pillow. A plush tiger plopped down right in front of me. "Where did you get this from?" I reached out and bopped its nose with a finger.

"I came into the house looking for you, found it in your room," Jack said, laying down behind me and wrapping an arm around my middle. "I wish I'd had more time. I'm glad you survived."

He was so warm against my back. The hot shower had helped, but not enough. Shivering, I pressed back against him, soaking in his warmth.

"Ev, your skin is like ice," Jack said, snaking his arm around my middle.

"Still thirsty," I admitted, not opening my eyes.

"Mmm, I figured." Jack chuckled. "I'll pick you up something at the office later today." Jack was silent for a moment, his warm breath tickling my ear. "Feeling any better? You were pretty morose on the drive back."

"I'll be better once I know Lin and Stephen are alright." I tried, and failed, to keep the quaver from my voice. "I abandoned them. I should have done more—"

"Done what, exactly, against four men armed with silver weapons?" Jack cut me off with a snarl, his arm tightening around my middle. "I saw one of the hunters when I got there. You did the right thing not trying to fight them. You called for help and then you bailed when you needed to." He hugged me close, burying his face in my hair, which muffled his next words a bit. "When I thought you'd died in the fire... it felt like I'd been cut in two. I don't know what I'd do if I lost another boyfriend. I'm so glad you're still here with me."

"Me too." I sighed and opened my eyes as Jack lifted his hand from my stomach, bringing mine with it. He turned his wrist so that the back of my hand faced him. The blackened and charred skin there looked shriveled in the light.

"Does it hurt?" he asked quietly.

"Now it mostly feels numb, like a scab. Hurt a lot at the time, though I was so panicked that it barely registered." I pulled my hand off his and tucked it to my chest. "Eric was helping them. He's the one that led them to the house; he followed me home from the picnic. So why kill him?" I asked.

Jack's fingers gently played down my stomach. "Look, Eric's not... He wasn't a bad guy. He probably really thought he'd be helping me by getting rid of you, but hunters just want to kill vampires. Any vampire. Eric probably tried to stop them from going after Lin and Stephen, so they took him out. Or William killed him."

"Is that why they burned the house? Because they couldn't find them?"

Jack sighed, blowing on my hair. "I hope so. I haven't heard back from Felicia or Colton one way or the other yet though. Now, I don't know about you, but I'm exhausted."

"Aren't you worried about sleeping with a vampire?" I hugged myself, pulling away from Jack.

Jack wiggled closer and molded himself to my back. "I'm not sleeping with a vampire, I'm sleeping with my boyfriend. So, no, I'm not worried."

I smiled. I liked that. Not a vampire, just another guy, but one that drank blood instead of dining on rare steaks. And unlike the cow, my meals lived after I'd dined on them. Their lives changed afterward, but so what?

Nothing stayed the same, no matter how much you wished it wouldn't.

We lay there in silence for a bit. "I love you," I mumbled.

"I love you too, Ev," Jack whispered back. I fell asleep grinning.

CHAPTER 23

MEET THE GODDESS

JACK WAS GONE WHEN I awoke. I rolled over and looked around. Judging by the coolness of the bed, he had been up for a while.

The room was pitch black. I could still see, but I could tell because the color had been leached out of everything and the edges of objects stood out sharply from each other. I could almost see better without the light, except for being colorblind.

Yawning, I crawled out of bed and went over to the bedroom door. Through the door I heard voices, a man and a woman, talking.

"Jack?" I called, knocking on the door in case he couldn't hear my sleep-roughened voice.

Soft footsteps thumped closer and there was a light tap at the door. "Ev, it's me. You decent?"

Blinking, I took a moment to process this. "Why? It's not like you haven't seen it all before."

Jack chuckled. "Yeah, but Felicia's here. I left some clothes for you on the chair. Come out after you get dressed."

I found the clothes where he said they'd be. A three-pack of new underwear and socks, and a few T-shirts and shorts in my size with tags from Goodwill attached. I popped the tags off my favorites and dressed.

I noticed a small black bag on the floor next to the chair. I opened it out of curiosity, but recoiled in horror at the sight of the metal cuffs and gag Colton had restrained me with the night before.

When I came out of the bedroom, I found Jack and Felicia sitting in the living room. Squinting against the brightness of the overhead light, I threw the black bag on the floor, where it landed with a solid thunk. I crossed my arms over my chest, not fighting my fangs dropping down at the sight of the warm flesh.

My fangs ached to pierce the thin skin and... No! I tore my gaze from Felicia's throat and swallowed hard. Felicia's eyes widened and she froze.

"Ev, you alright?" Jack asked softly.

"Fine," I managed to get out, though my tongue caught on my parched lips. I licked my lips and tried again. "Fine," I said again, mostly to myself.

The feeling of loss of control settled over me, and my body turned and walked towards the front door. I fought it, ordering my body to stop, to turn, to do anything, but it was like I was floating a bit outside myself, only an observer to my own actions.

Jack jumped up and ran after me. He caught me as I put my hand on the doorknob. He landed hard against the door, closing it with a bang. "Everett! Stop, talk to me!"

With a snap I was back to myself. I yanked my hand off the knob like it was burning hot. Shaking, I stared at my hand in horror.

"Look." Jack grimaced and stared down at his feet. "Remember how Colton took me aside before we left the house?" Jack glanced up at me and then quickly back to feet. He shuffled his feet, grimacing again. "He wouldn't let me leave unless I took those and promised to put them on you once you were asleep. But I swear, I didn't. I brought them into the bedroom, but then you looked so peaceful and innocent. I couldn't."

As he spoke, I slowly looked up from my hand as his words sunk in until I was staring at him. At first I didn't even remember what he was talking about; I'd still been pretty out of it at that point. I took his hand and pressed it against my chest until Jack met my gaze. I smiled at him and he smiled back. "I'm sorry I overreacted," I said softly.

"You didn't." Jack shook his head and pulled me into a hug. "I shouldn't have even taken them out of the car."

I leaned into his embrace, wanting to tell him about the sleep-walking feeling. But not in front of Felicia.

After a moment, Jack let go of me and stepped back to hold me at arm's length. "I warmed you up a drink; it's still in the microwave. Why don't you go grab that while I finish up with Felicia?"

I gave Jack a weak smile. "I look that bad?"

"I hate to say it, but yeah." Jack chuckled. "Plus the fact that your fangs are down."

I touched my tongue to my teeth. "Shit," I muttered as I started towards the kitchen. As I passed by Felicia on the couch I paused. "Thanks for your help last night." I shuffled my feet, embarrassed. "Sorry you had to see me like that." I paused. "Are all Jack's partners werewolves?" I joked.

Felicia gave me a tight smile that didn't reach her eyes.

Jack came up behind me and placed a hand on my back. "A coincidence. Wolves are the most common shifter type. Go eat while I finish up here."

I nodded and continued on into the kitchen. I found the blood in the microwave where Jack said it would be. I pulled it out, but didn't start drinking right away. When I popped the top off, the stench made me gag. I could tell just from a whiff that this wasn't going to help much. Normally, at least, it smelled somewhat appealing. I needed fresh. Something about it was just different, better somehow. But unless I was willing to bite Jack or Felicia, this would have to get me by for the next few hours.

As I was steeling myself to drink, the coffee pot clicked as the heating element turned on. I wondered...

I got down a mug from the cupboard and filled about half full with coffee, then I mixed in some blood from the bottle until the glass was full. I took a sip. Not bad at all. Without thinking, I gulped down the rest of the cup. My fangs clinked on the edge of the ceramic. I refilled it again, coffee with the rest of the blood, and put the coffee pot back in the coffee maker. Concentrating a moment, I put my fangs up then I went out in the living room, sipping on my drink.

Jack grinned at me and patted the couch cushion next to him. He lifted his arm as I sat and placed it around my shoulders. I snuggled up to him, soaking up the warmth from him and the hot coffee in my hands.

"Any word yet about Lin or Stephen?" I asked, bringing the coffee up to my nose to breathe in the scent of it. Being so close to Jack was making me hungry, but the tang of the blood in my coffee helped distract me.

Jack squeezed my shoulder. "Colton called me with an update at dark. They're fine. The hunters didn't find the secret door. Lin and Stephen were hungry, but unhurt."

I nodded and sipped my drink, smiling. "That's a huge relief."

"I should get going, Jack," Felicia said, standing up. "See you at work tomorrow?"

"Yeah, hopefully." Jack glanced at me then back to Felicia. "Feel free to call me if you have any questions tonight, but I think you've had enough training to be alright on your own."

"Will do. Night, Jack, Evan." She left, shutting the door firmly behind her.

I took another sip of my doctored coffee while Jack's hand drifted down my shoulder, his fingers brushing my outer arm. He leaned towards me, burying his nose in my hair for a moment. "I know you need to go hunting, but think you're up for a little one-on-one time first?" he whispered, reaching his other hand over and placing it on my thigh.

I gulped down a mouthful of coffee and giggled, leaning to the side to put my coffee cup on the side table. Then I fell back into Jack's arms.

"Definitely."

I straddled Jack, facing him. With me sitting up on my knees, it put us at eye-level with each other. I ran my hands up his chest and leaned towards him until our lips met.

We kissed. His lips were soft and warm, and I found myself pulling on his lower lip with my fangs. Stubborn things had come down again while we were kissing. Groaning, I leaned back to rest on my butt on Jack's legs and covered my mouth with one hand. "Sorry," I muttered.

Jack took my hand and gently lowered it, holding it between both his. "Ev, don't apologize for what you are. If you're too thirsty, we can stop. Or you can take a little from me."

"No to both." I shook my head and gave Jack a shaky smile. "The bottle was enough for a while. I can go hunting later." I pulled Jack's clasped hands to my mouth and kissed his knuckles. "I want this, you, right now."

Grinning, Jack pulled his hands free and put them on my hips, grabbing the bottom of my T-shirt. "Glad we agree on something."

I put my hands up, and Jack yanked my shirt up and off then tossed it to the side. Bare-chested now, I leaned back into him and we kissed some more. I pulled up Jack's shirt and ran my hands under the fabric. Still kissing, Jack wiggled to the side, leaning away from the couch so he could pull his shirt up. We broke off for a moment so Jack could get it over his head. He tossed it on the side of the couch.

Since we'd already broken apart, I slid backwards off Jack's legs. I unzipped and shucked off my jeans, leaving myself wearing nothing but my underwear, then crawled back into Jack's lap.

Jack grinned and cupped my butt with both hands. Butterflies fluttered in my stomach at the sight of Jack, shirtless, in front of me. We'd slept together several times now, but the sight of him still thrilled me.

I threw my arms around his neck, rested my head against his chest, and closed my eyes. Under my ear Jack's heart beat hard and steady. It was comforting.

The now-familiar, unwelcome sensation of loss of control swept over me. "No, no!" I managed to yell before it settled over me.

Under me Jack started. "What?" He took my shoulders and pushed me away so he could look at me.

I grinned, or more like my body grinned, opened my mouth, and lunged at Jack, sinking my fangs into the side of his neck. I fought as hard as I could to stop myself, but none of my internal flailing so much as twitched a single muscle. Warmth flooded through me as I gulped down Jack's blood.

"Ev, stop!" Jack yelled, grabbing my hair and trying to pull me off of him. I growled and dug my fangs in deeper.

Jack cried out and his form twisted under my legs. Fur sprouted up into my mouth. I finally pulled away, jumping up and backing off the couch as Jack's legs shrunk in his jeans.

I put my hands on my hips, cocking them to one side in a very feminine pose, one that I would never use myself. "Huh, I thought you were dinner." The words came from my mouth, but they were not mine. I licked my lips and regarded the jackal now sitting on the couch.

"Dinner?" Jack yelped, kicking out of his pants and rolling over to stand on all fours. His ears were pinned back against his head and his hackles were up.

"A jackal," I purred, though inside I raged. "A blessed sign indeed."

"Ev, what's gotten in to you?"

I flexed my hand and lifted it up to examine the burn marks on the back of my hand and wrist. "Interesting," I said, drawing the words out. "I'd wondered how you'd gotten out," I muttered to myself, or more that the person controlling me said it to themselves. I turned, cocking my head to the side, and held up a hand. "We'll have to catch up later, gorgeous. My ride is here." With that, I turned on my heel and dashed for the door.

I flung it open, and my body put on a burst of speed, getting me all the way to the sidewalk before I heard the bang of the door crashing into the wall behind me. However, that's as far as the meager amount of blood I'd taken from Jack got me before I slowed.

Staggering a little, I turned and jogged down the sidewalk away from Jack's house. My legs felt weak and shaky, and I shivered involuntarily as I ran. I wanted to stop, but my body had other ideas.

"Everett, wait, come back!" Jack called out.

I glanced over my shoulder to see the jackal run out of the house and jump down the steps after me. I blew a kiss at him, then turned back to watch where I was running. I was almost at the intersection of Jack's street with the main road.

An SUV pulled up to the curb at the intersection and the back door opened. A man looked out at me and gestured, as if he knew me.

I ran up to the car and was almost there when the controlling force bled away. I stumbled as I got control of my legs back. Momentum carried me a few more steps before I fell against the rear end of the car. The metal was cold on my bare skin.

"Everett!" Jack howled, the words turning into the bark of a jackal at the end. I pushed away from the car and twisted to see him pounding down the sidewalk after me, his paws a blur under him as he ran.

I took one step away from the car towards him. "Jack, help—"

Someone grabbed my arm and yanked me backwards through the open car door. I landed on my back, sprawled across the back seat.

"Get the jackal too!" a woman ordered.

A large-muscled Black man got out of the front door, scooping up Jack in his arms before getting back in. The car squealed away from the curb. I screamed Jack's name as I thrashed against the strong hands that had grabbed hold of my arms and legs, holding me down as the car sped off. I caught a dizzying view of the car's roof as I struggled to get free.

"Everett," a woman commanded in a firm voice, "calm down. I can explain."

Her voice sounded familiar, but it took a moment for the memory of where I'd heard it before to get through my panic.

I froze, an icy chill sweeping over me. The woman who'd been at our front door just a few hours before the house burned down. Either I was now in the hands of vampire-hunters, or something worse.

"That's better," she purred, letting go of my legs. She and the man holding me pushed me into a sitting position in the center of the backseat of the SUV.

The spicy tang of vampire in the air made me swallow and clench my jaw to keep my fangs from descending. In the front seat, Jack yelped as he struggled futilely against the vampire's grip.

I hugged my arms across my bare chest. "Stop, you're hurting him!"

The vampire holding Jack clamped one hand around his muzzle, and his other pinned Jack's body to his chest. Jack let out one small whimper, and fell silent and ceased struggling.

"That's better," the woman said, twisting in her seat to look at me. Her lips twitched as she looked me over. I blushed and crossed my hands my chest, but there wasn't much I could do with my hands to cover the fact that I wore nothing but a tight pair of boxer briefs.

She wore the same dress as when I'd seen her the other night.

"You're a hard man to track down," the woman said, twitching lips resolving into a smile. Her hand curled into a fist on her chin.

I squirmed in my seat and didn't reply, glancing at Jack.

"I see you have a jackal guardian." She reached a hand up to the front and grabbed Jack's fluffy tail, scratching her fingers down through the fur at the tip. Jack whimpered and wiggled, but the Black vampire's arms flexed, tightening further until Jack yelped and froze again. The woman smiled back at me as she petted Jack's tail. "I thought it a fluke that you were the one that woke me, but now I think it's fate."

"Woke you? I don't even know you. Who are you?" I swallowed as we came to a stop at a light, judging our chances of escaping. Close to none right now.

"Me?" She laughed, settling back into her seat and putting a hand to her chest, batting her eyelashes. "Why, I made you what you are, dear boy."

I stared at her, unable to articulate any of my swirling thoughts. "You?" I finally stammered out and swallowed, glancing one at a time at the other three vampires in the car. "Did you make them too?"

"No, these dear men are my loyal servants." She blew the vampire next to me a kiss. He blushed and inclined his head to her. "Now." She turned her attention back to me and extended her hand, uncurling her fingers one by one. "I'd like my amulet back now."

"Does it look like I have anything on me?" I pulled my hands away from my chest and gestured at my mostly-naked body.

"I see." She scowled and pulled her hand back. "Then tell me where it is and we'll go retrieve it."

I hunched my shoulders and hugged myself again. "I... don't have it anymore. It was taken from me."

"Ah." The woman frowned and clenched her fist. "That's why you haven't been feeding me this last week."

My head spun and I gulped. "Feeding you? It's just a hunk of gold, not a, a..." I ran out of words and curled forward over my knees and put my hands on the back of my head. Suddenly what happened to Trevor made a lot more sense.

"It's much more than that, as you should know." She snapped her fingers suddenly, making me jump. "Holt, follow my high priest's directions. We're going to get my amulet back.

"Of course, Goddess." He inclined his head to her ever so slightly. "Which way?" Holt asked as we came to the next light, glancing at me in the rearview mirror.

I pointed west, left, and he took the turn.

"Why did you call me your high priest?" I asked.

She quirked a smile at me. "You did the ceremony that woke me, so you more than deserve the honor."

My stomach twisted. I had a feeling I knew exactly what ceremony that had been. I'd wondered what the magical result had been, but the mages had not been sure either. I got the feeling that it might be a bad idea to admit that my involvement had been an accident. "Oh, yeah, of course. So, um, what should I refer to you as then?"

Her smile widened and she scooted a little closer to me. "You may call me 'Goddess', like the rest of my followers."

"Alright, Goddess." Saying that left a bad taste in my mouth, but I needed to placate her while she had me and Jack hostage.

She shifted to touch her leg to mine. I tried to discreetly move away from her, but bumped into the vampire on the other side.

"You don't have to be shy." The woman—I didn't want to call her Goddess, even in my thoughts—brushed my knee with a hand.

I gently brushed her hand off. "I'm not interested. I have a boyfriend. Please, take me, but let him go."

"Ah. The jackal." She crossed her legs and smoothed down her skirt. Her voice was even, as if she didn't mind my rejection, but her eyes glinted. Her eyes flicked up to the front seat, where the other vampire still kept Jack restrained and muzzled. "I'd rather prefer to keep him."

"Why are you so interested in him?" I said, mostly to divert her attention. I didn't like the expression on her face as she looked at Jack's tail.

"Did you know, where I'm from, jackals were considered the protectors of the dead?"

Yes, of course, if she was from the same time and place as the amulet. I nodded. I'd taken classes in university about the history of old Egypt. "Death dogs," I said. "The jackal-headed god, Anubis, is god of the underworld."

"Protector of vampires." She smiled and leaned forward to run a finger down Jack's tail tip again. Jack flipped his tail, but otherwise didn't react. "A strong portent indeed that you were with one when I found you."

I shivered and hugged myself. The woman's gaze roved up and down my body as we rode in silence for a moment. Her gaze settled on the crotch of my underwear. The pouch was deflated; my packer had been lost in the house fire. She frowned. I blushed and crossed both my hands over my crotch.

Then too fast for me to react, she moved with vampire speed that I couldn't match as thirsty as I was, and tore my hands away, twisting my wrists so hard that they popped and cracked.

"Hey!" I cried as she grabbed my crotch with her other hand.

"What?" the woman exclaimed when she found, well, probably not what she was expecting.

I pushed her hand away. Again. "Stop that," I snapped. "Look, I'm trans, alright."

She sat back and regarded me thoughtfully. "Trans?"

"I was considered female when I was born, but I'd prefer to be seen as a guy." I crossed my arms and tried, and failed, to keep the blush off my face.

She leaned back in her seat, looking thoughtful. "I'm familiar. We had such people in my time as well."

"If you've been... sleeping, all this time..."

She nodded her head, and flicked a finger for me to continue. I needed to learn more about her if I were going to try to escape with Jack.

"How do you speak such perfect English?"

She batted her eyes at me and smiled. "As my high priest, I'll teach you the secrets of your lineage in due time."

I sighed, trying not to scowl. I'd wanted to learn about my bloodline, but she was terrifying. Not to mention... "Does that include how you got me out to your car?" I asked, my voice quaking despite my best efforts.

She sighed and crossed her arms, rolling her eyes. "This modern world, magic is a lost art. My followers." She waved a hand, indicating the three vampires that rode with us in relative silence, except for Dolf's occasional requests for directions. "Even the oldest of them was born after magic started leaving the world. And you, you're a baby, comparatively."

I scowled. As someone who regularly got mistaken for a teenager, I did not like being called a baby, even if it was by someone that most likely was an ancient vampire. I looked around at the three men. "Your followers? You've gathered this many just since you woke up a month ago?"

She smirked. "I have more than just these three. Don't worry, I'll teach you my secret soon, since gathering new followers is one of your duties as my high priest."

"I'll direct you to the amulet, but then I would like to return home with my jackal to think over your offer of the position of high priest," I said, attempting to bargain.

Her eyes flashed. "It was not an offer, it was an order. I can see I'll be needing to work on your fealty to me."

I twisted my shaking hands in my lap and glanced away. Fuck. "Can I hold my boyfriend on the way to the amulet?"

She regarded me for a moment. "Kurt, release the jackal."

Kurt relaxed his grip. Jack wiggled free and scrambled back into the back seat to hop into my lap. He curled up there, trembling.

"You asked what I was doing out of town. I've been looking for them," Jack said, pointing his muzzle at the front seat, his ears perked forward. Then he swiveled his head towards Goddess. His ears flattened and his lips pulled back in a snarl. "You've left a trail of dead vampires behind you, including the partners of both of these men. Why would they serve you?"

She lifted a finger and bopped Jack's nose. "They belong to me now, just like your boyfriend."

Jack jerked back and I put my arms around him, cradling him to my chest. "What do you mean I belong to you?" I whispered.

She scooted over another inch so that her thigh pressed against mine. "The ceremony bound you to me."

I was trapped between her and the other vampire. I hugged Jack tighter, but he didn't complain. My gut twisted. "But I didn't..." I whispered.

"Darling, it's not my fault if you didn't read the fine print before you—"

"No, I didn't do the ceremony. I was the sacrifice." I shivered. "I have no idea what the spell even was for."

She threw back her head and laughed at that. "Oh my. Whoever did cast the spell then very much misunderstood it. And what happened to this mage?"

"I..." I swallowed. I didn't like to remember this part. "I kinda ate her..."

Jack whined and trembled in my lap. I stroked his head like he was a dog, but he didn't object.

She chuckled again, a throaty rumble, and leaned towards me. "Yes, not surprised. New vampires aren't known for their control."

"Why do you need your amulet?" Jack asked. "And why not get it yourself? You found Everett quite effortlessly, after all."

I lifted a hand and pointed still further west in answer to another of Dolf's inquiring glances.

Goddess inclined her head to me. "Only Everett can sense where the amulet is. When it raised him, it became his, but it also made him mine."

My head spun, and I felt like I was going to pass out. "You. At Jack's house, and earlier. That was you. You controlled me like a puppet."

Her smile could have cut steel. "I thought I made that clear earlier. I own you."

CHAPTER 24

DRAWN LIKE A LODESTONE

THE PULL OF THE amulet led us out west of Hillsboro, in Forest Grove out near the farms. As we got closer, the amulet's hold on me tightened, until I felt like a bowstring about to snap.

We finally located the farmhouse, but had to circle the roads around it while Holt looked for a place to park. It took him a few miles, since the narrow roads had ditches on either side to deal with the occasional heavy Oregon rains.

A second car pulled up a few moments later to park behind ours, a black town car sedan. I was too jittery and shaky to really care, but Jack stood up in my lap to look out the back window.

"Friends of yours?" he asked the woman, cocking his head.

"As a matter of fact, yes. The rest of my disciples." She put her hand on the door handle and paused, considering Jack. "We'll need to do something about you."

I shrank back from her, pulling Jack down, eyes widening.

"Give him to me, Everett," Goddess ordered.

I didn't want to comply, but my arms moved of my own accord, lifting Jack and handing him over to the woman. Jack struggled and barked, scratching and biting at her, but she ignored him even as he shredded her dress. Her skin healed instantly, white flesh peaking out through the rends in the bright red fabric. Kurt got out of the front seat and came back to open her door.

"Everett, stay there while I deal with this." She got out of the car, Jack pinned in her arms against her chest.

I felt glued to the seat, but I was able to twist my head around to watch. She carried Jack over to the vampires who got out of the second car. While she kept Jack still, one of the vampires wrapped duct tape tightly around his muzzle and front and back legs, trussing him like a turkey. A second man opened the trunk of the car, and she tossed Jack inside. He landed with a muffled yelp before the vampire slammed the lid shut.

"Jack!" I pushed at the seat, but her words kept me in place.

Goddess came back to the open car door. "Everett, get out. Come with me, but keep quiet."

I slid out of the car to stand next to her in the mud. All I could see in either direction were trees, but I could feel the pulse of the amulet nearby.

The vampires, all men, gathered in a semi-circle around her and me. I blushed, feeling exposed standing under the trees in nothing but my underwear. I crossed my arms across my chest, trying not to stare at the town car's trunk where Jack lay.

"The objective is a gold amulet around this big." Goddess held her hands, holding them in a circle the approximate size. "One side is a stylized depiction of my face, and the other has hieroglyphs on it. Everyone in this place is expendable. Feel free to eat whoever you'd like."

They all grinned. I really wanted to use the break in the conversation in ask if anyone would lend me a shirt, but Goddess' command of silence still had hold of me.

"Everett and Dolf are with me," Goddess said, putting a hand on my arm. "The rest of you are to create a distraction while Everett leads me to the amulet." She paused. "Any questions?"

Everyone was silent.

"Let's go." Goddess pulled me along, and we all entered the woods.

A group of vampires in the woods at night was the deadliest thing I'd ever seen. Or not seen, or heard. Our enhanced night vision let us avoid even the smallest twig. We raced through the woods quiet as the wind, which was really the loudest sign of our passage. This was even better than that night at the park with Jack and would have been fun except for the circumstances.

With vampire sight, even the darkest parts of the woods were lit up like what would have been the brightest day when I was still human. I'd never felt more alive, despite the exhaustion that pulled at me from still being hurt, and not having eaten tonight.

We came to a black metal fence about ten feet tall. We all cleared it easily, barely breaking stride.

The trees beyond it had all been cleared, leaving a rolling lawn with only spots of landscaping between us and the house visible in the distance. The porch lights were on and the windows dark.

The pulse of the amulet came from dead ahead, at the dark house. At this point I was in the lead. I'd been self-conscious about being just in my underwear, but the joy of running through the woods had blown that away.

About ten yards beyond the fence, I hit what I could only describe as an invisible wall. My head snapped back and I fell, landing hard on my ass. All around me were the groans of the other vampires who'd hit the same wall of force and now lay in the wet grass around me. Even Goddess lay sprawled on the grass next to me. She sat up and regarded the empty space between us and the house with a frown.

"What was that?" I asked, or at least I wanted to. I opened my mouth but I couldn't get any sound to come out, still held by her compulsion.

"Bloody hell!" Kurt stood and dusted off the back of his pants. "What is this?" It looked like he was performing a very good mime routine as he spread his hand out on the air and leaned against it. Muscles bulged under his white button-up shirt, and his shoes slid on the grass as he pushed.

"Magic. Stop, let me." She put a hand on Kurt's arm. He nodded and stepped back next to me.

She placed the fingertips of one hand against the barrier. She closed her eyes and began to sway. Then she balled the hand that rested against the barrier into a fist and punched. There was very little force behind it given that she already had her hand extended in front of her. Still, the effects were immediate and electric.

There was a pop, and a wave of energy fizzled out from her hand, washing over us all with a tingle and leaving me feel like I'd just gotten zapped by static electricity. My hair all stood on end, and I could see my bangs floating up out of my face before I smoothed them down.

She turned to look at us over her shoulder. "They'll know we're here now, so we'll need to be quick. You all know what to do." They all nodded and ran off, about half of them moving with superhuman speed.

"Everett, take me to the amulet." She took my arm and pulled me with her. Dolf ran next to us. I winced, but I couldn't disobey her. I resisted for only a moment or two before the order behind her words forced my legs forward. The amulet drew me like a lodestone; I would have run towards the house anyway with or without her orders.

As we reached the house, the first screams began coming from inside. I started to run along the side of the house, but Goddess grabbed my arm and stopped me.

"No detours." She pointed to a first-floor window.

Since we were both short, neither of us could reach the window to break it easily. I grabbed a decorative rock from the landscaping around the window and threw it at the window. It shattered into pieces, but the sound could barely be heard over the screaming coming from inside.

There was still some glass in the frame, but I wasn't worried; any cut would heal near instantly. I crouched and then launched myself at the window with my hands outstretched. I easily cleared the window, landed on my hands, and dropped into a roll. Some of the glass from the window got dug into my back as I rolled across it.

I jumped up to my feet just as Goddess came springing through the window after me. She had curled up into a ball, pulling her legs to her chest and wrapping her arms around them so she'd fit through the window, then once she cleared the broken glass fragments still in the frame, she unfolded and landed on her feet. She'd done that in heels and a dress. I was a bit jealous of how graceful she was, but more jealous of the fact that her entrance didn't leave her covered in glass shards. I could still feel a large piece lodged in my back, slicing me open further each time that I moved, but I couldn't reach it.

Dolf was less graceful than either of us. He was tall enough that he just grabbed the frame and hoisted himself inside, ignoring the cuts on his hands and arms. I turned away before he finished coming inside, the dual call of the amulet and Goddess's orders pulling me further into the house.

The screams were more intermittent now, and punctuated by pauses and pops of what I thought were gunfire. I ran down the hall, feeling the amulet to my left. Distantly I realized that I was leaving bloody footsteps on the cream carpet in the hall. I must still have glass in my feet too, but it didn't hurt. Or maybe it did, but the energy pulsing to me from the nearness of the amulet drowned out any pain.

The hallway exited out into a large great room with high ceilings and floor-to-ceiling windows that looked out over the backyard. The room was empty of people and dark. Two dark leather couches and a plush red upholstered chair were grouped around a large fireplace at the side of the room near where we entered.

The screams and sounds of battle from upstairs were louder here, and I glanced up to see that there was a second-story balcony that looked down over the great room we were in, although I didn't see any way to get up there from here.

Opposite me, on the other side of the room, it opened up into the kitchen and dining room area, also dark and still. Another hallway entered from that side as well. The amulet was somewhere near here, very close. I took two strides through the room and stopped.

The amulet was to my right, but that couldn't be right. That was just a smooth wall. But Pembroke had given the amulet to a mage. This house was probably laced with spells and illusions, like the one in Portland that protected the hidden road up to the PCA office in the park. I couldn't trust my eyes, so I closed them and reached out my hand to touch the wall. Brushing my fingertips along it at hip height, I paced forward until my fingertips hit a door frame.

I felt down around the door until I found the doorknob. I rattled it, but it was locked. Opening my eyes, I still couldn't see the door, but could feel the knob beneath my hand.

"Let me," Goddess said, shooing me aside. I didn't want to move away; her order fought with the pull of the amulet, and I hesitated. She frowned and grabbed my chin, jerking my face up to look me in the eye. "Move aside," she stated, enunciated each word carefully.

All I could see where her dark eyes, filling up my vision. My feet shuffled away without my conscious thought. It took me several long moments before my vision cleared and I could think of anything except pleasing the owner of those eyes. When it cleared, I could see her hands resting lightly on the doorknob. The illusion of a wall faded away to reveal the doorway.

The wooden door was carved with an elaborate motif of deer and acorns which I found a bit odd. Then again, what I knew about magic was basically nothing.

An empty feeling began in the pit of my stomach and slowly grew. "Oh, no..." was all I was able to get out before I collapsed writhing in pain. I tried to scream, but I couldn't get a breath.

My ears popped as I went limp, feeling like a puppet with my strings cut. The same thing that had happened when Isabella had performed that spell to seal away the amulet in the basement of the house.

Dolf crouched at my side, lifting one of my eyelids with one finger. I rolled my eyes to look at him, but that was as much as I could move.

"He's still alive," Dolf said, presumably to Goddess, although I couldn't see her or the door from this position. "But I don't know what's wrong with him."

"A spell, probably on the doorknob. Leave him. We'll retrieve him on the way out," Goddess said.

She was wrong, the mages were doing something to the amulet, but I couldn't move to tell her that.

Dolf pushed to his feet and stalked out of my field of view.

Unlike last time where the spell lasted only a few moments, this time it didn't let up. I could see the window past the edge of the leather couch. A few screams pierced the night, some close and some farther away. A flash of light came from outside the window, followed by a bang that shook the house.

CHAPTER 25

GUARDIAN OF THE DEAD

I STRUGGLED AGAINST THE tape on my legs, not caring how much fur I ripped out, no matter how painful it was. Everett was in more trouble than he knew. I wished I hadn't been so secretive about my trips, but I hadn't wanted to scare him.

The woman who claimed to be a goddess was very dangerous. I hadn't been able to figure out how to warn him in the car with her there listening. Then again, it seemed like he might have already figured it out. Still, I had a bad feeling that Everett was in trouble. I had to get him away from her.

I managed to get one front paw free. Blood trickled down from where patches of fur had been torn out. I used my claws to shred the rest of the tape on my back legs and muzzle. Luckily this one was a newer car with an emergency trunk release. A bit of a challenge to pull it without fingers, but I couldn't take the time—or the energy—to change back to human.

My teeth finally caught one side of the T-shaped orange handle, and a few tugs later the trunk popped open with a soft click. I scrabbled out, falling to the gravel in an undignified heap with a loud yelp. Shreds of duct tape flapped around my legs as picked myself up and limped after the vampires. I was just glad that the woman had been arrogant enough to not leave someone behind to guard me.

The vampires were easy to track; their strong scent burned my nose. In fact, it was so strong that I feared I'd never smell anything else ever again.

No sound marred the silence of the night other than my own panting breath. My stomach rolled. My legs hurt, and I went slower than I would I have liked.

I came to a metal fence. The bars were far enough apart that in my jackal form, I was able to wiggle through.

The lights of the house blazed; gunfire and screams pierced the night. I hoped I wasn't too late.

The scent-trail split here, and it took me a moment of nosing around to separate Everett's from the rest. I followed it to the house where I found a shattered window with blood on the windowsill. The bottom of the windowpane was almost five-feet up. I backed up and took a running leap, just barely making inside.

The trail here was easy to follow; bloody footsteps that smelled like Everett led from the room and down the hall. I crept carefully after them, swiveling my ears around listening for vampires.

I passed into a great room and stopped. Everett lay on his back on the floor directly in front of stairs leading down.

I dropped to my stomach, glancing around, but I didn't see any sign of any other vampires.

"Everett," I whined, inching across the hardwood floor towards him. I kept my ears pricked for any sound.

He didn't respond. I reached him and pressed a nose to his cold cheek. He twitched, his eyes fluttering, so he was still alive.

I needed to get him out of here before the others came back. With as little as he was wearing, there wasn't much for my teeth to grab on to. I'd have to risk taking the time to change back.

My joints popped as I transformed. The second change left me ravenous, but I powered through it, leaning over to scoop up Everett. A few stray pieces of tape still stuck to my face, arms, and legs.

Glass in his back scraped my arms as I hoisted him to my chest. His blood stung as it mixed with mine. Everett's skin was cool enough to shock me awake, when I wanted nothing more after my second change than to lie down and sleep for a few hours.

I staggered away with him, heading for the front door. I didn't dare call for help and risk alerting the vampires to my presence. The front steps felt like cliffs in my weakened state.

"Jack, put me down. Run," Everett moaned from my arms, struggling. I stopped to hoist him higher and tightened my arms.

"Shhh," I said, stumbling a little on the bottom step. "I've got you."

I got to the grass, cool with dew, but only made it a few steps before a woman's voice yelled from behind me. "Jackal, protecting your charge I see. Well, I'm back now. Hand him over to me."

I spun and backed away. The woman was there alone, the gold amulet hanging around her neck, bright against the dark red of her dress. Her straight hair was disheveled, and blood smeared her perfect makeup.

"Never," I growled, my vision narrowing as my intense emotions began triggering a change. Fur began sprouting on my arms.

A blur flashed by me on the left, and Everett screamed, "No!" and covered his ears for some reason, flailing so hard I could barely keep hold of him. The color started to bleed from my vision, but I fought the change with all my might. One mere jackal was not big enough to challenge even a single vampire.

I dodged to the right, and straight into a trap. Kurt appeared in a blur and a whoosh of air directly in front of me. I skidded to a stop and backpedaled, but the first vampire came up behind me and grabbed my arms.

"I'll be taking that," the woman said, stepping toward me and holding out her arms.

"I don't think so." I clung tight to Everett, but the vampire behind me grabbed my arms, wrenching them back. The woman took the fingers of both my hands in hers and, looking me right in the eyes, wrenched my fingers off Everett hard enough that I felt several snap.

I grunted and fell to my knees as Goddess yanked Everett from my grasp.

"No, don't hurt him!" Everett yelled, flailing against the woman's hold. It looked awkward, since she was actually an inch or two shorter than Everett, yet she was strong enough to hold him up and keep him contained.

"Hold still," she ordered, and immediately he froze. "Better, now stand up. I won't hurt him, or you."

"But I'll hurt you," I growled, stopping my fight against the change, letting it wash over me. Not only letting it wash over me, pushing all my anger and rage into the change.

I'd never been able to hold warrior form before, but really I hadn't had a pressing reason before.

My muscles bulged under my skin and the fur grew thicker. I spun on the vampire holding me, slashing down in an x-shape with my claws. He fell back, clutching at his chest and screaming. I kept my momentum going as I spun back towards Everett and the other two vampires. They had begun moving, but in this form I was almost as fast.

I slashed an oversized paw at Kurt, tearing a gash across the front of his shirt. He fell back with a scream, rolling on the grass. That would leave a mark, and probably take Kurt out of the rest of this fight; wounds made on a vampire by shapeshifter teeth and claws took a while to heal, although they were not as deadly as silver to a vampire.

I lunged at the woman with my jaws open in a howl, swinging my arm at her throat. She jerked back. A single claw caught her throat, tearing a thin line of red across the length of it.

Her face twisted in rage. She chanted under her breath, hooked her hands, and swiped back at me with talons nearly as long as mine.

I danced back from her, easily evading the blow. Blood leaked from her throat, slowing her down. She wasn't healing as quickly from this as she was from my claws earlier.

I circled around her, snarling, looking for a weakness to end this fight. Holding this in-between state was draining; my body constantly was trying to finish the change to jackal form. I'd already changed twice tonight, and my vision was narrowing at the edges.

Her eyes glowed red and she bared her teeth back at me, revealing a single fang. She backed away from me and began chanting, moving her hands in an elaborate dance.

Shit. I didn't know what spell she was doing, but I had to act fast.

Dodge back or lunge forward. Defense or offense?

I went with offense, charging towards her, arm raised to strike.

Bad decision. When I was almost on top of her and too close to change direction, she pointed her hands at me and let loose a gout of flame. I yelped and fell back, patting down the flames that had engulfed the fur on my chest, face, and head. I stopped and rolled in the dew-sparkled grass, trying to put out the fire.

That distraction was enough that I lost hold of the in-between state. My bones twisted and shrunk. By the time the fire was out, I was a regular-sized jackal again. It was all too much.

I staggered to all fours as the vampire woman stalked towards me, flexing her hands to show the claws tipping the ends of her fingers. And then I was falling sideways, the world sliding away from me into darkness.

EPILOGUE

THE WOMAN'S ORDER HELD me fast; I could not move as she advanced on the helpless Jack. He'd fallen over on his side, eyes closed. I think he'd fainted or passed out. He had to be as tired as I was. My legs shook; I was still recovering from the binding spell the mages had put on the amulet in their last-ditch attempt to slow down the attack, not realizing it only affected me and not the Goddess.

"No!" I screamed. "Don't hurt him!"

She stopped and turned to me, her lips twitching. "He's a guardian of the dead, Everett. I had not planned on hurting him." She turned back to Jack and crouched to pick him up. His head and tail lolled out of her arms, limp.

"No," I swallowed. "Please leave him, Goddess." My lips twisted as I forced the last word out.

"Why would I do that?" Her mouth straightened into a slim line.

One of the vampires from the second car zipped up to us, sliding to a stop next to the woman. "Goddess, we need to go, now. The mages are regrouping, pushing us back with their magic. We've already lost three."

"Everett, come with me." She whistled loudly, then turned and started running from the house. The remaining vampires—only Kurt and the other from the second car—fell in behind her.

"Where's Dolf?" I asked as my legs started moving after her of their own accord. But I could still speak.

She glanced at me over her shoulder. "He didn't make it out of the basement. The mages laid a trap for us there." She smiled. "Dolf sacrificed himself to save me, as it should be."

"Miss Goddess, can you leave the jackal?" I asked her. I couldn't bear to see Jack also captive of this ancient unpredictable vampire.

"And waste a perfectly good guardian jackal?" She laughed. "I think not. It was fate that he was there with you when I finally picked you up."

We'd reached the fence and Kurt had to pick me up and carry me over, as my legs refused to go further. I wanted to argue with her, but I didn't have the energy.

She pulled me into the back seat with her, while Kurt got back into the driver's seat. The other vampire got in the backseat with us, pinning me between them.

The car squealed off. She laid Jack's limp body across my lap, keeping his head on her leg so she could pet his head. I wanted to slap her hand away, but didn't dare anger her. Instead I twisted my shaking hands into Jack's fur and asked, "Where are we going?"

She smiled at me, reaching over to take my hand in hers. "To rebuild my church. In my day, vampires were rightfully feared and worshiped by the huddling mortals. We shall have that again."

Book 3: Jack and Everett struggle to stop the Goddess before she takes over all of Las Vegas. But can they stop her before Everett is pulled in too far to be saved?

Goddess of the Ancients is available to pre-order now at https://books2read.com/u/m2YpZo

ALSO BY ROAN ROSSER

The Changing Bodies Series
Book 1 - Ritual of the Ancients - Coming May 13, 2022
Book 2 - Bloodline of the Ancients - Coming July 13, 2022
Book 3 - Goddess of the Ancients - Coming August 16, 2022
Prequel - Jackal of Hearts – Newsletter Freebie
The Chaos Menagerie Series
Book 1 - Red Pandamonium - Coming June 13, 2022
Book 1.5 - Diamond in the Rat – Newsletter Freebie
Book 2 – Pandora's Fox – Coming Soon

About the Author

ROAN ROSSER

My urban fantasy novels mainly feature the trans and queer protagonists grappling with things like identity and found families that I wished I could have read about growing up.

I escaped from the bowels of Utah (namely Provo) and now live in the sunny Pacific Northwest of the United States.

When not writing, you can probably find me beating up pixel baddies or in front of one of my sewing machines adding to my overstuffed closet or my army of homemade plush dolls.

If you find yourself blinded by the vivid colors and loud patterns of my homemade shirts, know that I'm only trying to warn you that I may be poisonous. Or venomous? Or both? Probably both.

www.ingramcontent.com/pod-product-compliance
Lightning Source LLC
Chambersburg PA
CBHW022114170626
46808CB00002B/730